THE LOVELY

AND

DANGEROUS LAUNCH

OF

LUCY CAVANAGH

A NOVEL

STACY PETERSON

 FriesenPress

One Printers Way
Altona, MB R0G 0B0
Canada

www.friesenpress.com

ISBN
978-1-03-910595-9 (Hardcover)
978-1-03-910594-2 (Paperback)
978-1-03-910596-6 (eBook)

1. FICTION, HISTORICAL, AMERICAN

Distributed to the trade by The Ingram Book Company

There is a candle in your heart,
ready to be kindled.
There is a void in your soul,
ready to be filled.
You feel it, don't you?

–Rumi

For Lucy Cavanagh.
Thank you for haunting me for nine years,
and never giving up on me.

CHAPTER 1

———◆———

TRAPPED. THAT'S ALL LUCY could think as she gazed up at the white doves that had been brought in for ambiance. They fluttered about the high ornate ceiling, chandeliers, and closed windows, searching for an exit. The crowd hushed as the orchestra began, and the night was kicked off with dancers coming down the grand staircase in lavish costumes, performing the hobby horse quadrille, their faces powdered white like rare porcelain dolls. In the air, the scent of exotic flowers brought in from all over the world. Palm trees were draped with bougainvillea and orchids. The papers called it the ball that would change New York City: the Shaws' fancy costume ball. Twelve hundred guests, all of New York's high society. Lucy took a sip of her champagne and smiled back at two handsome men across the room, one dressed as the Count of Monte Cristo, the other, Thor, the Barbarian, in a steel-plated chest and bare arms. There were a few gasps in the crowd as Miss Fanny Morgan arrived wearing a taxidermy cat head atop her curls and tails sewn into her dress. Lucy choked back a laugh as she began making her way across the room to her.

"What's so funny, Miss Lucy?"

Lucy opened her eyes. She blinked a few times and looked around the stagecoach. Dark and damp. Her legs cramped. Grey daylight shone in through two small windows. A stench of whiskey, tobacco, and body odor. The sound of the hooves clopping along a road that grew more potholed and rockier each day. Her stomach turned, and she put a hand over her mouth. She wasn't sure if it was the mysterious meat she'd eaten at the station this morning or if it was motion sickness from the bumpy road, but it had been worsening all afternoon.

"What was so funny, Miss Lucy?" Seymour asked again. He sat across from her, on the middle bench, between Leroy and Gus. "I think that's the first time I seen you laugh."

"I was dreaming."

Seymour, Leroy, and Gus. They referred to themselves as the "gambling brothers," though she had come to learn they were not, in fact, brothers, nor very successful gamblers. Their clothing was ripped and stained and their trousers tucked into worn black boots to the knee like soldiers, though she never asked if they'd fought in the war. Never a straight answer as to where they were going or why. Seymour, the only other person awake now, was still staring at her curiously, grinning with a childlike innocence for his age.

On the front bench, beside Lucy, were the Holloways, young newlyweds from Missouri. Emily Holloway twitched and mumbled something in her sleep. Lucy looked down at her, cradled into her husband's arm. The Holloways had boarded outside of Julesburg, both waving as the stage approached, Nelson in dirty overalls and work boots, and Emily in her simple little cotton dress with the built-in apron. Lucy had thought they might be Amish at first, but they were just farmers down on their luck, cautiously excited for their new life with Nelson's uncle in the Colorado Territory.

Emily Holloway settled back into her husband's arm and snored softly now, her oversized bonnet pulled down over her face.

Lucy had meant to buy a practical bonnet like that in the rush to prepare for the journey—until she'd seen the little black lacy hat she was wearing on a mannequin in the store window. The salesgirl had showed her how to pin it off to one side and forward, almost covering an eye. Apparently, it was all the rage in Paris, and the French girls were wearing them like that, like they were keeping a little French secret. "*Gives off an air of mystery,*" the salesgirl had said. "*Slyness.*"

Lucy didn't feel very French or sly now, having nothing to protect her from the elements. Her dark hair was covered in a layer of dust. Her royal-blue silk dress with black lace detailing was muddied, smelly, and torn in two places along the hem. The matching lace gloves were soiled and ripping. She reached up, pushed the curtain aside, and looked out the window, out at the passing trees and puffs of clouds in the late-afternoon sky. The reflection of her face in the glass peered at her, lifeless and pale. Covered in a film of dust. Tired eyes. Her hair falling out of its chignon. She reached up and re-pinned a few pins and adjusted her hat. She was only halfway across the country and embarrassed to think what she would look like, getting off the stagecoach in San Francisco. She closed her eyes and pictured herself as her favorite Austin heroine, Elizabeth Bennet, in the scene where she arrives in disarray after walking through the field. Mud on the hem of her dress and her hair down and wild. Standing in front of Mr. Darcy and his companions so free-spirited and brave. Only in a book.

One of the horses whinnied, and the stagecoach jerked and went over such a bump that Lucy felt herself lifted from her seat, flinging an arm up against the wall to brace herself from ending up in Gus's lap. One of the oversized mailbags fell off the bench at the back, sending dust throughout the cabin. The coach jolted, and she thought she heard something crack near the back. Emily sat straight up now, her bonnet half over her face, and she looked down at the floor. Something had rolled past, and Lucy pulled the skirt of her dress aside and looked down. A whiskey bottle. Three-quarters full. Gus, Seymour, and Leroy all stared down at the bottle.

"Well, where did you come from?" Gus asked as he leaned forward to pick it up.

Lucy pancaked herself against the wall as his thin greasy strands of red hair brushed against the skirt of her dress. He sat up, unscrewed the cap, and took a long drink with his eyes closed.

Then Seymour grabbed the bottle out of Gus's hands. "Give me somma that," he said. He took a long drink, then wiped his mouth with the back of his hand and let out a belch.

"Fuckin' hell," said Gus, cuffing Seymour's head. "Mind your manners in front of the womenfolk."

Something about it struck Leroy as funny, and as he reached for the bottle, he laughed himself into a wheezing coughing fit.

In all the commotion, Lucy hadn't realized the stagecoach had been slowly coming to a stop. Footsteps rustled above, in the driver's seat, then two pairs of feet leapt down.

Barnet, the driver of the coach, passed by the window and bent down beside the rear wheel. His kind, weathered face was distraught.

The French guide, Jacques, joined him. "*Merde!*" Jacques shouted. "*Merde!*"

"That don't sound good," said Leroy. "What's he sayin', Miss Lucy? He cussin'?"

"Yes, Leroy, he's cussing," said Lucy, her eyes still on Jacques.

Jacques, the mysterious French guide. Thin strands of worn leather wrapped around his wrists. And hanging from his neck, a silver cross and some sort of animal tooth attached to it. Thick metal rings on three of his fingers. Half Métis, from Quebec. He'd come as a trapper and made a name for himself as a guide. He was fluent in five languages, though he hardly spoke at all. This was the first time in the entire ten days that she'd heard him raise his voice or use foul language. He had dark skin and intense green eyes that she found terrifying, in an exciting sort of way. He stood with his hands on his hips, watching Barnet and looking around, surveying the land; then he walked over to the door of the stagecoach and opened it.

"Everybody out, *s'il vous plaît,*" he said, offering a hand to Lucy. "*Vous d'abord, mademoiselle.*"

Lucy grabbed her parasol, bustled her skirt and crinoline, and shuffled toward the door. She took his hand and let him guide her down, then took a few steps out into the open air.

Rolling trees and evergreens as far as the eye could see. The breeze cooler than usual. She opened the parasol and held it up to shield the last few rays of evening sun. Grasshoppers leapt in and out of the tall grass, and she watched one. As she reached out to touch it, it fluttered off. The rocking movement of the stagecoach was still with her, and she wandered out farther away from everyone. Seymour called out and asked her if she was all right. Her stomach lurched suddenly; she brought the back of her hand up against her mouth and tried to compose herself. Her eyes watered, and then a sudden urgency came over her and she ran to a cluster of bushes and vomited.

Footsteps came running up from behind her. It was Seymour. He held a handkerchief out to her.

"Sorry," she whispered, as she took the handkerchief and dabbed at the corners of her mouth. It had a faint brown stain and reeked of stale whiskey and cigarettes. Her stomach lurched again, and she held her breath and tried to get her bearings. She felt weak and dizzy and couldn't stop shivering. Seymour took another step toward her and leaned in close to study her face. The smell of his cigarette wafted toward her, and she turned away from him.

"Don't be embarrassed, Miss Lucy," he said, taking her by the arm. "Come on. We'll get you all fixed up."

She let Seymour take her arm, and as he guided her back to the stagecoach, she handed the handkerchief back to him. He insisted she keep it. The men had all gathered around the broken wheel and turned to stare. She cast her eyes downward as they muttered amongst themselves. Nelson Holloway was certain it was cholera, and there was talk of her being quarantined. Emily stood quietly, peering out from under her giant bonnet, with her usual confused expression.

Gus spat a long stream of tobacco to the side and wiped his mouth with the back of his hand. "She ain't got the cholera," he mumbled. "I been feelin' sick after that breakfast this mornin'. That and this fuckin' road today."

"Shut up and toss me a canteen," said Seymour, still locked arm in arm with Lucy as he guided her to a nearby log and sat her down. "And someone bring me my coat," he added. "She's shiverin.'"

Leroy came hustling over with a canteen and draped a coat over her shoulders. It smelled of foul body odor but was lined with warm fur. She pulled it tighter around her as she took a drink from the canteen. "Thank you," she said.

Leroy took a drag from Seymour's cigarette, and the two of them stood on either side of her while the rest of the men continued looking over the broken wheel. An argument ensued over what to do. It would be after dark by the time it was fixed. Dangerous gangs of thieves rode this area, ex-Confederates. And they were in Cheyenne and Arapaho territory, a group of people displaced and retaliating by raiding settlers since Sand Creek, and rightfully so, according to Jacques. He demanded they continue to the La Porte Station no matter the hour. Barnet disagreed. If they continued on after dark, they were still at risk of an attack and of further damage to the stage or the broken leg of a horse on this terrible road. Lucy listened quietly. Barnet won in the end and climbed back up into the driver's seat. He drove the stagecoach off the main road and into the trees, broken wheel and all. Everyone followed on foot through the trees, looking for a hidden place to set up camp for the night.

It would be the first time Lucy had slept outside. Every other night, they had reached one of the stations, which were all the same—foul smelling and sometimes not much more than four walls and a grumpy station agent. If there were beds, they were hard and the mattresses full of stains. The bathing facilities consisted of a tin washtub and a bucket of cold water behind a thin sheet. There was little thought or need for privacy, as there were few female passengers that passed through. The food—condemned meat the stage company had bought for cheap, topped off with a murky beverage known as slumgullion. She was told it was tea and had tried it once, only to choke into a coughing fit. Now, as they walked through the trees in the middle of nowhere, under the huge open sky of Colorado Territory, she began to appreciate the strange sense of security that came with the four walls of a station.

When they reached a small clearing, Barnet was satisfied, and they stopped. Everyone went to work. Jacques tended to the horses, speaking to them in French as he brushed them down and looked over their hooves. Barnet, Nelson Holloway, and Gus worked on the broken wheel. Emily began unloading blankets and bedrolls. Leroy and Seymour went into the woods to collect firewood. They took the shotgun with them, just in case. Lucy wondered what *just in case* meant; she watched as they disappeared into the forest, then tucked her parasol away and helped Emily unroll bedrolls around what would be the fire. When they were finished, Lucy sat down on a log, hugged Seymour's coat around her, and opened her book, Homer's *Iliad*. Helen of Troy. A woman who could have had any man she wanted, yet she waited for the suitor who would sweep her off to an exciting land. An affair so dangerous it would spark the Trojan War.

Emily sat down on the log beside Lucy. "Your hat's slidin' off again," she said. "Just wait till I write my ma about you. My new friend from New York City. She won't believe me that dresses come premade. She'll say, 'What in tarnation?' She wouldn't even hear talk of puffed sleeves on my weddin' dress last year, and she wasn't the one doing the sewin'—I was. She said, 'That's a waste of material and wherever did you get such a devil's idea in your head?'"

Emily ran a hand absently over the sewn-in apron on her simple cotton dress as she spoke. An embarrassed look colored her face. "You probably think it's crazy, the thought of me sewing my own dresses."

"Not at all," said Lucy. "I wish I knew how to sew. I think it's a wonderful feminine quality."

Lucy studied the layer of dust on the satin of her own dress. The first and only other time she'd worn it was to the Lord & Taylor dress the destitute fundraiser. She was chosen to give the opening speech and had taken her father as her escort. She felt accomplished and on top of the world that day. Thrilled to be a part of a cause she cared about. Days later, there was a scandal when the money raised went missing; the culprit was never found. Lucy still had the feeling it was her father.

Suddenly, a shot rang out in the forest.

"Lucy," Emily whispered. "You think it's the Indians? Oh, my Lord in Heaven!"

Seymour and Leroy let out a woo-hoo of joy somewhere off in the distance. Their laughter echoed. Then they emerged from the trees, Leroy walking tall and smiling proudly, a limp deer over his shoulders.

The men clapped as he neared. The animal's tongue hung from its mouth and blood ran down its neck. Leroy tossed it down on the ground, took a knife from his belt, and cut a huge slit along its belly, then began to remove the guts. Emily put a hand over her mouth and looked away in horror, but Lucy watched on as Leroy and Seymour worked, blood up to their elbows now as they dug out the intestines. Leroy glanced over at the girls and smiled.

"Looky here," he said. "Farm girl can't handle a li'l blood and Miss New York City sittin' there like it ain't nothing. Better be careful, Miss Lucy. The wild'll make you wild."

Nelson came over to the girls and helped Emily up. As they walked away, Lucy heard him mumble that she shouldn't sit too close to Lucy. "She might have the cholera."

When they'd removed the internal organs, they strung the deer up to a branch by its hind legs, stood on either side, knife in hand, and began to remove the hide. Leroy let out a loud belch as he ripped and tugged. In the other direction, Jacques was still tending to the horses, cleaning out their hooves, speaking softly to them in French. Gus was on his hands and knees, working on the wagon wheel, his pants sliding down, exposing his crack. Luggage still was secured atop the coach, Lucy's carpet bag twice the size of anyone else's. At each station she'd been paranoid of it being stolen, her only remaining earthly possessions, including three thousand dollars cash, inside. She hugged the coat around her and thought about San Francisco and the things she'd get to see that she'd only read about. The shopping and theater district around Union Square. Lunch in Napa Valley, sipping wine. Nothing but rolling vineyards as far as the eye could see. Chocolate from Ghirardelli's. San Francisco's famous sourdough bread. Standing with her feet in the Pacific, looking out at the world-famous fog that blanketed the bay. She remembered her Aunt Louisa's eyes being the same as her mother's. She wondered if Aunt Louisa would recognize her, or better yet take her in her arms the first time she saw her.

"Miss Lucy," said Seymour. "You want me to save you somma the teeth and bones and make you a necklace?"

"No thank you, Seymour."

"Make the girl a necklace," said Leroy. "She needs a keepsake for her to remember us by."

The hide was pulled all the way down now and was dangling at the neck, covering the deer's face. Seymour had begun sawing at the ribs with the largest saw Lucy had ever seen. A dreadful sound. Leroy winced and walked away, back into the forest. When he returned, he had an armload of firewood and began building the fire beside where Lucy sat. Nonplussed that there were no matches to be found, Leroy set a piece of wood on the ground, flat side up. He made a groove down the center with his knife, and a groove at the end where he placed a ball of dried grass. Then he took a small stick and knifed the end into a point. On his hands and knees, he began rubbing the sharp end of the stick back and forth along the groove. His pants slid down, showing nearly half of his behind. Lucy averted her eyes and focused on the stick as he rubbed harder and harder, back and forth against the groove, until there was a spark and he stopped and bent down and blew on the ball of dried grass. Smoke appeared, then the tiny flame. With it lit, he added some newspaper and kindling. He stood eyeing the fire, his hands on his hips, and spat a long stream of tobacco juice downwind of Lucy.

Lucy looked back at Seymour and watched as he began to cut meat from the deer. She'd eaten venison only once before at the Chophouse on West 23rd, at a dinner with her father and a few of his colleagues. There had been a fondue with a plate of exotic meats, including alligator, which she'd found exciting. Her date, however, was not. He was Lane Briar, a young colleague of her father's, whom she'd been pressured to allow to court her. She pictured him here now, in his expensive suit, stirring his scotch on the rocks the way he did, smoking an expensive cigar, and ordering everyone around. He'd be just as useless as she was.

"Wood's too wet," Leroy said. "The newspaper ain't enough." Then, without another word, he went to the stagecoach and returned with one of the mailbags. He handed Lucy a stack of letters.

In confusion, Lucy looked down at them, all carefully sealed with handwritten addresses. "We can't open people's mail," she said.

"We don't get this fire going, we don't eat," said Leroy. Then he ripped a few open, crumpled the paper, and tossed it into the fire.

Lucy opened, unfolded one, and silently read:

April 5th, 1867. Dearest Friend. How long it has been since we last spoke! I intended on corresponding sooner but found myself fumbling to find just the right words for the sad news I have for you. . . .

"Miss Lucy," said Leroy.

Lucy crumpled the letter and tossed it into the fire.

It took half a bag of mail and a half an hour's time, but they had a roaring fire. Leroy cooked the smaller cuts of meat in a pan along with the last can of tomatoes, and the larger cuts smoked over a metal grate. Lucy was given the task of stirring the two cans of beans that heated slowly off to the side. She'd never sat so close to an open fire and marveled silently as it cracked and danced and spat. She removed her lacy gloves and sat with her hands reached out toward its warmth. Around her neck, she wore her new gift from Seymour. A necklace made of deer teeth dangling from a piece of twine.

By the time dinner was served, it was well after dark. The wheel was almost fixed, but Gus had grown tired of trying to work by lantern and decided to finish at daybreak so they could continue. The eight of them ate in a circle around the fire. Lucy barely ate, her stomach still not right. The last whiskey bottle was passed around communally now. The men pleaded with Lucy to take a few swigs to calm her stomach, though she politely declined.

Emily sat on the bedroll beside her, her bonnet hanging from her neck, her long brown hair in a braid that hung down the center of her back. "Oh, Lucy, how will I ever sleep tonight?" she asked. "I'm so nervous about tomorrow. I keep thinking what if his Uncle

Holloway don't like me? Or what if the house is awful or Nelson doesn't get that job at the mill?"

Lucy stared into the flames. After a while, she said, "There was a very wise ancient Greek philosopher by the name of Heraclitus. He said, '*The only constant is change.*' I think it's the reason behind every great novel, every great journey."

Emily shook her head, a confused smile on her face. "I never understand half the things you say."

"I'm saying you're brave, is all."

"You're the brave one. You promise you're gonna write from San Francisco? You'll tell me about reunitin' with your aunt? I can't read, of course. But I'll find someone to read it to me."

"I promise."

"You won't forget how to address it? Emily and Nelson Holloway, in Valley City, Colorado."

"I won't forget."

The men were still passing whiskey around, but Lucy lay back on her bedroll and pulled Seymour's coat over her. Somewhere off in the distance, a coyote howled, the sound haunting and beautiful.

When she closed her eyes her mind drifted back to the night of the Shaws' fancy costume ball. She'd kept dancing when her father was escorted out in handcuffs. Everyone had. There had been dozens of arrests since the war; none of them amounted to anything. And so, she was shocked to arrive home at four a.m. to buggies lined up outside and reporters on her doorstep. Then to make her way up the stairs inside the house to find her father's lawyers in his office, going through drawers and destroying papers. Over the next few days, she wasn't allowed to see him in jail, though she wasn't sure she wanted to. She was only informed of the plan for her to marry Lane Briar to secure her future. It shouldn't have come as such a shock to her, the idea of marriage. It was the very thing all young women were primed to do, the goal in everything they did, from the parties they attended to the way they did their hair. And yet Lucy could not do it. Not like this, not now, not to Lane Briar. And so, in the chaos of those few days, all she could see was her chance to do something else, something she'd dreamed of for so long—to find the answers her heart had always needed, even if it meant being disowned.

The howling had grown louder, several coyotes in chorus now. Lucy looked up at the stars.

Seymour burst out laughing across the fire. "Hey, Leroy," he slurred out, "'member that blond, the feisty little thing you was whorin' round with in Carson City? The one with the temper on her? I dunno what just made me think of her. 'Member when she came into that saloon and threw that fuckin' bottle at us, called us 'no good drunken hooligans'?" Seymour laughed and let out a sound between a hiccup and a belch.

Leroy chuckled quietly. "Yeah, she was quite a woman," he said. "Quite a woman indeed."

"Tell 'em the story of that poker tournament you won in Santa Fe," said Seymour. "Tell 'em."

Lucy looked up at the stars, half listening as Leroy carried on in his slow and methodical way, recalling with pride how he'd won, even though a full-figured lady sat on his lap with her titties in his face. "Nearly broke my concentration," he kept saying. "Nearly broke my goddamned concentration." His quiet chuckle was the last thing she remembered before she fell asleep.

When she woke sometime later, it was still dark. Quiet, save for the dull chorus of snoring around what was left of the fire. Her stomach turned, and she put a hand over her mouth. She got to her feet and stumbled away from the camp, into the darkness. She went a ways until a branch hit her face, and she fell to her hands and knees and vomited.

As she slowly stood back up, dizziness overwhelmed her again. Still no movement around the fire. She could no longer hear the snoring from where she stood. Her stomach lurched and turned. Maybe it was cholera. Maybe she was going to die out here. She took a few steps back and sat down beside a tree, shivering. An owl whoo-whooed. Crickets were chirping and trees rustled in the breeze. After a while she lay down, rested her head in her hands, and fell asleep beside the tree.

In her dream, a horse was galloping toward her. A black horse in the moonlight. She couldn't turn and run, and fear gripped her as she stood there, alone and helpless, listening to the sound of hooves hitting the earth, beholding the darkness of the horse's eyes as it neared.

Her body twitched, and she woke and sat up and looked around. It was still dark. The campfire had died down, and she could barely see the campsite. She hadn't realized she'd stumbled off so far in the night. The sound of horses galloping in the distance broke through her thoughts. Then branches cracking. Bodies rustled around the campsite and someone stood, but she couldn't make out who it was.

"Indians!" someone shouted.

She heard Emily scream.

Then the shouting, screaming, and whooping. Like no human sound she'd ever heard. Bits of moving torchlight shone through the trees.

"Wake up!" someone shouted.

A gunshot went off.

Lucy crawled back beside the tree and ducked down.

The torchlight grew brighter, then dark men on horseback appeared out of the forest, riding fast. Bare chested, their bodies streaked in paint. Emily screamed out again, and it echoed throughout the forest. More gunshots fired. One of the dark men rode through the camp, hanging sideways from his horse, firing a bow and arrow. One of the horses reared up, its rider swinging a rope with a rock on one end. Another rider leapt from his horse and swung an axe to the ground near the spot where Emily and Nelson slept. After a few swings, he held the axe in the air and yelped, then wiped the blood from the blade and smeared it across his chest.

And then everything quieted. One by one, they dismounted and tossed their torches into the fire. Three of the riders climbed up onto the stagecoach and began tossing luggage down while the others looted through it. She could see trousers, whiskey bottles, a dress, all the belongings of the passengers suspended in the firelight, then tossed into the fire. She watched helplessly as her oversized carpetbag was opened, rummaged through, then heaved into the flames. One of the dark men stopped and stared in her direction, then started walking toward where she lay crouched down in the grass. Her heart pounded wildly. A giant in the moonlight. He was bare chested, clothed only in dark trousers and an axe that hung from his belt. On his head he wore the pelt of a bear head with the eyes and teeth still in tact. She could see his broad, muscular chest heaving as he neared. He held a torch in one hand and a gleaming knife in the other. He kept coming, slowly, stopping every few feet to look around.

Lucy held her breath. He was only a few feet from her now.

One of the others shouted out, and he turned around. He took one last look in her direction, then walked back to camp and mounted his horse. The group of them rode off, with the stage-coach horses in tow.

Not a stitch of movement from the heaps that lay around the now roaring fire. The sound of galloping horses faded in the distance. Dead quiet.

"Jacques?" she whispered. "Seymour? Gus? Leroy?"

Nothing. She slowly began making her way to the fire.

"Barnet?" Her voice cracked. "Nelson?! Emily?!"

She kept walking.

Emily lay as though she were sleeping, except for the trickle of blood at the side of her mouth. Lucy gingerly pulled the blanket back. "Em?" she whispered. The blanket was wet, and she dropped it and looked at the blood on her hand. She wiped it on the skirt of her dress. Emily Holloway had been decapitated. Blood pooled around her throat. Nelson too. Lucy took a step to the side and vomited. The acid burned her throat, and she wiped her mouth with her wrist. The fire was hot on her face.

She walked slowly around the fire. Jacques lay with his skull crushed in. A large blood-stained rock sat upon the ground beside him. Barnet was facedown with his arms out to his sides, an arrow in his back. Blood everywhere. Gus lay with his eyes open. She knelt and placed her fingers on his neck. His skin was still warm, and she held her fingers steady, waiting, even though there was no pulse to be felt. Leroy lay on his side. Blood poured from a hole in his chest. Something floated out of the fire and landed beside her. The charred corner of a dollar bill. Her carpetbag was burning in the middle of the fire, melting and disfigured and barely recognizable. She picked up a branch and tried to lift it by the handle, but it disintegrated into ash. She quickly dropped it and stood back from the flames. It was no use. She thought she heard a branch crack in the distance and scanned the dark forest for movement. Nothing. A little ways off, Seymour lay on his back with his mouth open, as though he were yelling. She went to him, fell to her knees, and watched his face in the firelight. That was not sleeping.

Lucy sat there on the ground beside Seymour a while. Before today, she'd seen a dead body only once. It was over fifteen years ago now, but it all came rushing back to her as though it was yesterday, as though time was not linear. She was barely eight years old when she found her mother and, while standing by the bed, tried to wake her. Too young to understand fully but she remembered knowing her mother was gone, curling up against her still-warm body, closing her eyes, and wishing with all her might she could go with her.

Her eyes darted at every strange sound from the forest. A coyote howled. Then another. She went to the stagecoach and reached under the driver's seat where Barnet kept an extra gun hidden. She found it and sat beside the stagecoach amongst the few littered items not thrown into the fire. A few tools. Someone's bag, maybe Leroy's. An empty whiskey bottle. The gun in her hands had an ivory handle and Barnet's initials, BEB, carved into the side. She'd watched Barnet clean and open the cylinder once. She flipped it open now. Six bullets. She didn't know why, but she found comfort in holding it just now, turning the revolver, pulling the safety back and forth.

The first she saw of the coyotes was their eyes cutting through the dark, staring her down, pacing the tree line across the way. Three, maybe four. Braver and braver, until one came skulking in from the trees, keeping low and making its way into the camp. Lucy aimed the gun and clicked the safety back. Her finger trembled on the trigger. Two others followed a few feet behind.

"Get!" she shouted.

The lead coyote froze in its tracks, eyeing her. Then it took a few steps toward her. She fired. The shot echoed through the forest. The coyote leapt and yelped, and the pack of them scattered off through the trees. Her ears were still ringing, and she sat staring at the gun in her trembling hands.

The date was May 28, 1867. A Tuesday. That was the day she fired a gun for the first time.

CHAPTER 2

IN BOARDING SCHOOL, SISTER Mary Catherine had taught the girls that blackbirds used to be white, like doves, but God had cursed them because of their intelligence and trickery, turning them black and making them into scavengers—purveyors of death, a connection to the underworld, and a bad omen.

The ravens began to swarm at dawn, landing, one by one, to peck at the bodies. She threw rocks at them, and they flew off but continued to circle. Their caws echoed throughout the forest. She still sat beside the stagecoach, the gun in hand. The fire had burned down to the last remaining coals, heaps of the dead around it unearthly motionless. Her mouth was dry, and her head ached.

Lucy stood and went to the fire. She picked up a stick and poked at the remains. All that was left of her carpetbag was the charred metal clasps. The blackened-metal lid from her moisturizing cream. The chain of a necklace. She picked it up with the stick and set it aside, then walked around the camp. A knife lay on the ground near the body of Jacques, and she picked it up. Dried blood stained the blade and handle, but she carried it around as she continued walking, in search of anything useful left behind. Nothing else of value. A hammer and a few tools on the ground. An empty canteen. Rolling papers and tobacco. A dirty pair of trousers. In the stagecoach, two remaining mailbags and an empty whiskey bottle. Another empty canteen. No water anywhere. With no idea which way the road was, she walked into the woods in search of it, looking back every so often to see the red of the stagecoach through the trees. Her stomach turned, and she felt sweaty and clammy. She wiped her brow with the back of her wrist and looked up at the sky.

"Help!" she called out. "Someone, please help me!"

She collected branches and sticks for the fire as she walked. Branches cracked from somewhere to her right, and she dropped the bundle of sticks and pulled Barnet's gun from the pocket of her skirt. She pointed it at the trees but could see no movement. The ravens swarmed overhead, now joined by large vultures. She went in every direction, as far as she could without losing sight of the stage. No sign of the road. No sign of life in any direction.

Back at the campsite, the fire was dead. She dropped an armful of branches and sticks beside it, then went to the stagecoach and dragged the second mailbag out. She did exactly what she'd seen Leroy do. The groove in a piece of wood. The ball of dried grass. She sharpened the end of a stick into a point with the knife, then rubbed it against the groove, harder and harder, creating as much friction as she could.

Nothing happened. She kept going, working until her hands ached and there was blood. She studied the cut and squeezed it, watching as drops of blood dripped to the ground. Then she wiped it on her dress and tucked a stray piece of hair behind her ears. She suddenly wondered what happened to her little lacy hat. Or her parasol. She rubbed the stick against the groove—harder and faster this time—until more blood drew from her hands.

Still no hint of smoke, nor a flicker of a flame. She sat back and looked around at her comrades laying in their dried pools of blood. Their bodies were yellowing and puffy now. Maggots crawled from Leroy's eyes and mouth. And Seymour's chest. Gus's wispy strands of hair blew in the evening breeze.

The day she'd first met them in St. Louis would be forever etched in her memory. It was like nothing she'd ever seen, and nothing like she'd expected, stepping foot off the train in St. Louis. The sign as she exited the train station read: "WELCOME TO ST. LOUIS, THE EDGE OF THE FRONTIER!" The chaotic streets teemed with pedestrians and wagons piled high with luggage. She saw a hardware store on every corner. Men selling supplies out of wheelbarrows and wagons shouted out prices. Every café window had a sign that Lewis and Clark had eaten there. Loud steamboats rolling past brick buildings shrouded in a heavy cloud of black smoke. The stagecoach station was even more chaotic. Travelers speaking every language. German. Swedish. Japanese. Maps showing dozens of different routes in every direction. It took her the better part of an hour and all the courage she could muster to fight back tears while figuring out where to go, which ticket to buy, and how to get someone to help her with her heavy carpetbag, only to find out each passenger was only allowed twenty pounds, a rule strictly enforced. She was fighting back tears again when Gus, Seymour, and Leroy arrived, carrying tickets for her same stagecoach and traveling all the way to San Francisco. They reeked of whiskey and foul body odor, but they stepped in and argued with the management on her behalf. In the end, she paid an extra fare while the three men secured her carpetbag atop the stage for her. *"Don't worry, darlin'. We'll take real good care of ya."*

And they had.

She reached up and ran her fingers over the deer tooth necklace.

A raven cawed out overhead. Lucy looked up. Nearly dark now. She stood and looked around for a blanket that wasn't covered in blood, but there weren't any. Just the jacket of Seymour's and she took it, went to the stagecoach, and curled up on the front seat.

The bodies were beginning to smell by the next morning. Something had scavenged on Jacques in the night, his shirt torn open, intestines exposed. She stood over him, trembling. With the gun in hand, she went out in search of the road again. When she wandered too far and lost sight of the stagecoach, she became gripped with fear and turned and went back. They'd been due to arrive in La Porte yesterday. Surely help would be dispatched by now for the missing coach?

After another failed attempt at making a fire, and the swarming and cawing of the ravens and vultures beginning to drive her mad, Lucy sat beside the stagecoach, the mailbag beside her and the gun in her hand, five bullets in its chamber. She kept counting. Opening and spinning it shut. Clicking the safety back and forth. Half the pins had fallen from her hair. She set the gun down and she took the rest out, tousled it, and let it fall down her back, matted and dirty. A cramp intensified in her leg now. Her head pounded, and her eyes were sore. She reached into the mailbag, pulled out a letter, and took the knife from her pocket and opened the seal.

The next in the pile was in feminine handwriting, addressed to Sara Peterson in Carson City.

I pray this letter finds you in good health, as I am at present, thanks be to God. . . . You missed the opening of Othello and

I dare say it was exquisite! . . . And you'll never guess who had the honor of attending the Jordan Marsh fashion show . . . moi! Showcasing the most divine dresses of the season, of course I went home with four of them. . . .

Lucy set it down and opened another. And another. Letters from the East, letters of love and news, deaths, marriages, children born. More fashion shows and galleries attended. Letters professing intentions to visit, to make the journey west.

My dearest Josephine,

Please reconsider my offer in your hand in marriage. . . . I dare contest that your rejection is only a ploy to further my affections, and I shall soldier on, marching toward the prize that is you my darling . . . and I write to remind you of my connections. And that since our last meeting, my wealth has accumulated.

Lucy crumpled the letter. Why did it always seem men married out of desire, but women for security? What if the passion and love stories of great novels had ruined her with a longing for something that didn't exist? Maybe she'd been foolish to turn down Lane Briar. Or the others who had attempted to pursue her. She could still hear her father telling her to get her damned head out of the clouds, even with over fifteen hundred miles between them.

A bird cawed out overhead. She looked up at the sky, her eyes feeling funny now, a dizziness overwhelming her.

Suddenly there was a loud crack of a branch behind her, followed by more cracking and rustling through the trees. Her heart raced. Something was coming. She grabbed the gun, stood and peeked around the stagecoach.

A lone horseman, a black bandana around his neck, was making his way toward her. She scurried to hide in the bushes.

The horse was jet black, with a patch of white down the center of its face.

"Whoa, girl," the rider said, stopping the horse about twenty feet from her. He wore his tan hat low, shading his face, and for a while, he just sat there, surveying the scene. A few vultures had landed, pecking at the body of Jacques. The rider reached down and pulled a shotgun from the saddle and aimed in the direction of the vultures. The sound of the shot made her jump. One of the giant birds fell with a thud and lay limp on the ground, and the others flew off. He re-holstered the shotgun into the saddle, dismounted, and took his hat off as he continued surveying the scene. His hair was dark blond and unkempt, his face dirty and unshaven. He looked to be in his late twenties or early thirties. The calf of one of his pant legs was soaked in blood. A leather belt hung low on his hips, a gun hanging from each side.

Lucy kept as still as she could.

He patted the horse's neck and tossed the reins loosely over the branch of a tree. He untied a canteen and took a long drink, then poured water over his face and hair, and gave his back a stretch. He pulled a cigarette from his shirt pocket and lit it with a match. Then he went to the stagecoach and looked inside before coming out empty-handed. He kicked at the ground and picked up a hammer and studied it, then tossed it aside. From Leroy's bag, he took tobacco and rolling papers and pocketed them, then went to the bodies, spurs jangling as he walked.

Lucy looked back at the horse. The canteen hung from the saddle. She looked in the direction he'd come from. Had he come from the main road? A bug fluttered beside her in the grass and tickled her hand, and she lifted it ever so slowly while it crawled across her knuckles.

The man went first to Emily's body, knelt over her, and lifted her hand. Lucy slowly pulled the branches away for a clearer view. Why was he touching her? Then she realized he was working

Emily's wedding ring off, his foot on her chest now, pulling up on her ring finger. Lucy looked away. When she turned back, he was holding the ring up to the sun. Then he wiped it on his pants and pocketed it. He went and knelt over Nelson and worked his ring off. He continued to search every corpse. From Jacques, he took the cross from his neck, the leather from his wrists, and pried the rings from his fingers. From Barnet, a pocket watch.

When he finished he took one last drag on his cigarette while he scanned the area, then stomped the cigarette out with the toe of his boot. He started to walk back to the horse.

A bead of sweat ran down Lucy's forehead and into her eye, but she didn't move. She blinked her eyes and tried to focus, but her headache throbbed so badly her vision was beginning to blur. A sudden sharp cramp in her leg caused her to wince. She was starving and aching with thirst. If she didn't have water soon, she would die. Whoever this terrifying man was, he might be her only hope.

The man reached the horse, and it whinnied and shook its mane. He spoke softly to the animal as he untied the reins from the branch.

Time stood still for a moment. Her hands shook violently. Slowly, she stood, raised the gun, and pointed it at him as she stepped out from behind the bush. "Excuse me, sir?"

He turned and drew his gun on her. "Drop your gun."

"Please, sir, I need water."

He motioned to her gun, slowly walking toward her now. "Drop it."

The gun trembled in her hands, but she kept it pointed on him.

"Lady, I'll shoot you," he said, still coming at her. "Drop your gun."

She bent down and lay the gun on the ground in front of her, then stood with her hands up.

He stopped just in front of her and stood there, his gun still pointed at her. His face was dirty. So was the bandana around his neck. There was blood on one of his hands. He was tall, at least six feet, with a lean but muscular build. His eyes met hers intensely for a moment. Then he looked past her, scanning the forest, then surveyed the massacre and the stagecoach again. He turned back to her.

"Indians?" he asked.

"I believe so."

"Yeah, who knows. Wouldn't surprise me if it was white men dressed as them. Nothing's ever as it seems out here. You the only one survived?"

She nodded. "Sir, I beg you. A drink of your water."

Her eyes felt out of focus again, and she rubbed them and looked up at the sky. She could no longer see the ravens or vultures, and her hands were trembling. She looked back at the man. He was eyeing her strangely now. She could hear his voice and see his lips moving, but it was muffled, and her body felt weighted, as if she were being pulled down into a tunnel. She took a sidestep to try to balance herself. She turned and looked for the coyotes, but everything was going black and she felt herself falling.

Chapter 3

———◆———

SHE WOKE TO THE soft crackle of a fire, with her cheek resting on the cold ground. She tried to sit up, moaned and rolled onto her back, looking up at the stars. Something covered her, a piece of clothing that smelled of cigarette smoke. Her mouth was dry. She wanted water. Footsteps came toward her, and a hand lifted the back of her head. A canteen was put to her lips. She couldn't make out a face in the dark.

"Thank you," she whispered and drifted back to sleep.

When she opened her eyes again, darkness had begun to give way to light and the sky was overcast. The fire was down to the last remaining coals. The smell of smoke filled the air. She shivered and pulled the coat around her, a tan trench coat she didn't recognize.

"Mornin'," said a man's voice. "How you feelin'?"

He sat on a log a few feet from her, eating something out of a can. His gun belt and guns sat beside him, and one of his pant legs was rolled up, revealing dried blood on his calf. He stopped eating and looked over at her. His eyes were almond-shaped and dark hazel. A piece of his dirty blond hair lay across his cheek and he reached up and tucked it behind his ear. She looked around for the stagecoach, but it was nowhere in sight. She didn't know where they were. Just the two of them, and the black horse with the white patch on its face tied to a nearby tree. She looked back at the man. With an unreadable expression on his face, he tossed her a canteen, and she caught it in her lap and unscrewed the cap and took a drink.

"I'm not gonna hurt you," he said. "Figured I couldn't just leave you there. There's a town called Thompson 'bout fifteen miles from here. It's on my way."

She said nothing and looked back at the horse. Had she ridden that thing with him? The man stood, put his gun belt on, and held the can out to her.

"You should eat," he said.

"Thank you," said Lucy as she took it. It was a can of beans half eaten. She spooned a bite. The man went to the horse and adjusted the straps on the saddle. She wondered if he was some sort of trader or a guide maybe, like Jacques, even though he wore guns and had stolen valuables off the dead. She looked around again at the trees and the black horse. "Where are we?"

"We've ridden a few hours south, about a day or two's ride to Denver."

"What'd you say the name of the next town is?"

"Thompson."

"Do you know if there's a stagecoach station in this Thompson? Or somewhere I can send a telegram?"

He lit a cigarette and studied her. "You lose family back in that massacre?"

"I'm traveling alone."

"Where you headed?"

"San Francisco."

He was checking the hooves of the horse now. "The West isn't a place for a woman to be traveling alone."

Lucy ate the last few bites and set the can aside.

He came to her and held out his hand. "We should get going," he said.

She let him help her up. Her legs ached. Dizziness overwhelmed her again. He kept a grip on her arm as he walked her to the horse.

"Thank you," she said. "Forgive me, I don't think I've gotten your name."

"Will."

"Pleased to meet you, Will. I'm Lucy. Lucy Cavanagh, and I'm very grateful for your assistance."

"Grab the horn of the saddle," he said. "And put your left leg in the stirrup."

She bustled her skirt with one hand and reached up and grabbed the saddle with the other. She started to lift her foot but couldn't quite reach, so she bustled her skirt a little tighter, and as she tried again, she felt his hands on the back of her thighs and he hoisted her up onto the horse, forcing her right leg up and over. She sat straddling the saddle now in the most unladylike position. He leapt up behind her, his body pressed against her backside, and he reached around her and grabbed the reins that lay over the saddle horn, his hand grazing hers. A filthy, calloused hand. Dried blood across his knuckles. He made a clicking sound and spurred the horse into motion. They rode through the forest, through the overgrown bushes and trees.

She'd ridden a horse only once before at a charity polo event on Long Island, sidesaddle, like a proper English lady. That was the day she'd met Walt. She'd thought he was a vagrant at first, or that he'd wandered in by accident. He wore the most eccentric plaid pants and suspenders and had a long grey beard and wild hair. She couldn't remember now how she'd started conversing with him, but he'd turned out to be quite interesting. He was there at the event as a journalist but had just published his first collection of poetry. The name of it eluded her now, something about leaves. What she did remember, clearly to this day, was his unusual wisdom and the last thing he said to her: "*Never believe anything without first searching for veiled intent, my darling. Re-examine all you've been told at school or church or in any book, and dismiss that which insults your soul.*"

When they reached a small stream, Will stopped to water the horse and stretch his legs. Lucy crouched down beside the water and washed the dust from her hands. The water was icy cold, and she cupped it in her hands and drank. Will was standing beside the horse, rummaging through his saddlebag, and she caught a glimpse of the ivory handle of Barnet's gun.

"I'd like my gun back, please," she said.

He lit his cigarette and shook the match out. "No can do, little lady."

She stared at him incredulously.

He lifted one of the horse's hind legs and cleaned the hoof with a tool he'd produced from his pocket. "Different rules out here, sweetheart," he said. "If you point a gun on someone, you best make damn sure they don't get their hands on it or it's theirs to keep."

At dusk, they rode up a ravine onto a worn-out trail that widened into a road. The first building they saw was a wooden shack that stood alone. A dog slept lazily on the porch and didn't look up as they rode past. Farther down, a general store appeared on the right, then a brothel with "Lou Lou's House of Ladies" painted across the window in giant swirly letters. A man in a top hat and three women in white transparent lace dresses stood outside of it. One of the women blew a kiss and waved. She felt Will's arm go up in a wave behind her.

A wagon passed them on the left. A dog and three children sat in the back and stared at her with their dirty, solemn little faces. They rode past two houses that were boarded up and abandoned. Foreclosure signs on the door. A bank. A livery. More houses. Farther ahead, five horsemen rode toward them, spurs, bandanas, and trench coats flapping open in the breeze, exposing the guns that hung from their hips. One of them had no facial hair, and Lucy did a double take, realizing it was a woman. *A woman. On the horse by herself. Dressed in trousers and a hat and guns just like a man.* Lucy watched her pass out of the corner of her eye, never so intrigued by something in all her life.

Will stopped the horse a little farther down, on what seemed the main street. There were a few buildings. A bakery, with a few customers inside and a parked wagon across the way. A livery and a grain and feed store, with three men on the porch standing with their hands in their pockets, eyeing Lucy.

Will dismounted and helped her down. "That's a café called Magda's. She's got a few rooms upstairs she rents at a good price. Or used to, anyway."

Lucy studied the building he'd pointed out. It had a broken window and no sign.

Will reached into his pocket and held out two gold coins to her. "This should cover a room for the night and a meal. Sorry I can't help you more."

Lucy paused and eyed the coins in his hand, then reached out and took them. "You've done plenty. I don't know how to ever repay your kindness."

"No need," he said. "I best get goin'. Good luck to you, miss."

"Good luck to you, too, Will. And thank you."

He gave a curt nod, turned, and began to walk away in an easy stride, as though he had nowhere to be. The gun belt rode low on the hips of his blood-stained pants and sweat marks sullied his grey shirt. His spurs jangled as he led the horse down the street. Lucy reached down and rubbed a cramp out of her left thigh. Her legs, bottom, and lower back were sore from the saddle. What a story this would be to tell one day, riding into a dusty western town on a horse with a desperado. The girls back in New York would scarcely believe her. It was all so surreal, she barely believed it herself.

A door chimed, and a woman exited the bakery.

"Pardon me," Lucy called out. "I'm looking for the stagecoach station and telegraph office? And the name of a hotel?"

The woman looked at Lucy with a confused expression on her face, then she looked her up and down and shook her head.

"Ain't no hotel," she said. "Just Magda's. No stagecoach or telegraph office neither. Not in these parts. Have to go to Denver for that. But if you're in the need of some sourdough bread, we got the best baker in Colorado Territory. But hurry, they sell out fast."

Lucy bid her good day and looked back down the street where Will had been, but he was nowhere to be seen. A dog was barking from somewhere in the distance. Two horsemen were now riding toward her. One was overweight and wore a badge. As they passed, he flashed her a strange smile that gave her chills. Suddenly, she felt very alone. Maybe more alone and helpless than she had at the stagecoach in the middle of nowhere amongst the dead. She turned and walked toward the deserted looking building.

She could see the tiny sign on the ground beside the door as she neared—MAGDA'S, carved in a piece of driftwood. She peered through the front window. Two men and a woman were sitting around a table, eating and playing cards. She went to the door and started to open it, but something blocked it—a man lying asleep on the floor. Smoke billowed out. A woman was laughing and speaking in a low, raspy voice. "You sonofabitch Hadley, I knew you was bluffin', you Goddamn sonofabitch."

Lucy poked her head inside. "Hello," she said.

The woman paused from shuffling the deck and looked up at Lucy, with uninterested eyes. "Well, come on in then, don't be shy," she said. "Just step over Lawrence. He won't hurt ya. He's just drunk."

Lucy pushed on the door a little more. The body rolled over, and he let out a snorting sound. A chair slid back, and the woman walked over to Lucy in the doorway and kicked the man on the floor.

"Get up, you ol' drunk. You're blockin' the fuckin' doorway," she said. "Go home to your wife. You ain't sleepin' under my roof again, you fat bastard."

The body on the floor didn't move.

"Is he all right?" asked Lucy.

"Oh sure," said the woman, taking a drag of her cigarette. "What can I do ya for?"

She had wild blond hair, long and cascading down her back, backcombed and tousled, as though messy on purpose. And she wore a patchwork dress of multicolored silk and tweed. The woman blinked and shrugged at Lucy, as though hurrying a response.

"I was told you might have a room available?"

"Sorry, darlin', don't got anything left. Check down at the saloon. I think Gilbert's still got a few rooms available. He'll be the one bartendin'. Tall. Big mop'a dark hair."

"A saloon? No, no. Please, I know I must look a fright, but I can pay." Lucy took the coins from her pocket and showed her. "Please, a bed. And a meal. I'm so hungry."

The woman took the coins, inspected them, and put them in her pocket. Then she punched Lucy in the stomach, so hard it knocked Lucy back into the street.

Lucy heard the door slam, and she lay coughing and gasping for air. Eventually, she stood, dusted herself off, and started to walk. Her stomach throbbed and her eyes stung with tears. A sign creaked from somewhere above, and she jumped. She passed a store window and looked at herself, barely recognizing the reflection, everything about her filthy. She brought her sleeve up and wiped something off her cheek. She tried to smooth her hair a little, comb it with her fingers. Then she walked on.

The saloon was near the edge of town at the end of Main Street. A giant canvas with big bold black letters: THE LONELY DOVE SALOON. She slowed her pace as she approached. The building was bullet ridden, and the front window was shattered. Smoke billowed out above two large swinging doors. All she could see of the inside was a wooden chandelier lit with candles. She could hear a drone of conversation. Laughter rang out. She smoothed her hair again, crossed the street, and entered through the swinging doors.

Men were sitting around a few tables, smoking and drinking and playing cards. Ten or twelve, and they all looked up as she entered. One of them lewdly waved his tongue out at her and she quickly turned away. There was a piano in the corner, but no one was playing it. Three prostitutes beside it. Dresses gaped open, their breasts showing. If they were embarrassed or in any way ashamed, they did not show it. Candles were lit everywhere. A blood stain on the floor. Mounted animal heads of antelope, deer and bear decorated the walls. A burly voice from one of the tables asked if she needed a lap to sit on, but she didn't look. At the back of the room was the bar. Three men sat off to the right of it, and a lone man with a thin grey ponytail sat on the far left. Behind the bar, shelves lined the wall, brimming with whiskey bottles, and the bartender, with a mop of shaggy dark hair, stood ready to serve.

Lucy started making her way back to the bar, and a girl in red, carrying a tray of drinks, came out of nowhere, nearly colliding with her but just brushing her shoulder. She wore a low-cut, tight, red-velvet dress. Cleavage spilling out. Black kohl lined her intense green eyes. Her hair was pinned up, loose and chaotic.

The girl looked Lucy up and down with a scowl. "Watch where you're fuckin' goin'," she said.

Lucy said nothing and continued making her way across the room to the bar. The bartender was pouring a long line of whiskey shots.

"Excuse me, are you Gilbert?" Lucy asked. "Magda said you might have a room available. I also am in need of a ride to Denver, to send a telegram. I was hoping you could help."

The bartender motioned for the girl in the red dress to come over while he finished pouring the whiskey.

The lone man with the ponytail at the end of the bar scooted a few chairs over and sat closer to Lucy. "If they don't got a room," he slurred, "you can come home with . . . with me."

The way he said it made Lucy's skin crawl and her hands tremble, but she pretended she didn't hear him.

Piano music started. A fast beat with complicated chords, like nothing she'd ever heard before. One of the prostitutes was playing it. Another began to move to the music, smiling as she danced as though she hadn't a care in the world. Lucy was fascinated. The ponytailed man slurred out something she couldn't understand and then stood from his chair and grabbed Lucy's arm.

She pulled away and stepped back out of his reach. "Sir, please!"

As the man tried to sit back down on his stool, he knocked his glass of whiskey over. He let out a wheezy laugh. "Shit," he said. "I'm all flust-flustered."

The girl in the red dress came to the bar and wiped up the mess and poured the man with the ponytail another whiskey. The bartender asked her if that Boston fellow had checked out of Room 3. She'd go check after serving whiskeys to Sheriff Mason and that handsome stranger he was talking to. The room would cost a dollar for the night, she informed Lucy as she poured the whiskeys.

Across the bar, the prostitute in white danced erotically, making her way from table to table. Someone smacked her on her backside, and she turned back and winked at him. The ponytailed man slurred something out again and took a step closer. Lucy ignored him and turned her focus away from him to the other end of the bar. The girl in the red dress was now carrying a tray of whiskeys over to the three men at the end. She set a whiskey in front of one of them, then ran her hand along his face and tucked a piece of his shaggy blond hair behind his ear. Then she leaned in and whispered something in his ear. The man turned ever so slightly toward Lucy.

Lucy leaned forward for a better look. "Will?"

He took a bite of his steak and ignored her. Surely it was him.

"Will!" she said it louder this time and waved. "Will! I thought you'd be long gone by now!"

Still, he ignored her.

"Will? Will! It's me, Lucy!"

She took a few steps toward him, then stopped. The fat man beside Will stood and looked back at Lucy. He wore a sheriff's badge. It was the man she'd seen in the street with the unnerving smile. He drew his gun as he turned back and jabbed it into Will's side. The younger one, standing behind them, drew and pointed a gun at Will's back. Will sat calmly, looking down at his plate, with a strange grip on his steak knife. Then in a move so swift she'd have missed it had she blinked, Will jabbed the steak knife into the sheriff's throat, then reached back to rip the gun from the kid's hands and shot him between the eyes.

The piano music stopped. A few screams rang out. Chairs scraped across the floor. Blood pooled around the sheriff and the deputy kid that lay dead on the floor. Will leapt over the bar and disappeared from view. A few patrons ran out the swinging doors. Others flipped tables and took cover behind them, then peered out with their guns and fired at the bar. Will stood behind the bar, a gun in both hands, returning fire. Glass shattered and sprayed everywhere. Lucy ducked and covered her head. Bullets pelted the bar inches from her face. She began moving back along the bar.

"Come here, girl," someone hissed from behind a table.

Lucy turned to see the man with the ponytail waving her over, and the girl in the red dress ducked down behind him. Lucy kept moving backward, and when she reached the end of the bar, she peered behind it. The floor was covered in glass and whiskey. Bleeding from the neck, the bartender lay on the floor not moving. Will was crouched down, reloading his gun. He spun it shut and looked at her. His face strangely calm. He reached a hand out to her. She looked back at the townsfolk, hiding behind tables, then took Will's hand and crawled over the bartender's lifeless body. One of the shards pierced and lodged into her hand as she crawled, and she gasped as she quickly pulled it out. Blood ran down the side of her palm. She kept moving and crouched down beside Will. "What's happening?" she whispered.

"Stay down," he said. Then he stood, a gun in each hand, and fired again.

Lucy covered her head as gunfire returned and whiskey bottles smashed to the ground all around her, raining glass. Then the gunfire slowed, and all went quiet again. She lowered her arms. Will was crouched back down. He retrieved a few bullets from his pocket and reloaded again.

"Will Shanks!" a man shouted from outside. "I know that's you in there."

She heard heavy footsteps; then the doors swung open. In the reflection of one of the bottles that remained on the shelf, she made out a large man entering, holding a shotgun pointed at the bar.

"US Marshal Cliff James," he said. "The fun's over, son. Stand up nice and slow with your hands up."

Will stayed crouched down. He rubbed his face and looked at Lucy. Everything quiet for a moment.

The marshal took a few steps closer, and she heard the cocking of a shotgun. "I'm not gonna ask again," he said.

Will holstered one of his guns and opened the chamber of the second and spun it shut. He studied Lucy's face. Then, without warning, he grabbed her by the forearm and yanked her to him violently, his arm around her middle pinning her against him, her back pressed up against his chest. The cold iron end of his gun dug into her temple.

"Don't shoot. I've got the girl!" Will shouted, his voice ringing in her ear as he stood them slowly.

Lucy cried out in pain. Everywhere she looked, guns pointed at her. Everyone stood still. No one fired. She tried to writhe out of Will's grip, but it was no use.

"Drop your weapons! I swear to God I'll kill her. Drop your weapons now!" Will dug the gun harder into her temple. The heat from his breath lingered on her cheek.

Will clicked the safety back. Lucy closed her eyes. When she opened them, every gun pointed at them was slowly lowering to the ground.

"Keep your hands where I can see 'em," Will said, dragging her backwards over the bartender's body. He kicked a backdoor open, backed through it, and let out three sharp whistles. They were outside on a porch in an alleyway. Will whistled again. He was dragging her toward the railing. The galloping hooves and quiet neighing of a horse sounded. He lowered the gun from her temple and fired at a rooftop across the way. She looked up but couldn't see whom he was shooting at. Then his black horse came around the corner and was galloping toward them, saddled and riderless. Will let go of Lucy for a split second and leapt up onto the railing, then he reached down and took her by the forearm and lifted her to him, grasping her by the midsection again like a rag doll with her legs dangling in the air. They jumped. For a moment, they were airborne. As they landed on the horse, her face crashed into its neck and the wind was knocked out of her.

Will spurred the animal into a gallop. Gunshots rang out from somewhere behind. Then the sound of horses in the distance. Dogs barking. Blood ran down her nose and mouth, and she wheezed and struggled to catch her breath, grasping to get a grip on the horse's mane as its hooves pounded the earth beneath her.

It felt like an eternity before the gunshots grew faint, and Will slowed the horse. When they came to a stop, he loosened his grip on her, and as the horse stopped, he let her slide down to the ground.

She stood bent over with her hands on her knees. The world was spinning. Darkness had almost fallen upon them. Still struggling for breath and with an aching side, she ran a hand along her ribcage but couldn't tell if anything was broken. Will dismounted and stood beside her. He poured water onto his handkerchief and held it out to her.

"Are you all right?" he asked. "It was the only way outta there alive. I didn't mean to hurt you."

Lucy took the handkerchief and dabbed at her nose and mouth.

"I'm so sorry," he said. "I didn't mean to hurt you."

Her eyes were watering, and her tongue felt swollen. She moved it around in her mouth to make sure all of her teeth were intact. She leaned over and spat blood.

"Can I have the canteen?" she asked.

He untied it from the saddle and gave it to her. She took a long drink, then poured some more water on the handkerchief.

"What the hell were you doing in that saloon anyway?" he asked.

"There was no vacancy at Magda's. And no stagecoach station or telegraph office. I have to get to Denver."

A dog sounded in the distance, and Will looked back in the direction they had come from.

"They're not far behind," he said. Then he took the canteen from her and tied it back to the saddle. "I'll take you with me to Denver if you want."

Lucy looked back in the direction of the town.

Will leapt up onto the horse. "I gotta keep moving," he said. "You can come with me, or you can wait for the townspeople. I'm sorry again, for what happened back there." He waited a moment, then spurred his horse and started riding off.

Darkness was falling fast. The night was still, and there was no rustling of leaves or crickets chirping. Just the sound of him riding away. And the barking of the coon dogs in the distance, growing closer. She was shivering now and pictured them coming at her, baring their teeth and foaming at the mouth, along with unruly drunken townsmen on horseback. She'd be at their mercy. The taste of blood lingered in her mouth. She spat again.

"Wait," she said, and started after him.

CHAPTER 4

———◆———

THEY RODE LONG AND steady into the night. She had a vague memory of dozing off and Will catching her as she nearly fell from the saddle. She lay now with her face against his chest, cradled in his arms, his trench coat draped over her. It was dark, and she looked up at the outline of his face in the moonlight. His eyelids fell in long slow blinks.

He pulled back on the reins and they stopped.

"We're gonna stop here for a few hours," he said and lowered her down off the horse.

"What time is it?" she asked.

"Two or three in the morning, I reckon."

"Where are we?"

"'Bout a day's ride from Denver," he said as he dismounted and gave his back a stretch. He tied the horse to one of the trees, then began to walk away. "Stay here with the horse."

"Where are you going?"

He kept walking and disappeared through the forest.

She was still holding his trench coat and wrapped it around her shoulders and sat down beside a tree. The sky was overflowing with stars. The sound of a stream trickled from somewhere in the distance. She lay down on the cold ground, rested her head in her hands, and closed her eyes.

She woke to the smell of food. It was still dark, the glow of a small fire the only light. Will was on his knees, holding a small carcass, ripping meat off with his pocketknife. A pile of feathers lay beside him.

"What is that?" she asked.

"Chicken."

She stood and went to sit beside him, the coat still wrapped around her shoulders. She reached her hands over the flames. A few pieces of meat cooked in a small pan near the edge of the fire. Smoke wafted at her, and she closed her eyes for a moment, then looked over at Will.

"Where did you get a chicken?"

"We passed a farm about a half mile back," he said as he scraped more meat from the carcass and added it to the pan.

Lucy looked back in the direction they'd come from. "Did you steal it?"

"Are you hungry, Lucy?"

She said nothing and pulled the coat tighter around her.

Will rolled his pant leg up and inspected his wound in the light of the fire. A circular wound, the size of a coin. He dug into his saddlebag and produced a tin of salve and smeared it across the wound.

"What happened to your leg?" she asked.

"Bullet."

"Who shot you?"

"I robbed a bank."

"You robbed a bank."

"Yes." He flipped a few more pieces of meat, stabbed a piece with the end of his knife, blew on it, and held it out to her.

She took it and ate it. It was surprisingly delicious, charred yet moist.

"What happened to your hand?" he asked as he reached out and gently took her wrist in his hand and inspected the blood on her palm.

"I cut it on the glass, crawling across the floor of that saloon."

He took the canister and dipped his finger in and gently rubbed it into her cut. It stung slightly, but to her surprise, he leaned closer and blew on the cut. His gaze lifted from her hand and held her eyes for a moment. Then he released his grip and sat back down beside the pan of meat.

She studied his face across the fire, as he flipped a few more pieces of chicken. The walls of the stagecoach stations had been littered with wanted posters. They were terrifying, mean looking sketches of cheats, thieves, and murderers. Most of them with ugly, pocketed faces and scars. Will had well-defined cheekbones. Full lips. Almond-shaped eyes. Take away the dirt, sweat, and unwashed hair, he was actually rather handsome, in a rugged sort of way. She thought back to the shootout at the saloon. Now she understood why Will had ignored her when she'd used his name. She thought of how effortlessly and quick he'd killed the sheriff and deputy, and the way he'd used her as a human shield after she'd crawled to him for safety. Would he have killed her, if it had come to that, to get himself out alive?

He handed her another piece of chicken, and she ate it. She hadn't realized how hungry she was.

As it cooked, they continued to eat piece by piece with their fingers, staring quietly into the fire. When they were finished, Will packed up the horse and threw water on the fire.

"Let's go," he said.

At dawn the darkness lifted into rolling grey clouds. As they rode quietly through the morning, the terrain gradually became rockier and Lucy clung to the saddle as the horse traversed the ravines. Amazing how the horse was able to keep its footing. Sometime in the mid-afternoon they rode out onto a small cliff. Will stopped and pointed out at a spot in the landscape.

"If it weren't so cloudy, we'd be able to see the snow-capped peaks of the Rockies from here," he said.

What she could see was magnificent. Rolling hills of tall majestic evergreens and streams winding amidst the rocks. The Rocky Mountains had only existed for her in a painting until this moment, and now here she was, in the foothills, with the highest peaks just beyond the clouds. They stared out in silence for a while.

"I don't like the look of those clouds," Will said. "We're not going to make it to Denver tonight. I've got to try to find us some shelter."

He spurred the horse and they rode on.

By evening, the sky had transformed to a seamless dark grey and the wind turned to powerful gusts. Will guided the horse through the trees, up onto a road. Eventually, they came to a fork in the road, two small wooden signs marking the way. Straight ahead, the main road to Denver. To the left, a narrow, overgrown trail. Lucy stared at the sign as they rode past.

"Valley City," she said. "That's where the young couple from my stagecoach was headed."

"The couple wearing the wedding bands?"

"Yes."

"Did they have family out here or something?"

"An uncle of Nelson's. They were going to stay with him while they got settled. Nelson had a job waiting for him at a local lumber mill."

Will eased back on the reins and slowed the horse. "You remember their names?"

"Emily and Nelson Holloway."

"You sure about that?"

"Yes. Why?"

Will pulled back on the reins, turned the horse around, and began guiding them down the narrow trail toward Valley City.

"We just found our shelter," he said. "Tell me everything you know about them."

What she knew wasn't much. They were newlyweds, farmers from Missouri. Nelson was planning to work at the lumber mill until he could get their crops in. He'd fought in the war, though he never spoke of it, but Emily did. She'd missed him terribly and thought him dead and never wanted to let him out of her sight again. Emily was illiterate, never having attended a day of school. Lucy had never met anyone who hadn't attended proper school and had struggled to maintain composure when Emily had told her so matter-of-factly. But apparently, she could bake a pie and had won local awards for it. She was homesick for her parents in Missouri.

Lucy thought of Emily's parents now, eagerly awaiting word from their daughter.

Will stayed silent, taking in everything as he guided the horse down the trail. Before them, the sky, a mix of dark clouds, melded with a strange light, as though something prophetic was unfolding. She closed her eyes and whispered words she hadn't said in years: "Our Father, which art in heaven. Hallowed be thy name. Thy kingdom come. Thy will be . . ."

"Lucy, stop that," Will said. "And here, hold these for a second." He put the reins in her hands.

It took him three tries to light the match in the wind when finally, the smell of cigarette smoke wafted past her and he reached back and grabbed the reins as the horse took them down the overgrown path. After they'd ridden in silence for a while, he said, "We'll say we were traveling with them, just wanted to pay our respects, tell the uncle in person, in case the stagecoach company hadn't. Hopefully, he'll take pity on us, let us stay the night."

"Do you mean to tell this Uncle Holloway that we're a couple?"

"Brother and sister."

A gust of wind came on, and she tucked her face into her arm.

As they neared the town, the path widened into a pitted road. A few small buildings came into view. A white-washed building with bars over the windows and the word "JAIL" in big bold black letters. An empty, lone wagon parked outside. Farther down, they rode past a livery stable. A welder. A sign that read "Kelly's Mill" and pointed down an alley. A hotel. A few deserted-looking houses.

Light was coming from one of the windows up ahead. Will slowed and rode the horse up to the porch as they neared Hanson's general store and Mercantile. A candle lit up the windowsill and a dark-haired woman stood at the counter inside.

"I'm gonna ask directions to the Holloway place," he said.

They dismounted, and he tied the horse to the rail.

"I'll give a good performance," said Lucy. "I've always loved the theater and thought I'd make a great actress."

"Let me do the talking," he said.

They ascended the steps to the door, and as he opened it for her, he held her arm for a moment. "Don't forget I'm armed under this trench coat."

The store was packed with rows of shelves piled high with all kinds of merchandise. Fabric. Canned goods. Tins of jerky. Candy jars. Pots and pans. Guns. Ammunition. The woman they'd seen in the window looked up. Her hair and eyes were jet-black and set in a round, plump face.

Will took his hat off. "Evening, ma'am," he said. "I was wonderin' if you could give me directions to the Holloway place."

The woman threw her hands to her cheeks and gasped. "Nelson and Emily!" she shouted. "Oh, sweet name of Jesus, you're here! You're finally here!"

"Oh no, ma'am," said Lucy. "We're . . ."

Will put his arm around Lucy and gave her a squeeze. "Yes, ma'am," he said. "We're here."

The woman rushed around the counter, a wide smile across her face. "Well, welcome, welcome! I'm Luvinia. Luvinia Hanson. Call me Vinnie, though. Everyone does." Vinnie peered past them out the window. "Where are your things?"

"Our stagecoach was attacked, ma'am," said Will. "We lost everything."

Vinnie just stared at them, wide-eyed. A stricken look crossed her face as she gave them both another once over. Lucy's heart started to race as she searched the woman's face for any hint that she was on to them.

"Oh, you poor, poor dears," Vinnie said, with tears in her eyes. "I'm afraid I have more bad news. Your uncle passed away a few days ago. We buried him just the day before yesterday. Gave him a real nice funeral. Sang 'Onward Christian Soldiers.' I hope he liked it, even though he wasn't a church-going man. Course, I never cared much for church either. Oh, listen to me rambling on. You must be starving. I'm going to go upstairs and pack you up some stew. There's plenty extra. Don't you move a muscle. I'll be back in a jiff," she said, then disappeared behind a side door.

Lucy stood still, listening to her footsteps ascending a set of creaky stairs to somewhere above them. "Have you gone mad?" she asked Will. "Why would you let her think we're the Holloways?

We'll never pass as a couple, or farmers from Missouri. Heaven help us, she's probably going for the sheriff."

Will said nothing and went down one of the small packed aisles to a shelf with guns and ammunition. He opened a container and took a handful of bullets and pocketed them. Above them, pots and pans clanked around, then the sound of footsteps descending the staircase, and Vinnie's smiling face came through the door.

She carried a small box wrapped in a dishtowel.

"Now, I'm a Texas girl," she said. "I hope it's not too spicy. It's called chili *con carne*. A Spanish stew with peppers. And a small loaf of cornbread."

Lucy clutched the box to her chest. "Thank you so much, Ms. Hanson."

"Oh no you don't, it's Vinnie. Now, you best get riding if you're going to beat this storm. Your uncle's place is back the way you rode in, first left out of town just before the jail. Follow that road about a mile, past the Anderson farm."

Vinnie flung her arms around Lucy in a big bear hug that she could not return for fear of dropping the box of stew. Vinnie smelled of musky perfume. Lucy couldn't remember the last time someone hugged her like that.

"I'm so happy you're here!" said Vinnie. "And don't you worry none about your things. We take care of each other around here. We'll get you all fixed up in no time."

Will gently took Lucy by the arm. "Thank you kindly," he said, and guided her to the front door.

The wind gusted as he opened it.

"Don't be strangers now, you hear?" Vinnie shouted as they went outside. "Oh, and Wesley's got your uncle's horse and cow at the livery. He's been takin' real good care of 'em for ya."

Will grabbed the door just as it was about to slam behind them and looked back at Vinnie.

"Thank you, ma'am," he said.

CHAPTER 5

———◆———

THE SKY DARKENED AS they rode. Lightning flashed in the distance and thunder rumbled. Lucy clutched the box of food in front of her, her hair whipping across her face in the wind. Will's arm came around her and clutched her to him as he spurred the horse into a gallop.

The Holloway property reminded her of something out of an Edgar Allan Poe story—a long, overgrown drive, with a giant cottonwood at the end, and a desolate building on either side. To the right stood a lopsided barn, with a large door that creaked loudly as it swung open in the wind, then slammed back with a bang. Beside it was parked an old wooden wagon with rusting wheels. Surrounding the barn was a run-down fence made of wood and chicken wire.

To the left of the property was the house. A small square structure that had a front porch with a few broken rail posts. A rocking chair was moving back and forth with the wind, as though a ghost sat there, expecting them. There was a crack in the front eye-like window. A few of the shingles on the roof flapped in the wind. A chimney rose from one side.

Will guided the horse to the porch where they stopped and dismounted.

"Get inside," he shouted over the wind, then grabbed the horse by the halter and began leading it across the yard to the barn.

Lucy went up the porch steps. Something ran out from beneath the rocking chair, and she jumped and nearly tripped. A cat. A skinny, grey little thing. It ran off across the yard. She opened the front door, left it ajar to let some light in and took a few steps inside. A stale smell. An unredeemed dreariness. A small brick fireplace, built into the wall on the left, had a few logs piled in it, ready for a fire. On a mantel above hung a rusty shotgun and a stuffed fox, its eyes gleaming in the darkness. Straight ahead on the back wall stood a black stove and a counter with a small washbasin. To her right, beneath a large window, she saw a small wooden table, with a bench on each side.

She set the box on the table and unpacked it. Vinnie had packed them a feast. Two giant bowls of the chili *con carne*, two spoons, and a loaf of cornbread. She cut herself a small slice of the cornbread and spooned a bite of the chili. Flavors of meat stewed in tomatoes, onion, garlic, pepper and something very spicy. It was the best meal she'd eaten since leaving New York. She watched out the window while she ate. Will emerged from the barn and struggled to shut the large door. At last, he shut it and started across the yard toward the house.

He entered and set his saddlebag and lantern on the table. He struck a match and lit the lantern. "How's the chili?" he asked.

"Delicious. I still don't understand why you let that woman believe we were the Holloways."

Will took a few bites, then went and knelt before the fireplace, arranged the logs, and lit them. As the fire began to smoke, he stood and took the shotgun down from the mantel. He opened the barrel, took the shell out and inspected it, reloaded it, and cocked it back. Then he brought it to his shoulder and closed an eye and aimed at the back wall. "You know what the first rule of lying is?"

"I try not to make a habit of lying."

"Figure out what people already want to believe," he said. Then he put the shotgun back on the mantel, stoked the fire, and came and sat down at the table across from her and continued eating.

A hostile rain began pelting the roof. A drop of water landed on the table. Then another, and another, forming a small pool. Lucy looked up to see cobwebs and a few cracks where rain seeped in and was now dripping down. They ate fast, and when they were finished, they warmed themselves in front of the fire, sitting side by side, on a blanket Will retrieved from the bedroom.

Will's saddlebag lay on the floor beside him and he took the tin of salve from it, rolled up his pant leg and unwrapped his wound. Lucy could see the small red circle of a bullet wound.

"I take it the bank robbery wasn't a success?" she asked, regretting it as soon as she asked.

He took papers and tobacco from his bag and began rolling a cigarette. "No, it wasn't."

"Are there wanted posters?"

"Yes."

"What is it you're headed to Denver for? Is it the next job?"

He lit the cigarette, took a drag, and exhaled a long stream of smoke. A dull scent of hickory, black licorice, menthol in the air that she found strangely calming.

"Can I ask you something?" she asked.

"I'd rather you didn't."

"That day you came across me, at the massacre. Why did you help me?"

"I couldn't have just left you for dead."

"But you killed that deputy and sheriff. And the bartender and several others."

"They meant to arrest me, and see me hang. Killing isn't a choice; it's an instinct. You know when someone or something means to kill you. In a flash of a second, you know it's kill or be killed. Out here, it's survival."

Lucy held her hands out to the flames and thought about it. What was this barbaric world she'd stumbled into?

"It's no different where you come from. The civilized are just better at hiding it." He took a drag on his cigarette and grabbed the canister of salve. "Let me see your hand."

She held her hand out to him, and he gently held her wrist, turning her hand to the side to inspect the cut in the light of the fire. He rubbed a dab of the salve into it. His hands were an unexpected combination of calloused and soft. She felt her face flush. "Thank you," she said and pulled her hand away, then gazed into the fire. Feeling warmer now.

"You still have those coins I gave you?"

"Magda took them."

"I can sell the jewelry I took off your comrades in case the lines are down and you need a hotel for a night or two. You have someone you can telegram for help?"

She remained quiet and thought about it, then decided to tell him about her father being arrested and their assets frozen, in case he had any ideas of holding her hostage and demanding ransom. She told him of her father's history with fraud, how he'd always said there was nothing you couldn't buy or talk your way out of. But this was different. This was the first time her father had tried to marry her off, tried to secure her future. He was still in jail awaiting the trial date when she'd left, so to answer Will's question—yes, she did have someone to telegram: his attorneys. That was all she'd meant to divulge. But then, unsure whether it was a need to fill the silence or a need to speak it out loud, she found herself reminiscing about the night she'd left New York. She'd sat at the train station alone, feeling a strange combination of fear of the thought of getting on that train all by herself and confidence because she'd read once, in a book by a philosopher whose name escaped her now, of his deep-seated belief that if one followed their heart, everything would work out for them. All she had was some cash and an old letter with the last known address of Aunt Louisa in San Francisco, her only living relative, the sister of her long-deceased mother whom Lucy's always had unanswered questions about. In leaving, Lucy had rejected her father and the marriage proposal he'd arranged, and in that she'd rejected security.

"You must find me the most naïve fool," she said. "But all I could think was, what was the point of security if I knew I would drown in it?"

He flicked his cigarette into the fire. "There's nothing foolish about deciding to depend on yourself."

There was a loud bang outside that made them both jump. Will grabbed one of his guns and went to the window.

"What is it?" she whispered. "Are you worried we were followed?"

He stood quietly gazing out at the darkness for awhile. "I think it's just the wind," he said.

She stood and went to the door in the back of the house. It opened onto a small room with a bed in the center of it, a window beside it.

"I'm taking the bed," she said.

"We *are* married now," said Will.

She looked back at him and said nothing, then shut the door behind her and went and climbed into bed.

She was still awake when the door opened and Will walked in carrying the lantern. She lay the other way and listened to him take off his boots, then undo his gun belt and set it down on the floor beside him. Then he lay down on the floor and blew out the lantern. Lucy grabbed one of the pillows and handed it down to him.

"Thank you," he said.

Lucy woke the next morning to the sound of a wagon coming down the road. Will was asleep on the floor, lying on his stomach. The sheets on the bed were yellow and stained and smelled of something she couldn't quite explain. She quietly got up and tiptoed past him to the window. Coming toward the house was a two-horse hitch, pulling a flat, uncovered wagon. Two people sat atop, one of them in an oversized red hat.

"Will," she whispered.

He didn't move, save for the slight rise and fall of his chest.

"Will," she whispered again, then carefully crept out of the room, closing the door behind her.

The dirty bowls of stew from last night still sat in the washbasin. The house looked even more dismal in the light of day. Cobwebs. Dirty walls. A layer of dust on the counter. The fire burned down to coals and ash. She went and opened the front door and went out onto the porch.

The day was overcast. A lingering smell of rain filled the air. An evergreen tree had snapped at the base and now leaned against the side of the barn, slightly caving one of the walls, but the building still stood upright. Will's horse, Zeta, was outside in the small fenced-in area. Past the barn, the rolling hills and trees, lay the mountains, barely visible through the clouds. The wagon was coming closer and turned up the drive toward the house. As it neared, she recognized Vinnie from the general store last night. Vinnie was smiling and waving frantically at Lucy.

"Valley City Welcome Wagon!" Vinnie shouted out.

As they reached the porch, the man beside her pulled back on the reins and halted the wagon. Vinnie hopped down. Her oversized hat was adorned with roses and feathers, and she wore a red-and-white checkered cotton dress, high at the neck with lace detailing and ruffles across the bodice. The man was slender, with reddish, greying hair and a gentle demeanor. Vinnie was talking a mile a minute. She introduced the man as her husband, Thomas, and told Lucy how she'd been up all night worrying and woke early to tell Thomas to hitch up the wagon, knowing she wouldn't have a moment's peace until she saw for herself that they'd made it all right and were getting settled in.

Thomas went to the back of the wagon unloaded a wooden box.

"A few things to get you started," said Vinnie, giggling with excitement.

"My goodness," said Lucy. "You didn't have to do that."

"Thomas," Vinnie said, "take it in the house for her."

"Oh no, that's not necessary," Lucy said as she reached out to take the box. "I can take it from here. I'm much stronger than I look."

"Fiddlesticks!" Vinnie said. "Out of the way, lady!" Vinnie was beaming as she came up the porch steps and brushed past Lucy into the house, Thomas just behind.

Lucy followed them inside and glanced over at the bedroom door. It was cracked open, and she could see the shadow of Will's feet behind it. Were there wanted posters of him in this town? Would he be recognized now in the light of day? She pictured Thomas and Vinnie laying on the floor with blood pooling around them like the sheriff and deputy back at that saloon. Her heart was pounding. Thomas set the box down on the counter, and Vinnie opened the cupboard. She gave a "tsk-tsk" and shook her head. She took a rag and wiped down the cupboard as Thomas unpacked the box onto the counter. Two jars of tomatoes. A bag of flour. Sugar. Jam. Vinnie's famous blueberry jam, a first-prize winner at the annual town picnic four years running now. The counter was piling up. A few cans of beans. Eggs. Vinnie was putting items into the cupboard, carrying on about how they take care of their own around here and keep a donation box in the store for occasions such as this. Then she stood, holding one of the cans, and looked around the room. She asked where the mister of the house was. Lucy looked at the shadow beneath the bedroom door.

"He's still asleep," she said.

Vinnie howled and covered her mouth, as though it was the most scandalous thing she'd ever heard. "What a rascal!" she said. Then she stopped loading the cupboard and turned to Lucy with her hands on her hips. "Why, with these empty cupboards, what on earth have you managed to find for breakfast?"

"Oh, I hadn't gotten around to breakfast just yet."

Vinnie stared at Lucy for a moment, then turned and grabbed the pan from the cupboard, set it atop the stove, and told Thomas to hand her the matches.

"Sit your pretty little self down at the table right this minute, young lady," she said. "Vinnie Hanson is about to cook you up some of her famous flapjacks." She winked, then turned and lit the stove.

"Honestly, Vinnie, please don't trouble yourself. I can't let . . ."

"Uh-uh-uh, not another word. Sit."

Lucy slowly sat at the table. She shouldn't have answered the door. Now she pictured Will standing behind the door, a gun in each hand. Her hands were clammy and she was starting to perspire as Vinnie rattled on, telling Lucy how she'd been counting the days till their arrival and looking forward to some new faces in town. She knew they were going to be the best of friends. She just knew it.

Then the bedroom door opened slowly. Will stood in the doorway, dressed, with his boots on. It was the first time Lucy had seen him without his gun belt. He gave Vinnie a charming smile, then walked over and shook Thomas's hand. He never looked back at Lucy but stood with Thomas, who began a brief history of the town, of its founder, Alister Kelly, and the annual picnic he threw each year in honor of the people who made the town possible, which was always a hoot. There was a lumber mill, with jobs available. He wondered if Will was planning to plant a crop and they talked of farming here verses farming in Missouri. The difference in soil. She was surprised at Will's knowledge of Missouri and of farming and crops. And breeds of horses. Zeta was an Arabian, and he'd had her for two years now. He still hadn't looked over at Lucy. She looked him up and down, surprised still that he had no guns on him, then stared at his boots. Something stuck out the back of one, causing his pant leg to bulge out slightly at his calf. His gun.

Vinnie dropped batter into the pan, then holding the handle of the pan and using the dust rag as a potholder, she gave it a healthy swirl before setting it back down on the stove. She whistled happily as the men discussed livestock. When she had two plates piled high with flapjacks, she set the pan aside and handed one to Will, then set the other in front of Lucy.

"Breakfast is served," she said, with a self-satisfied smile.

Will came to the table and sat across from Lucy. She took a heaping bite of her flapjacks. Their fluffy texture melted in her mouth. Buttermilk. Just the right amount of sweet. And real maple syrup. She told Vinnie between mouthfuls how divine they were and that this was even better than the Sunday brunch they served at the Regency Royal Hotel on the Upper East Side. She froze as soon as she said it and looked at Will. He'd stopped his fork halfway to his mouth and looked at her with the coldest stare. Vinnie let out a boisterous laugh and said there was a secret ingredient, but they'd never get it out of her. She'd take it to the grave with her. They shouldn't even try.

"Okay," she said after a moment of silence. "It's cardamom. But just a pinch."

Thomas went to open the front door. "Looks like it's gonna rain again," he said. "Me and the missus best be gettin' back to town."

Vinnie wiped down the counter, then pulled out a book from the wooden box. For a moment, Lucy's heart leapt. Then she read the front cover. *A Bible study on the Book of Ruth.* Vinnie set it on the counter, with a wink, and reached back into the box to pull a few shirts out. "Old shirts of Thomas's," she said. "They might be a little tight, but they'll do for now." Then she pulled out a dress for Lucy. It was one of Ava's, the quiet girl in town who ran the café.

The dress was simple and made of cotton. Pastel blue with polka dot ruffles around the high collar.

Vinnie came to the table with the dress. "Stand up, missy," she said. "Let's see if it'll fit."

Lucy stood.

"Arms out," said Vinnie as she held the dress up to Lucy's front. Then she tucked it against her, holding it at her armpits, and pressed it tightly against her breasts. She cupped them upwards slightly with her hands, then measured around Lucy's waist before turning her around to measure hip to hip, pulling the fabric around her backside.

"Oh, to be young and have a great physique again," Vinnie said. Then she reached across the table and playfully smacked Will on the shoulder and laughed. "Get your jaw off the table, mister," she said and gave Lucy a little wink.

Will looked back down at his plate, his face flushed, and took another bite of flapjacks.

"Vinnie," said Thomas, "let's go and let these two eat their breakfast."

Will stood and went to the front porch. Lucy followed and stood beside him. Vinnie was still talking as Thomas helped her into the wagon. She told them she was getting a big shipment later today and to be sure to come start up a bill at the general store and come get anything they need. And she already told Wes at the livery that they'd be coming for the horse and cow. But she hadn't seen the sheriff yet; he'd want to come out and meet them soon as he could.

Will put his arm around Lucy and waved as Thomas flicked the reins and set the buggy off down the driveway.

"Bye for now!" Vinnie shouted.

When they were out of earshot, Lucy whispered, "Are you angry I let them in?"

"Finish your breakfast and let's go."

CHAPTER 6

IT WAS EARLY AFTERNOON by the time they reached Denver, the streets filled with the hustle and bustle of pedestrians. Wagons and buggies of all sizes pulled by horses, mules, or oxen. Gunslingers on horseback. More sheriffs and badges than she'd noticed in other western towns. She felt Will reach up behind her to adjust his hat lower, shadowing his face. Brick and stone layers were at work almost everywhere; it was a city under enormous construction and growth. Will told her about the fire that had devastated the downtown as they rode. From the ashes, emerged building codes and larger, grander buildings than the previous ones made of pine. Large canvas signs, tied across store fronts, told them what was what. Saloons. Gaming houses. The Bank of Denver. Levi's Storage and Commission. A drugstore. The Denver Pioneer. But it was the way they dressed here that intrigued Lucy most. She saw women in everything from puffed out crinoline dresses to simple cotton, many in long delicate gloves and lace-trimmed umbrellas to shield them from the hot sun, and men in dirty trousers and work boots, axes and shovels over their shoulders. It was the high society of

New York City mixed with all the grittiness of a dime store novel's portrait of the Wild West. She loved it.

Will stopped the horse in front of a saloon and they dismounted. He handed Lucy the reins. "I'm going to go pawn that jewelry." He spoke under his breath. "Stay here with the horse."

There was an old man on a chair outside the saloon doors, smoking his pipe. He eyed Lucy curiously but said nothing. Zeta shook out her mane. Lucy patted her on her neck and continued to take in the bustle of the thoroughfare. A wagon carrying several squealing pigs in cages passed her, leaving behind the smell of manure. She drew the back of her hand to her mouth and held her breath for a moment. Two women on horseback were riding toward her now, on her side of the street, conversing and laughing as they rode. She knew the bad etiquette in staring but couldn't help herself. Both wore pretty yet simple satin dresses, their hair worn with a few pieces in the front loosely pinned up, the rest cascading down their backs. Elegant laced-up boots rested in the stirrups. One wore a gun belt, the copper shiny butt of a gun sticking out of the holster. Around her wrist she wore thin strands of leather braided together to create the most interesting bracelet.

Lucy jumped when Will took the reins from her hands. "Let's go," he said.

Lucy and Will continued down the street on foot, the horse following behind on the lead as they made their way down another busy thoroughfare. In the distance, she could see stagecoaches lined outside of a large brick building. A large canvas sign read: "The Overland Stagecoach Company."

They stopped at the end of a long line of stagecoaches. Will reached into his pocket and handed Lucy a few coins. "I wish I had more to give," he said. "You sure you're going to be all right?"

"I'm sure. Thank you, Will. I wish there was a way to repay your kindness."

"You take care of yourself, Lucy Cavanagh. I hope you find what you're looking for in San Francisco."

"Thank you. And good luck to you too, Will." She felt a strange urge to reach out and hug him, but she resisted.

He mounted the horse. Then he tipped his hat to her, jabbed his spurs, and rode off down the street. Lucy watched until he disappeared into the crowd, then she walked past the coaches and entered the stagecoach office.

Inside, the wall was lined with benches and luggage. A few families congregated in small groups throughout the room. To the far right was a long wooden desk with an older gentleman behind it, whom Lucy approached, sparing no details of the massacre nor the troubles she had endured because of it.

He listened with an uninterested expression that Lucy did not care for and stopped her with a wave of his hand. "Proof of payment, please."

"I just told you everything was burned in a massacre while under the care of your company."

"Ma'am, if I had a nickel for every time I heard a story like yours, I'd be a wealthy man. I know of that massacre. There were no survivors. Next." The man waved the next customer in line forward.

"Excuse me, sir, but I will not be dismissed, and I'm not leaving unless it's on a stagecoach bound for San Francisco."

Lucy did leave, eventually, but not on a stagecoach. Instead, she was escorted out by two large employees, who threatened to have the police lock her up for harassment if she returned with another cockamamie story. She stood in the street alone for several minutes, holding back tears, before asking a group of passersby for directions to the telegraph office. She'd have to resort to doing the very thing she'd been dreading since the day she set foot on the train. She was going to have to ask her father for help.

The United States Telegraph and Postal Services was a grand-looking building with a wrap-around porch, just off a busy downtown street, the corner of Fifth and Columbus. Steps led up to the main door. A bell chimed as she entered. She saw red brick walls. Polished wooden floors. To the right-hand side, a long marble counter and a telegraph machine. Behind the counter, the wall was littered with wanted posters, and she searched the sketches for Will's face.

A young man came out from behind a curtain she hadn't noticed near the end of the counter, startling her. His dark hair was greased neatly back, and a thick moustache, gelled up on each side in little whorl, adorned his face.

"What can I help you with, sweetheart?" he asked.

"I need to send a telegram to New York."

"All righty," he said and reached under the counter for a piece of paper and a quill pen. He dabbed it in the ink a few times in an effeminate fashion and shook his wrist in the air, then gazed at her expectantly.

"Please say, 'In distress. Stage attack. Stranded. Denver. Send money.'"

The telegraph operator wrote a few words, then paused and looked up at her, wide-eyed. "A stage attack!" he gasped. "Land sakes, no wonder you look such a fright! You know, my cousin had this friend who saw someone get run over by the wheel of a stagecoach. Dead. Right there on the spot. Can you imagine?"

Lucy wasn't sure what to say and couldn't help but smile. He had a lisp that she found endearing. She searched the wanted posters again behind him. Her heart leapt at the sketch of his face. *Will Shanks. WANTED. Dead or alive. For war crimes. Armed robbery. Murder. $2,000 reward.* It was the most she'd ever seen on any wanted poster. The sketch was not a good likeness, his face vengeful and unpleasant, and his eyes were all wrong. But it was him.

Lucy's heart was racing. She averted her eyes to the counter where a pile of the newspaper *Denver Pioneer* lay. She grabbed the top one and began to read as the operator fiddled with his feather pen and continued to write on the paper. The front-page story was about the upcoming railroad to connect them to Cheyenne, set to commence this fall, and included interviews with business owners excited for what it would do to the economy. The investor was a war hero turned banker from Missouri, General Lewis B. Hall, whose stagecoach had been stalled in Julesburg and delayed a few weeks. A ball was being held in his honor, the date postponed until his arrival. Lucy rifled through the next few pages. Two new dress boutiques were opening on Washington Street. An annual fair was coming up. A goat milking competition. Steer wrestling. A fiddler duo from North Carolina performing. She turned the page.

THE SHANKS-KANE GANG STRIKES AGAIN

Will Shanks narrowly escapes shootout at the Lonely Dove Saloon in Thompson. Possibly in cahoots with a woman. She has dark hair, slender figure, and an Eastern accent.

Lucy brought a hand to her mouth. "In cahoots?" she said aloud. "Excuse me?" asked the operator.

She read on silently:

Will Shanks is the leader of the Shanks-Kane Gang, an armed and dangerous group of ex-guerillas, wanted for armed robbery, murder, and war crimes.

Shanks and the woman are now believed to be staying in the area in or around Denver.

Ten more Pinkerton Detectives have been dispatched. Reward for any information that leads to their capture is 2,000 dollars.

Justice will be served to these men and anyone harboring them.

Below the article was the Pinkerton Detective Agency emblem of an eye, with their slogan: "We never sleep."

Alongside the sketch of Will was one of Silas Kane, a blond with a scar on his left cheek; Patrick "Irish" O'Brien, a clean-cut fellow with an Adam's apple and a flashing, debonair smile; and the Rindone brothers, Oscar and Cal Rindone, both depicted with stern expressions and wild mops of dark hair.

She could go to the police right now and set this straight. Tell them everything. Two thousand dollars would be more than enough for stagecoach fare and new luggage, a new dress. But what if they disbelieved her, just as the stagecoach company had? She studied the sketch of Will's face. She'd seen him kill with her own eyes and knew it should have invoked fear, but all she could see was the person who'd helped her. A certain kindness in his eyes.

The operator leaned across the counter to see what she'd been reading.

"Have you heard of this gang?" Lucy asked.

"Yes, they're making a lot of headlines lately. Very naughty," he said. Then he pointed at the sketch of Will with his feather pen. "But I'll tell you this for free: I'd harbor and abet this one anytime if he's looking for volunteers," he said in a hushed tone, then went into a fit of giggles before returning to the task at hand. "Now, to whom are we addressing this telegram?"

Lucy studied his face for a moment in shock, then gave him the address of her father's attorney, and paid him. She told him she'd check back in the morning for a response and asked if he could direct her to a low-budget accommodation for the night.

He grimaced. "Larimer Street," he said. "It's in Lower Downtown. And be careful."

Larimer Street was a main thoroughfare that ran north and south through the city. As Lucy walked south, farther into Lower Downtown, the elegant brick buildings of the city became fewer and then suddenly she was surrounded by the odd wooden building amongst shanties constructed of tarps. People living out of wagons. Dogs barking. Signs in English, Spanish, and Chinese. A small general store with a dark-skinned woman wearing an exotic blue head wrap unloading milk jugs off a wagon outside. A brothel called Bessie's, where a red-headed girl leaned off an upper balcony smoking a cigarette. Eventually Lucy stumbled across a small hotel where a middle-aged clerk and his sheepdog showed her to a small room at the end of the hall. It was plain with a single bed and a chair. A small window with bars looked out into the alley. The bath was in a separate room and cost ten cents extra. Water had to be heated in kettles on the stove.

"I'll take it," Lucy said.

Five heated kettles and half an hour later, Lucy lowered herself into the tin bathtub. The walls were thin, and she could hear people in the hallway. Doors slamming. A baby crying. The lock on the door was flimsy, and she didn't trust it. She washed quickly with the sponge and toweled off. She wrapped herself up in the towel and when the hallway was clear, she carried a bucket of water back to her room with her to spot clean her dress. With no desire to go back outside, she skipped dinner even though her stomach growled and she felt lightheaded with hunger.

She slept with her window cracked open, and sometime in the night, she woke to men's voices outside. She sat up in bed and looked down at the floor for Will. Forgetting, for a moment, where she was, she sat there looking around the empty room. She stood and tiptoed to the window. A half dozen or so men had congregated around a fight. She stood, watching, her hands on the bars of the window as they rolled around in the dirt, wrestling and throwing punches. Lucy slunk to the floor and sat against the wall, then hugged her knees to her chest and cried.

The next morning at the telegraph office, the same quirky fellow, Albert, she learned was his name, had not received a response for her. And no, there were no lines down; he'd investigated that already this morning.

"I still can't believe your stagecoach was attacked," he said. "I was telling a customer about you. She said she'd heard of a girl being kidnapped and held captive, forced to wed a warrior chief or something like that. Got me to thinking, though; it might not be all that bad. Running around in beaver furs and pelts and leathers. And you'd learn to weave and smoke the peace pipe and sleep in a teepee with your big fierce warrior husband."

Lucy stared at him, dumbfounded for a moment.

"Anyway, is there someone else who can help you?" he asked. "Shall we send another telegram?"

"No. There's no one else, I'm afraid. I'm sure he's just very busy. I'll check back in later."

She went out onto the porch and stared out at the street. Her father could be the most charming person in the world, yet anyone who dared go against him, even in the smallest way, knew his coldness and wrath. She'd seen it all her life; she'd learned not to get too attached to staff, even people he considered friends. How could she have been so naïve to think it would be any different for her just because she was his daughter? She reached into the small pocket of her dress and felt the last coin. It was only enough for one more night in the hotel. A rider in a tan hat, on a black horse coming toward her caught her eye. As he neared, she felt disappointed when she searched his face and it wasn't Will.

Farther down was a group of young girls in uniforms, skipping along gaily, carrying their lunch pails and a few books. Lucy thought back to all those years in school, trying so hard to follow the rules and please the sisters, listening and trying to learn the subjects whether they interested her or not. Algebra. French. Literature. Moses and his ten commandments. She wished she could lean down to that little girl who'd tried so hard and whisper in her ear, *"learn something useful."*

She continued to check in with the telegraph station at least once a day. Still nothing had come from her father. Albert was more concerned for the bags forming under Lucy's beautiful eyes. He once heard from the mayor's wife, the most gorgeous woman he'd ever seen who was forty but looked twenty-five, that the key to her beauty, she'd told him, was to sit with an orange slice on each eye for an hour each night. Albert put his hand up, as though testifying in court, and swore on his grandmother's grave it was a true story. He had been doing it for weeks now and could see a difference already.

Lucy thought endlessly about her options. Without any money, there were few. She couldn't go back. Not to New York and certainly not to her father or Lane, now. There was that Uncle Holloway's house in Valley City. It kept crossing her mind, but Will and his gang were all over the papers, surely they'd have figured out who he was by now, and what if they believed she was in cahoots with him? She wanted to continue out West, but her only option was to hitch a ride with strangers, which felt too vulnerable and dangerous.

She roamed the streets by day and when the sun went down, crouched beneath a set of stairs in an alleyway, listening to the sound of rats scurrying about throughout the night, squeaking and fighting. Though the days were warm and sunny, the nights were cold, and she shivered as she stared up at the moon through the slits of the stairs.

Back in New York, immigrants were arriving by the thousands through the harbor at Castle Garden. Lucy had spent many an afternoon watching them take their first steps onto new land. Many of them would seek housing in the already overcrowded shanties and tenement homes that lined the streets of boroughs like Little Germany and the Five Points. And they would take back-breaking labor jobs or work as servants to the rich for very little pay. She'd always wondered what made it worth it, and what it must have been like where they'd come from to make the arduous trip to America to live such a hard life.

Now, as she lay on the cold ground, listening to the eerie sounds of the alley at night, she thought about how naïve she'd been. The real hardship had nothing to do with the tenements those new immigrants resided in, or the jobs they took. People could survive hard and humiliating things, just like she would survive shivering beneath the stairs with the rats. What she may not have survived was if she'd stayed in New York, living a half-lived life, never listening to that inner voice that knew there was something more. The real hardship isn't about what we face, but in never having set out on the journey in the first place, a quiet suffering in the knowing we lacked the courage to try. Lucy was halfway and though it felt hopeless, she was not going to give up now. She had to keep going.

She was getting more desperate to find food. Scraps from garbage canisters and the rare apple she slipped into her pocket from a street vendor were not enough, and she felt weaker by the day. It was mid-afternoon, and she followed a crowd to what she thought must be a street market. She felt horrified when she turned the corner to realize they were gathering for a hanging, to jeer as an elderly man on a plank pleaded for his life and wept. The sheriff slid a burlap bag over his head. The preacher read a passage from the Bible. Several jeers came from the crowd in anticipation. The sound of the plank releasing and the snapping of his neck resonated through Lucy's ears. Legs dangling. Lifeless. "He pissed himself," a woman's voice shrieked above the crowd, followed by a cackle of laughter. Then the crowd began to disperse, going about their day as though nothing had happened.

Lucy spent the rest of that afternoon with a stray cat, who followed her through the alleys as she looked for food, weaving in and out of her legs and tripping her. She found nothing edible in the garbage she rooted through. Empty bottles. Bags. Tins. When she came upon a sleeping man, who smelled of alcohol and belched in his sleep, the cat hissed and scurried off.

Dizziness was overwhelming her now. As she passed an alley, something came running out, startling her. A skinny dog. It looked up at her, licking its chops, then scampered off down the street. It had found something to eat. Lucy started walking down the narrow alley until she spotted flies on something. The carcass of a rat. She lifted her skirt and stepped over it. At the end of the alley, she stopped and peered around. To the right, a set of stairs ascended to the back door of Bartholomew's Brothel. To the left, a small set of stairs came out from the kitchen of a café, with wooden garbage bins beside them. Lucy tiptoed over and behind the bins and ducked out of view, poking her head up just enough to peer into the garbage. A half a sandwich. She dusted it off, smelled it, and took a bite.

Across the alley, the back door of the brothel opened, and two girls stumbled out. Ivory colored dresses of lace draped open. Cleavage. One had dark, almost black hair that she wore down in loose waves. She stumbled down the stairs and caught herself on the banister at the bottom, then swung around it and laughed as she tipped her head back and brought a bottle to her lips. The other, a blond, laughed at her friend as she sat down on the top step.

Lucy took another bite of the sandwich, staying low and as still as possible while peering out from behind the bin. The blond rolled up her sleeve and tied something around her arm, just above her elbow. She tapped the inside of her elbow a few times with her fingertips, then reached down and fished a needle out of her skirt pocket. Lucy had heard about soldiers becoming morphine addicts after the war but had never pictured a woman doing such a thing. She inched herself forward for a better view as the woman stuck the needle into the inside of her forearm and pushed the end down with her thumb. A slow, pleasant smile creased the woman's face, and she loosened the tie on her upper arm and let the sleeve of her dress drape back over her arm. She set the needle to the side and leaned back on her elbows, her eyes half open.

Suddenly, a few feet from where Lucy crouched, the back door of the café's kitchen opened, and a cook in a white hat walked outside and lit a cigarette. Lucy ducked farther down.

"Hey, who's back there?" he shouted.

Her heart raced, and she felt her hands begin to shake.

"I see you! Behind the garbage! Get the hell out of here!" Heavy footsteps came toward her.

Shaking, she dropped the rest of the sandwich, stood, and put her hands up. "Please don't hurt me. I was just hungry. I'm so sorry, sir."

The man lunged forward, grabbed Lucy by the arm, and marched her toward the alley. "I oughta call the sheriff on you. We don't take kindly to trespassin' back here, you hear me?"

"Let go of her, you fat fuck," called out a woman's voice from behind her. Lucy turned to see the dark-haired woman walking toward them. Her dress gaped open in the breeze, revealing a black leather corset. With the whiskey bottle still in her hand, she had a calm, steady expression.

"Take your hands off her 'fore I break this bottle over your fucking head."

The man's grip loosened on Lucy's arm, and Lucy pulled herself free.

"I don't want no trespassin'. You whores keep to your own side," he said, then he spat and went back into the café, slamming the door behind him.

The girl stared at Lucy with beautiful, intense dark eyes rimmed with kohl. She had defined cheekbones. Full lips. "He was just tryin' to scare ya's all," she said. "Come sit for a minute; you're shaking."

"I'm fine," said Lucy. "Thank you."

The girl took a swig of the whiskey and looked Lucy up and down a few times. "You need work?"

Lucy shook her head no and felt the tears coming. "Thank you," she said quietly and started to walk away.

"Hey, girl."

Lucy stopped and looked back.

"You want some free advice? Stand up straight and stop fuckin' cryin'. Only thing of value my mama ever told me," she said. "You can come in for a meal if you want. It's on me."

"No, thank you," Lucy said, then turned and slowly continued walking down the alley.

"Suit yourself. I'll leave the door ajar in case you change your mind. Ask for Esther," she shouted out after Lucy.

"Esther, leave her be," the blond slurred from the porch.

"Well, she's eatin' out of the goddamned fuckin' garbage . . ." Esther's voice trailed off as Lucy kept walking.

Lucy stood at the end of the alley, looking out at the thoroughfare. A group of three elderly ladies was passing by, speaking Spanish. One of them let out a bellowing laugh. A wagon passed by with a fierce looking dog in a wire cage. Then another wagon with five children in the back of it. Their solemn little faces stared at her. She stood there for what felt like a long time. Then she turned and walked to the back porch of the brothel. The door was propped open with a crate. Lucy walked up the stairs and went inside.

CHAPTER 7

———◆———

THE BACK HALLWAY WAS dark, lit only by a few candles on wooden candelabra sconces hung along the wall. Lucy could make out two doors, both closed. Someone was moaning behind one. Lucy stared at the closed door as she passed. At the end of the hallway was the main room, where men were drinking and gambling, sitting around tables littered with whiskey bottles and poker chips and the odd gun. Everyone was smoking. A few of the men turned and looked at her as she entered. A long bar stood to the right of the room. Esther was standing and leaning up seductively against it.

"Well, looky what the cat dragged in," she said. "Well, don't just stand there, come on in."

Lucy went and took a seat at the bar.

Esther studied her as she blew out her smoke in rings. "What's your name, girl?"

"Lucy."

Esther reached over the bar and produced a wine glass and bottle of wine with a cork half sticking out, which she removed with her teeth, and poured Lucy a healthy glass.

"You like roast beef, Lucy?"

Lucy nodded.

Esther turned to the bartender. "An order of roast beef with mashed potatoes," she said. "Extra gravy. Put it on my account and don't let anyone fuck with her."

"Thank you," Lucy said quietly. "You see, my stagecoach was attacked and . . ."

"You don't gotta explain yourself," Esther said, then turned and sauntered toward a table of men playing cards and took a seat on a gentleman's lap. Lucy noticed two other prostitutes standing near the front door, smoking cigarettes with long elegant holders. One was the blond she'd seen outside earlier, still looking foggy, laughing in the corner with a gentleman. Esther let out a laugh and lit a cigarette for the man whose lap she was sitting on. Lucy watched as the man ran his hand along the inside of her thigh, pushing her dress up past her knees. The table of men Esther was entertaining were young and attractive and dressed in expensive-looking clothing. One of them was smoking a pipe. He looked up at Lucy, and she quickly looked away and took a sip of her wine. It had a slight vinegar aftertaste from the bottle either having been open too long or corked, but it reminded her of New York and she eagerly took a second sip. She noticed a few shelves lined with dusty books, whiskey, and beaver pelts were on the back wall behind the bar. Candles everywhere. A drawing of a nude woman, sitting on a chair with her legs spread, a mischievous smirk on her face.

"Your roast beef, milady," said the bartender as he set down in front of her a plate of roast beef covered in dark rich gravy, a scoop of mashed potatoes dripping with butter at its side. It smelled heavenly. She forked a bite and reveled in the warmth and flavor of the meat. She took care to eat slowly.

Someone let out a whoop of joy and collected a stack of chips at one of the tables. The dealer collected the cards and continued dealing.

When she was finished, the bartender took her plate and topped off her wine.

Esther came over to the bar and poured two glasses of whiskey. She set one in front of Lucy and held hers up for a cheers, then she drank it in one gulp and elegantly set the glass down.

Lucy lifted her glass and smelled it, then took a sip. It was so strong it made her eyes water.

"You smoke?" Esther pulled two cigarettes out of her corset and held one out to Lucy.

Lucy paused and stared at the cigarette. She'd never tried it but was curious.

"Sure," she said. She took it and lit it with the candle on the bar, then took a long inhale deep into her lungs. It burned and gave her a head rush, but she liked the way it felt to exhale. "Is it true that smoking helps keep your figure nice and slender?"

"Where'd you hear that?"

"They have this column in the *New York Tribune*, gossip and tidbits about royalty. I read once that Empress Sisi of Austria attributes smoking cigarettes to how she stays trim. She's obsessed with her looks and her figure, has a gymnastics room in her house, and sleeps with veal on her face. She claims it's anti-aging."

"She sounds crazy," Esther said. "Crazy in a good way." She took a long drag on her cigarette and blew her smoke out in rings again. "You don't got a man?" she asked.

"No."

"Where was this stagecoach attack?"

"Near La Porte."

"How'd you get to Denver?"

"There was this man, a thief, who happened to come along and . . ."

"I knew you had a man," Esther said, smiling now. "Where is this thief?"

"He's gone."

"Well, fuck him. I'll give you work here. I'll guarantee you'll make more money in a day than any man in this room. Four dollars a trick. Five to twenty tricks a night."

Lucy sat quietly staring at the bar. That was an average of forty dollars a night. One week of work, and she'd have stage fare and money to spare. She tried to imagine being naked with a man she didn't know, possibly one she was repulsed by, and couldn't. The furthest she'd ever gone with a man was a kiss from Lane; she'd found it rather unenjoyable and pulled away from him.

A man called out for Esther from across the room. She waved him off and poured them each a little more wine. He shouted louder for her to come sit on his lap. Esther slammed her hand down on the counter and turned to him. "I said I'm fuckin' busy."

Past the tables of men, in the far corner of the room was a piano that sat empty.

"How come nobody's playing that thing?" Lucy asked.

"You know how to play?"

"I used to," she said, leaving out the part that she got her musical start by playing for the school choir when they needed a replacement after the elderly Sister Mary Angelica's arthritis got too bad.

Esther gestured toward the piano. "Be my guest," she said.

Lucy started out playing Beethoven's "Für Elise." As she played, she began adding a few chords and picking up the tempo, pounding the keys faster and louder. A blond prostitute sat down on the bench beside Lucy. She took Lucy's wine glass and took a sip, then set it back atop the piano. After a while, she turned back to Esther, who was dancing now with a gentleman. "If she plays poker as good as the piano, we're in trouble."

"I don't know how to play poker," Lucy said, over her piano music.

Esther laughed and kept dancing. "You will by morning."

Esther's first poker lesson: "Don't calculate, play by instinct. Poker, like life, has an element of risk. Face it." The second lesson: "Know what you're holding. Play the hand you've been dealt, not the hand you wish you had. A full house beats a straight. Three of a kind beats the highest pair. Four of a kind beats a flush, but a *straight flush*, that beats everything." Third lesson: "Act on reason, not emotion. Always, always keep your composure."

The blond's name was Mississippi Kate, and there was a redhead named Dahlia who joined them. Esther won almost every hand. The brothel, quiet now, was closed for the night, with just the girls left playing. Lucy looked out at the dark street. She had no idea what time it was, but time no longer mattered. She had nowhere to go; no one was worried or expected her. She thought of Will and wondered where he was now, if he was okay. She pictured him sitting at the bar, eyeing her from across the room. Quiet and alone. And ruggedly handsome.

The girls were full of questions for Lucy, and she answered them all. They listened without judgement as Lucy told them that she had never known the real reason her mother died, hated the mystery surrounding it, and how much she needed to know who her mother was, and in turn, who she was. They seemed to understand, in a way that didn't need to be spoken aloud. They admired that she was traveling alone, but felt a girl should protect herself. They gasped when they found out she was traveling without a gun or weapon of any kind. Esther had an extra knife that she retrieved and gave to Lucy. It was a tiny but sharp dagger that fit snugly into its leather sheath, made to tuck into a woman's corset. The girls showed Lucy how to pull the knife quickly and discreetly from between her cleavage and where to stab someone.

Mississippi Kate used Esther as a human example and went through the motions, touching each spot on Esther with the tip of the knife as she spoke. "Number one, the jugular. If possible, always go for the side of the throat. Number two, the eyes. Number three, the gut. Mind you, the heart and lungs are also fatal jabs, but too risky with all the ribs in the way. But the gut, right here, is surprisingly effective, and if the victim doesn't receive immediate help, they'll bleed out. Got it?" asked Mississippi Kate, still pointing with the knife. "Jugular, eyes, gut. Jugular, eyes, gut."

"Enough," said Esther. "Jesus, you nearly poked my goddamned eye out."

"Well, how else is she gonna learn?"

Esther sat back down and began shuffling the cards. She took a drag on her cigarette and blew the smoke out in rings. "All right, who's in? All or nothing this hand."

At dawn, the only two remaining at the table were Lucy and Esther. Esther took a long drag and blew smoke out in rings.

"All due respect, Lucy Cavanagh," she said. "I get wanting to meet your kin, the sister to your dead mother and all. But she ain't got nothing to do with who you are, and if you think she does, you're settin' yourself up to be sorely disappointed."

Lucy took a drag on her cigarette and stared out the window.

"There's a hotel on Main Street called the Harrison," Esther said after a while. "Busiest hotel in the city. So busy that you could swipe a few suitcases off the back of a buggy and disappear into the crowd without anyone noticing."

"You mean to steal someone's belongings? Have you done it?"

"Watch for one with good style. About your size," she said, looking Lucy up and down. "Get yourself out of that torn dress. People like that always travel with cash. Use it and go. Go find this aunt or whatever it is you're needing to find."

Lucy suddenly remembered the knife in its sheath and started to pull it out from her cleavage.

Esther put a hand on Lucy's and stopped her. "Keep it. I'd best get on upstairs and get some sleep. Good luck to you, Lucy."

"Thank you so much, Esther. I'll wire you the money from San Francisco once I'm settled. For the dinner. And the drinks. And cigarettes."

"You'll do no such thing," said Esther. "But you'd better write and let me know how it is there. You never know, maybe I'll make my way out there one day. They say it's booming so fast out there, even women can own their own business. I could open my own café. Can't you just see it? Esther's Place. Anyway, enough about my silly dreams. Give me a hug and off you go."

Esther had been right. The Harrison was bustling. Lucy sat across the street on a bench, watching. Each time a wagon pulled up, the valet attended to the luggage and horses while the doorman escorted the guests inside. Five wagons and a row of horses were parked outside now, a few of them unattended, luggage sitting in the back while the busy valet made his way down the line. A few businessmen smoked cigars on the veranda. An elegant buggy with a couple pulled into the row of wagons. Lucy was disappointed when the woman hopped down. Too big. Her dresses would be swimming on Lucy. One more buggy arrived. A lone man wearing a suit. And then she saw them. Coming down the street in a sharp red buggy. The driver was an older gentleman; the girl beside him much younger. She was about Lucy's size and wore a stylish peach dress and an exquisite little hat and gloves. They parked beside the others and leapt down. The girl kissed him and hung on his arm as he escorted her to the front door. The doorman greeted them at the door, and they went inside.

Lucy watched for a few minutes while the wagon sat unattended, the valet busy with another guest's luggage. Then she summoned the courage to stand and cross the street to the buggy. When she reached it, she peered inside. On the back seat were a few pieces of luggage. Lucy glanced both ways, then opened the back door, reached in, and grabbed two, a garment and a carpetbag. Her heart had never raced so fast. A bag grasped tightly in each hand, she began to walk away. She'd only gone a few steps when she heard a scream from behind her. She turned around. The girl had come back outside and had a horrid look on her face, wailing for help and pointing at Lucy. The valet was running toward her. Lucy dropped the bags and started running as fast as she could.

"Thief! Stop her!"

Then there was a hand on her arm, and he yanked her back. She tripped and fell to the ground. The valet was standing over her now, and he pulled her to standing. "I gotcha!"

"Please, sir, it was a misunderstanding. Please let me go."

Everyone had stopped and was staring, their scowling faces a blur as Lucy's eyes watered. The valet clutched her arm and began walking her down the street.

"To the sheriff's office with you, you little wench," he said.

The jail smelled of stale urine and some sort of vinegar cleaner. To the left of the main room was a small desk and a sheriff behind it, with his feet up. The middle-aged man eyed Lucy up and down and stood as she was dragged into the room. He laughed when she told him this was a mistake, a wheezy laugh that shook his belly and made him cough. He took Lucy by the arm, thanked the man who'd delivered her, and walked her down a hallway to the cell, which was nothing more than a few filthy blankets strewn about the dirt floor, and a pail in the corner. Two males sat in separate corners of the cell, an old man and a kid, who couldn't have been more than fourteen or fifteen.

"Got company, fellas," said the sheriff as he unlocked the door and slid the metal bars open.

The sheriff pushed her into the cell and shut the door behind her, whistling as he walked back to his desk.

"Might as well sit down," said the kid. "He ain't coming back for a while."

Lucy went and sat in the corner and huddled her knees to her chest. She was shaking. She felt the kid's eyes on her.

"First time?" he asked.

"Yes."

"I been in here six times," the kid said. "I'm in the business of stealin' horses."

"I see."

The kid gestured toward the old man. "That's E.B. Shot his son-in-law. He's waitin' to meet the gibbet."

"The what?" Lucy asked.

"Waitin' to hang."

The old man's eyes were on Lucy now, but he said nothing. He was thin and looked unwell and had the most wrinkled skin she had ever seen. He had only a few strands of short, greasy, grey hair and a long sparse beard. He struggled to stand up, then went to the bucket in the corner, unzipped his pants, and began to urinate.

Lucy put a hand over her mouth and held her breath.

"Don' worry, miss," the kid said. "When you need to piss, we'll look away. What are ya in for?"

"Stealing," she said quietly.

"Shit. What'd ya steal?"

"A carpetbag from a wagon."

The kid nodded and rubbed his chin, as though contemplating something. "You been caught stealin' before?"

"No."

"Might not hang ya then."

"Hang me?"

"Where ya from?"

"New York City."

"What brings ya to these parts?"

"I'm traveling to San Francisco. My stagecoach was attacked, and I've been trying to contact my family. This is all a huge misunderstanding."

The kid made a strange face, then burst out laughing. He laughed so hard he wiped tears from his eyes.

"Oh," he said after a while. "Pardon me. Pardon my fuckin' manners. I don't know what struck me so funny 'bout that."

The hours passed slowly. There was a small window in the corner that faced the outside. Daylight shone through, and she could hear sounds of the street. The ground was hard and cold, and her back ached. The old man sat quietly in his corner, and the kid fell back asleep. When he woke, he sat against the wall. He hummed a tune she didn't recognize, then made popping sounds by pulling at his cheek with his finger. She could feel his eyes on her, but she ignored him. When she had to relieve herself so badly it hurt, she finally went to the bucket in the corner. The men did as they said and turned away as she held her skirts and squatted over it.

Dinner was served in three metal bowls, passed through the door and set inside the cell on the floor. It was served by the same sheriff, wheezing and hacking as he informed Lucy a public attorney would be by to see her in the morning. She shouldn't get her hopes up, though. Four witnesses had seen her take that carpetbag from the wagon.

"I'm not sure where you come from, lady," he said. "Around here, we hang thieves."

Then he walked away.

The meal was mush with a small crusty piece of bread on the side. Lucy took a few bites, but the taste was too rancid and she set it aside. The other two cell mates ate theirs hungrily. The kid finished hers.

Hours later, a lone fly buzzed the empty bowls that sat beside the cell door. Lucy stayed huddled in her corner as darkness slowly came upon them. She was dozing off when she heard the old man get up again. He came to her and stood over her. Then he gently set a blanket over her and went back to his corner.

They say your mind plays tricks on you when you think your life is coming to an end. Floods of memories. Epiphanies. A sense of clarity about life, about what really means something, and an awakening of how we might have lived differently. Lucy felt nothing of the sort, mindful only of the cold floor beneath her and the stench of the bucket of piss. The sound of her cellmates snoring. Hunger pains and a throbbing headache. Nothing mattered. She didn't care if she ever saw her father again, or if she ever laid eyes on her aunt or California. The sounds of the crowd jeering and laughing at the man dying by noose replayed in her mind no matter how hard she willed it to stop. Dying suddenly in the massacre might have been better than this. She wished Will was here. He would know what to do.

She woke to the sound of footsteps in the darkness. Spurs jingling, coming down the hall. She sat up. Moonlight shone through the bars of the tiny window. The footsteps stopped at the door of the cell. There were two of them, but she couldn't see their faces in the dark. One of them lit a match and she met his gaze. Now she knew she must be dreaming. She stood and went to the door and grasped the bars.

CHAPTER 8

———◆———

WILL STUDIED HER FACE in the dim light. "Are you all right?" he asked.

She nodded.

The kid and the old man were standing beside her at the bars now.

Will's comrade held the sheriff's keys and was trying them in the lock, one by one. In the candlelight, she could see he was around the same age and had blond hair and a scar under his left eye. Suddenly, the lock made a clicking sound, and he opened it and slid the door open.

Will reached in and took Lucy by the hand. "Let's go," he said.

Lucy stepped out of the cell and followed Will and his friend down the hallway. The old man and kid followed closely behind. The sheriff's body lay face down on the floor in a pool of blood.

Will led her through the front door and out onto the porch.

The street was lit by a few dull torches. Empty, save for a drunk stumbling across the street, who stopped and studied the group of them as they exited the jail. Will took a few steps forward and held his gun up. "Keep walking, mister," he said.

The drunk said something Lucy couldn't make out, then continued stumbling down the street, quickening his pace now.

The kid stood, blinking his eyes, looking between Will and his friend in amazement. "Are you guys who I think you are?"

"Look, kid, you're free," said Will. "Good luck to you."

"Fuckin' shit! You are! You're Will and Silas . . ."

"Shut up," said Will. "You want to wake the whole goddamned street? Now go on."

The kid turned and took off running down the street. The old man limped after him.

Will and his friend guided Lucy down a dark alley to where Zeta and another horse were waiting. Will helped Lucy mount Zeta and leapt up behind her, then they all set off. The three of them rode in silence. They came to a fork in the road and stopped. "Thank you, Silas," said Will.

Silas studied Lucy for a moment, then gave Will a nod, spurred his horse, and rode on down the smaller side road without a word, disappearing into the darkness.

Will and Lucy continued on the main road. Feeling the breeze on her face, she began shivering. Will took his coat off and put it over her shoulders.

"Thank you," she whispered.

Then he handed her something wrapped in brown paper. "It's a sandwich," he said. "Figured you'd be hungry."

She took it, unwrapped it, and took a bite. Turkey and cheese and the most delicious bread. "Thank you," she said between bites.

The city fell farther and farther behind them as they rode. The night grew still and quiet, the only sound, the clip clop of Zeta's hooves. Lucy studied the majestic outline of the mountains in the moonlight.

"They were going to hang me," she said.

"I know."

"How? Better yet, how did you find me?"

"A lucky accident."

"Where are we going?"

"Back to the house."

"The Holloway house?"

"Yes."

"There's wanted posters of you everywhere. Surely they must know we're imposters by now."

"There's no wanted posters anywhere in town, and they still believe we're the Holloways."

"But I don't understand, why are you still here? I thought you'd have done whatever job you meant to do and be long gone by now."

He didn't answer, and they rode on in silence for so long it surprised her when his voice came from behind her. "After the war, we thought we'd just ride home and carry on with our lives, but the government had left soldiers stationed in Missouri. It was made to look like an effort to keep the peace, but they were there to run out anyone who'd fought for the Confederacy. One of them was General Hall. He made himself a rich man by investing in the banks that were stealing and reselling our land. He's en route to Denver, with a stage full of cash."

"General Lewis B. Hall, the railroad investor. I read about him in the paper. They're throwing a ball in his honor, but his stage has been delayed, so . . ." she said, and thought about it a moment. "You're going to rob his stage?" she asked in a hushed tone, even though they were alone on the road.

"I'm going to take back what's mine."

As they rode the darkness lifted, giving way to the first signs of dawn. By the time they reached the house, the morning sun was shining. A tan horse whinnied and trotted in from the pasture and stood at the fence beside the barn. Farther out in the pasture, a black and white cow let out a long moo. A tiny goat was baaing while leaping around a small pen beside the barn, its brown ears flapping.

"Where did the animals come from?" she asked.

"The livery. They belonged to the uncle."

In the middle of the yard, just behind the oak tree, was a scarecrow standing over a small square patch of dirt.

"You planted a garden?"

"Vinnie did."

A light breeze rustled the leaves of the cottonwood and waved the night dress on the scarecrow. Lucy studied the mop used for hair. One of Vinnie's oversized hats. Buttons sewn on for eyes. Lips drawn in large and crimson red.

"Is that scarecrow wearing lip rouge?" she asked.

Will stopped the horse and dismounted before helping her down. "I'll untack Zeta and be in in a minute."

Lucy went into the porch and sat on the front step. When Will was finished with the horse he crossed the yard and sat on down beside her.

"I'm sorry you never heard from your father."

"How did you know…? Never mind, it doesn't matter."

Will lit a cigarette. "What'd you do to end up in jail anyway?"

"The prostitute who bought me dinner assured me it was so busy outside the Harrison hotel that I could lift a carpet bag and no one would notice."

"Prostitute? You were in a brothel?"

"The girls were actually quite lovely. They taught me to play poker. And how to exhale cigarette smoke out in rings."

Will stared at her curiously but said nothing.

"The papers describe me as being in cahoots with you. With the Shanks-Kane Gang."

"How much am I worth now?"

"Two thousand dollars."

"You could have gone to the authorities and told them what you knew. What stopped you? Two thousand dollars could have solved all your problems."

"I can't say it didn't cross my mind. I wasn't sure they'd believe me, and it didn't feel right after you'd helped me."

Will took one last long drag of his cigarette. "I don't know how long that stage will be delayed for, but I'm planning on staying here as long as they keep thinking I'm this Nelson Holloway fellow. Hopefully until I can pull off this robbery. If you stay on and help me keep up pretenses, farmwife stuff like helping with the chores and cooking, and making the odd appearance in town, I'll give you some of my share. I'll pay you what I'm worth, two thousand dollars."

Lucy sat quietly, letting what he'd just proposed sink in.

"Goddamnit, what now?" said Will. His gaze fixed on the road.

Lucy turned to see a rider coming up the drive. As he neared, she could see a badge on his vest.

"Will," she whispered, "do you think he's here for me? What do we do?"

"Just stay quiet. I'll get rid of him," Will said.

They both stood.

The rider stopped the horse a few feet from the porch. "Both of you stay right where you are. You're under arrest."

Lucy felt the color drain from her face and her heart raced so fast she felt as though she might pass out. She could see Will's hand slowly hover over the gun tucked into the back of his pants.

"Just kidding," the rider said, laughing now. "I always like to have a little fun with the new folks in town. You should have seen the looks on both your faces."

His voice had a raspy quality to it. An Irish brogue. He was tall and broad in stature. He dismounted, took his hat off, and held a hand out to Will. "The names Lyman Walsh. I'm the sheriff around these parts. I was attending to some business up north, else I'd have been here sooner to welcome you folks."

"It's a pleasure to meet you, sir," said Will, shaking Lyman's hand. "I'm Nelson Holloway and this is my wife, Emily."

The sheriff gave Lucy a nod, then looked around the property. "Your uncle sure loved this land," he said. "Was such a shame, his death. I was the one who found him, you know. I knew something was wrong when he didn't come into town for his weekly bottle of whiskey, so I rode out here to have a look see. He looked peaceful, you should know. If it weren't for the stench in the house, I'd have taken him for sleeping."

Lucy looked back through the house at the bedroom door. "He died in that bed?"

"He'd be real happy to know you're taking the place on," the sheriff said. "Speak of." The sheriff reached into his saddlebag and produced a piece of paper and a pencil and handed it to Will. "It's the title to the place, all you have to do is sign and it's yours now."

Will looked over the piece of paper, then held it against a rail post and signed near the bottom.

The sheriff took the paper from Will and signed near the bottom himself. Then he slapped Will on the back. "Congratulations, folks. You're officially the owners of fifteen acres. And a real fine house," he said, studying the house now. "A real fine house indeed."

Lucy watched as Lyman folded the signed document and tucked it into his saddlebag. It wasn't a fine house, nor was she an official owner. Things had not come very far from the mid-century idea of coverture, or the idea that when a couple married their property became one entity, under control of the husband. She'd read that a few of the Nordic and European countries were starting to pass laws to change that, allowing women to hold jobs outside the house and control their own money. But not in the United States. In Sheriff Lyman's eyes and the eyes of the law, Lucy was just as much Will's property as the house and the land it sat on.

The sheriff mounted his horse. "I best get back to town. Got a pile of paperwork on my desk and a few US Marshals coming through this week."

"US Marshals," said Will. "There some trouble we should know about?"

"There was a shootout in a saloon up in Thompson little over a week ago. The marshal thinks it was one of the Shanks-Kane Gang. Apparently, he took a woman hostage. You probably haven't heard of them, being new out here, although I think they're native Missourians like yourselves. Anyway, they been causing a bit of a ruckus around these parts lately; those boys have robbed over fifteen banks and stagecoaches now."

"Haven't heard of them, no," said Will. He put his arm around Lucy. "I try to keep to my own business."

"Me too," said the sheriff. "Me too. But we're lucky here, not much happens in our sleepy little town, and that's just the way I like it. Anyway, I best be off. See you soon."

"Thanks for coming out," said Will. "Good day now."

They waved the sheriff off, and when he was out of view and earshot, Will removed his arm from Lucy's shoulders and lit a cigarette.

Lucy took it from him and took a drag. "After my mother died, I overheard a conversation between my father and aunt. She wanted to take me back to San Francisco with her, raise me there. My father wouldn't hear of it and I remember feeling so happy that he wanted me. In the end they sat me down and I was allowed to decide. I chose to stay with my father. A month later he dropped me off at boarding school. I was eight, and I remember watching him drive the buggy away without looking back. I was clutching my carpet bag as the nun gently tried to coax me inside. I made the wrong choice. It has haunted me and I've never felt like I really belonged anywhere since. The prostitute who bought me dinner told me in searching for my aunt, I was setting myself up for disappointment. I fear now she may be right, but I can't give up. I can't go back." She gazed out at the foothills as she spoke. "How much railroad money is that stagecoach carrying?"

"Enough."

"What are you gonna do with your share? Where will you go?"

"Do we have a deal?"

The vision of his wanted poster on the wall flooded her mind. And the crowd jeering all around her as that man dangled from a noose. If she stayed on here with him, the papers would be right about her being in cahoots. There would be no going back, and if she was caught, she would hang. She took another drag of the cigarette, then handed it back to him.

"I'll do it. But I'll need at least three thousand," she said, expecting a negotiation.

"Done."

Will went down the porch steps, then turned to her. "I've got to go into town. I took Nelson's job at the mill to keep up pretense. I'm sure you want to get some rest today. And wash up. I found an extra trough in the barn."

Lucy looked over to where he was pointing. A metal bin barely large enough for a person to fit in sat empty.

"There's a spring-fed creek," he said. "Just past the tree line. Just takes a few trips with the bucket."

Lucy was still looking out at the tree line. Would there be wild animals out there?

"The dress from Vinnie is hanging in the bedroom," Will said. "Along with a second one she found for you. And a pair of more practical shoes."

"I was thinking I could try and mend this one. Wash it up a little."

"Lucy. What you read about me on those wanted posters and in the paper is all true. Had that sheriff actually been here to arrest me, he wouldn't be on his way back to town right now. So please, go and put the farmwife dress on and don't do anything to blow our cover." He turned and started walking to the barn.

"You've really robbed fifteen banks?" she asked after him.

"Twenty-one," he said, without turning around.

She'd never worn anything so simple. No corset or tulle. Still shaking from the freezing cold bath in the trough, she studied her reflection in the bedroom window as she buttoned the last few buttons of the pastel blue dress. The dress fit her fine. The polka dotted collar a little tight around her neck. Long sleeves, cinched with a tiny bit of lace at each wrist. A cross-stitched flower at the bottom. She didn't know the first thing about chores or cooking or how to be a farmwife, but how hard could it be? The Bible study from Vinnie lay in the box in the corner of the room. Lucy picked it up, opened it to page one, and read:

The story of Ruth is one of love. A love so strong and bonding it is above even the law.

CHAPTER 9

SHE SLEPT THROUGH DINNER but woke in the night from a dream that she was still in jail, and she sat up in bed with a start. In the candlelight, she could see Will sleeping on the floor beside her. She lay back down and pulled the blankets over her, then relaxed into the sound of his slow and steady breathing.

She drifted in and out of an unrestful sleep until the cow started mooing at dawn and she got out of bed. Will was already gone. He'd left her a cup of coffee on the table that was lukewarm, and she took it and drank it on the porch steps. There was a chill in the air, but the sun was already filling the sky with pink hues of promise. The cow was out to pasture, mooing beside the fence. When she finished her coffee, she went to the barn, retrieved the bucket and lead rope, and walked slowly through the muddy field to the cow.

"Here, cow. That's it. I'm not going to hurt you."

When she reached the cow, she slid the rope around its neck and began to lead it to the fence surprisingly easily until a few steps in, the cow mooed and jerked back on the rope, causing her to lose her footing and fall face first into the mud. Slowly, she stood. She left the milk bucket and rope out in the pasture and turned and went back to the house.

The cow let out another long moo as she walked away.

A little while later, freshly bathed and in the spare dress from Vinnie, she set up the laundry bucket and scrubbing board in the middle of the yard. Holding the same bar of soap she'd used on herself, she sat on her knees, a pile of laundry beside her. The muddy dress. The sheets. Will's extra pair of trousers and socks. She picked up a pillowcase and scrubbed it against the board, ran the bar of soap over it, plunged it in the water, and scrubbed again. The morning sun was hot overhead. She reached up and wiped her brow with the sleeve of her dress and tucked a piece of hair back, feeling something crunchy in it—a dried piece of mud maybe? She wrung out the pillowcase and held it up.

"You're not doing that right," came a voice from behind her.

Startled, Lucy turned around to see a little girl, no more than eight or nine, with a dirty face and stringy, tangled blond hair. A tattered dress. Bare feet.

"Where in heaven's name did you come from?" Lucy asked.

The little girl pointed in the direction of the town. "That farm over yonder. Phoebe Anderson's the name. I know yer name." The little girl motioned for Lucy to move aside. "Well, go on and move over then," she said. "Let me show you how to get it clean."

Lucy stood and stepped aside, then watched as the wiry little thing knelt and scrubbed the pillowcase hard and fast against the washboard, then plunged into the soapy water, then repeated.

"Shouldn't you be in school or something?" Lucy asked.

"Pa says ain't no time for me to be sittin' all day in front of a chalkboard when there's work to be done." Phoebe wrung out the pillowcases and hung them over a branch, then looked around the property and shook her little head. "And there's work to be done round here, missus."

"Does he know you're here?"

The cow let out a long morbid moo.

"That cow needs milkin," Phoebe said.

"Yeah, well. That cow is the devil. I'm sure of it."

"Pa and my brothers are planting the back three acres today. Thought I'd come see if you needed help."

Lucy watched in awe as Phoebe scrubbed Will's trousers clean in minutes, wrung them out, and flung them over a branch of the cottonwood.

Phoebe stood with her hands on her hips and surveyed the property. Then she turned back to Lucy. "You got anything to eat, missus?"

"Do I have anything to eat?" Lucy asked.

"I don't work for free. I'll take something to eat, then we can get after the chores. Milking that cow and mucking out the stalls, for starters."

Lucy looked in the direction of the Anderson farm. She hadn't met the Andersons but knew from her time with the real Emily Holloway that many families in rural communities put little stock in formal education. She decided missing a day of school was probably not worth alerting the parents.

"All right, then. Let's go in the house and fix us up a snack. Tell me though, child, what's 'mucking out the stalls'?"

For Lucy's eighteenth birthday, her father took her to the Opera House on East 14th and Irving. Box seats. The premiere of Giuseppe Verde's *La Traviata,* the tragic love story of famed courtesan, Violetta. Torn between the lavish parties as a socialite in her

Paris salon, and the quiet country life with Alfredo, the man she loved. Lucy had thought it seemed so romantic at the time, the idea of a quiet country life.

Now she wasn't so sure.

Mucking out the stalls meant shoveling out the manure with a pitchfork. Such a foul task, Lucy sought out one of Will's handkerchiefs wore it around her nose and mouth.

"It ain't just chores needs to be done, the reason I'm not in school," Phoebe said as she tossed a shovelful of manure into a bucket with shocking strength and speed for such a wiry little thing. "There ain't no school here. Class met for a while in John Stark's Saloon, but after three teachers came and went, they shut it down. Pa even let me and my brothers go for a spell. I got two older brothers, Hank and Albert. They're a pain, but one time, when Barret Laringer took my doll, Albert grabbed him by the shirt and punched him right in the kisser. Made him apologize and everything. You got any brothers, missus?"

Lucy shook her head no. The stench of the manure was so pungent it burned her nostrils and she could taste it even through the handkerchief. She focused on not vomiting as she dumped her last shovelful of manure in the bucket. She tried not to feel angry at both the task and the idea of a town that didn't appreciate the education of its youth.

Next, they filled the water trough for the horse and cow by carrying buckets from the creek. Phoebe showed her how to carry two buckets at once, by placing a log across her shoulders and a bucket dangling from each side. She studied Lucy with a puzzled look as they walked. "Pa said you was farmers from Missouri, but you ain't like any farmer I ever seen."

Lucy opened her mouth to answer but Phoebe cut her off. "Forgive me, missus. Pa's always tellin' me to quit meddlin'. If he heard me askin' you so many questions, he'd whoop my ass all the way to Dakota Territory. I suppose Ma didn't like it here neither.

She ran off back East with another feller almost as soon as we got here. Course, I don't remember. I was a baby, or still shittin' in my bloomers—that's the way Pa tells it. Pa don't like me talkin' 'bout it, though, says, 'Phoebe, quit yer goddamned useless babblin' and get to work.' Do you like it here, missus?"

Lucy thought about it and gave the girl the most honest answer she could. "No, Phoebe. I don't like it here. But a wise person said to me, just lately, that the only way to survive is to play the hand you've been dealt, not the hand you wish you had."

When the water trough was filled, they chopped wood. The axe was too heavy for Phoebe, so she put Lucy to work, showing her how to swing back and aim for the middle of the piece of wood. Just when Lucy thought her work was done, Phoebe came out of the barn, carrying a large bundle of chicken wire.

"It's for the garden," said Phoebe. "So the rabbits don't eat all your carrots."

"I don't care if the rabbits eat my carrots," said Lucy.

Phoebe ignored her and dragged the chicken wire across the lawn. "Grab a shovel, missus. And a hammer."

"Lucy?" came Will's voice.

The last thing she remembered was sitting down in the rocking chair on the porch after Phoebe had gone. Lucy opened her eyes now to see Will standing over her.

"Lucy?" he asked. "Are you all right?"

"Yes," she said, and gave a stretch. "I must have dozed off. How was work?"

"It was fine. We all left a little early because of the heat today, though." Will looked back out at the property. "Did you do all this?"

"A little neighbor girl came by, from that Anderson farm. She's little, but works like the dickens."

"She chopped the wood?"

"The axe was too heavy for her. I did it."

"The stalls are mucked, and there's fresh water in the trough."

"What time is it? I haven't even started on dinner."

Will stayed quiet for a moment, studying her. Then he said, "Never mind that. I think we could both use a walk."

"Where to?"

"The stream you're getting water from widens into a river a little farther down. It's a pretty spot; I think you'll like it. You can even bathe there sometime if you wanted."

"Are you saying I need a bath?"

Will smiled and held his hand out to her. "No," he said. "But I think being away from this house for a spell would do you good. Too much sudden change can turn a person hard."

The river was lined with trees and rocks jutting out. Lucy sat on one of the larger ones, took her shoes off, and let her feet touch the water. Will rolled his pants up to his knees and waded out into the water with a fishing pole. Casting back and forth, the long line gliding across the water. Lucy sat staring out at the water, the way it flowed between rocks and rippled in the breeze. Will's line made a small splash each time he cast back out.

"Who taught you to fish?" she asked.

"Some neighbors I grew up with. The Rindone boys. Their pa used to take us."

"Your father didn't fish?"

"He died when I was nine."

"I'm sorry. Was he ill?"

"House fire."

"And your mother?'"

"She and my brother died in the same fire."

"I'm so sorry. What did you do after they died? Where'd you go to live?"

"The neighbors, the Rindones took me in. They were real nice people. Their boys, Cal, Oscar, and Johnny, were around my age, and there were two younger girls."

Lucy pictured Will as a nine-year-old boy, sleeping in a strange house. Life as he knew it, gone. She wondered if he'd silently cried himself to sleep most nights for a while, too, just as she had.

Will was quiet for a while and cast out a few more times. Then he said, "Mr. Rindone would never let us complain when we didn't catch anything. He said the test of a real fisherman isn't how many fish he catches, or how he catches them, but what he's caught when he's caught nothing."

There was a splash, and Will jerked the pole back. The pole was bent and he reeled the line in a few cranks, paused, then let a little of the line back out. The fish jumped. He reeled in again, then stopped, letting the fish tire. Gradual. Patient and deliberate in his movements. Back and forth, reeling a little closer each time. "Luce," he said, "can you grab the bucket?"

Lucy climbed down from the rock to retrieve the bucket and stood behind him on the shoreline.

When he reeled the fish in close enough, he reached into the water and held it up. It was striking. Over a foot in length and long and lean. Brown with speckles on its body. "Trout," he said.

"It's beautiful."

"It's dinner," said Will. Then he unhooked the fish and tossed it into the bucket.

Lucy looked at the fish struggling in the small amount of water in the bucket.

"Come here," said Will. He was back out, knee deep in the water.

Lucy lifted her skirts and gingerly walked to him.

He put the pole in her right hand and positioned himself behind her. "Keep your wrist firm," he said. With his hand over hers on the pole, he guided her back, stopping her arm just behind her head. "Stop here. Feel that? Now forward again. Back and forth. Back and forth."

Lucy felt a wave of chills running through her body at the closeness of him and struggled to focus on what he was telling her.

"Use the weight of the fly line as your guide," Will said. "If you feel a nibble on the line, jerk back to set the hook."

He stayed close behind her, helping her until she felt a nibble. She jerked back and felt something fighting with the line.

"Stay steady now. Slowly pull the line. Let it wear itself out a little, come to you."

After a long fight with the fish and doing exactly as Will instructed, she caught the first glimpse of it and watched as Will scooped it into the net.

"It's bigger than yours," she said.

Will laughed. "It sure is," he said as he tossed it in the bucket.

Lucy handed him the rod to look at the two fish in the bucket; they were both struggling and flailing in the small amount of water, hitting the sides of the bucket.

The nuns had always taught a life of ritual, principle, and convention. A *modus operandi*. If you lived with faith, and were strict enough in your beliefs and actions, you'd be in control of your life and it would be plentiful.

But that was not true.

Life changes and it changes in the most ordinary moments, when you're least expecting it. Dancing at a fancy costume ball. Riding a horse through the forest. Or swimming down a river in pursuit of a worm.

CHAPTER 10

———◆———

SHE WOKE THE NEXT morning to the smell of coffee, the floor where Will slept empty. She stood and dressed and went to the kitchen. Will sat at the table with his coffee cup and the Bible study from Vinnie. Lucy went to the stove and poured herself a small cup of coffee before sitting at the table across from Will.

"Morning."

"Morning."

"I hadn't realized you could read."

"I can read."

"Where did you attend school?"

"Missouri." He turned the page. "This book is boring."

"I know. I might look and see what Vinnie has to read when I go into town today for some food. And hopefully she sells hairbrushes. Look at my hair, it looks like I've given up on life."

Will smiled. Then he put the book down and stood. "I've got to get to the mill. You want a ride into town?"

"Something that little child said to me yesterday is still bothering me. Do you know there's no school here? Or teacher? How can they not see the importance of educating children?"

"I think there's probably more to it than that, like needing help around the farm. Needing to put food on the table. Did you want a ride to town?"

"No, thank you. I think a nice walk will do me some good."

It was mid-morning by the time she reached town on foot. Main Street was quiet, save for a few horses and wagons that passed her. A giant banner was strung across the street outside of the general store:

SEVENTH ANNUAL VALLEY CITY
PICNIC AND BARN DANCE
4PM, JUNE 28th AT THE KELLYS' MILL
Lace up your dancing shoes . . .
Live music from the Valley Banjo Boys!

A dance in a barn? With banjo music? She'd never been to a party without an orchestra or a dance card or waltzing. She felt a surprising twinge of excitement, imagining herself dancing freely to banjo music as she made her way up the steps to the general store.

Vinnie was helping another customer at the desk but let out a scream of delight as Lucy entered. "Well, looky who it is!" she shouted. "Loretta, this is her! This is my Emily. Emily Holloway."

The woman standing at the desk was a tall middle-aged woman with grey hair tied back in a tight bun. She eyed Lucy warily and gave a curt nod.

Vinnie's smile made up for the both of them. "Come here, dear," she said. "Come and meet the reverend's wife, Loretta Polly. I was just telling her, not more than a few minutes ago, that you should be back any day and *voila!* You come breezing through my door."

Lucy approached the desk and shook Loretta's hand. "Thank you, and I'm so pleased to make your acquaintance, Loretta," Lucy said. Then she took a basket and started to walk down one of the aisles.

"I thought you said she was from Missouri," Loretta said to Vinnie. "She sounds like an Easterner."

"Well, she's a Valley City girl now, that's all I care!" giggled Vinnie.

Loretta gave a small smile and looked her up and down, then turned back to Vinnie, continuing the conversation regarding the upcoming picnic. Loretta was of the opinion that Martha Bailey cheated and bought her pies from a baker in Denver. Lucy wandered down one of the aisles, found some beauty items and added curlers, pins, and a small handheld mirror into her basket. She racked her brain thinking of the historical beauty rituals of women of long ago. Cleopatra was said to have traveled with a pack of donkeys so she could bathe in their milk. She was also known for her masks of grapes, egg whites, and honey to keep her skin radiant. Lucy added a few eggs, grapes, and a jar of honey to her basket. And a small sewing kit, so for something to do she could try and mend the dress she'd left New York in. That reminded her, and she went and rifled through a stack of books. A lot of Bible studies on various books of the Bible. A book on raising God-fearing children. Finally, one near the back intrigued her, and she pulled it from the pile. *Taming Lord Ferguson.* On the cover was a scantily clad woman in the arms of a muscled man in a kilt. Lucy turned it over and read the back:

Forced into wedlock. She was the daughter of a penniless merchant. He, a fierce conqueror of both the battlefield and the boudoir. She was prepared to tame the beast that raged within him. What she wasn't prepared for was the one he would awaken within her.

"Speaking of picnics and pies," Vinnie said, startling Lucy. "Is there something you want to tell me, you sly boots?"

Vinnie and Loretta were both staring at her, Vinnie with her hands on her hips and a huge grin across her face. She turned to Loretta and pointed her finger at Lucy as she spoke. "Seems we have an award-winning pie baker on our hands. That's right, the secret's out, little missy! I've heard all about your pies! That handsome husband of yours has been braggin' you up."

"Pardon me?" asked Lucy. "He told you what?"

"Oh no, don't be little Miss Modest with us now. He told us all about it. Why, we can hardly wait to see what you'll dazzle us with." Vinnie beamed as she continued bagging Loretta's groceries.

"How wonderful," said Loretta. "She's entering the contest for the picnic then?"

"Of course, she will!" said Vinnie. "And I plan to put her first-place ribbon right there, above the cash register for all to see." Vinnie looked over at Lucy as she spoke. "Martha Bailey from Rosetown has won four years in a row. No one from Valley City's ever taken home first place. But each year we're hopeful!"

Lucy forced a smile. "Well, I'll certainly do my best," she said.

She tossed *Taming Lord Ferguson* into her basket and continued rifling through the books for a recipe book. What was Will thinking, telling Vinnie something so absurd? What if they were still here for the picnic? Now on top of all her chores, she'd have to learn how to make a sodding pie. She pulled a book from the pile. *The Exemplary Housewife: The Art of Cooking and Womanhood.*

Over five hundred recipes in the table of contents. How to prepare any kind of meat. Turkey, pheasant, partridge, pigeon, rabbit. How to make gravies, sauces, fricassees, pies, puddings, jams, and custards. The best methods of collaring, drying, and pickling. Proper table arrangement. Sunday picnic menus. How to remove grease spots, clean pearls, and tackle other domestic concerns with a smile. How to welcome your husband home from the field. There was even chapter on relations in the bedroom. She paged through it and found a section on pies. "Land a Husband Strawberry-Rhubarb Pie." She looked over the list of ingredients and directions and kept it open to the page as she walked up and down the aisles, placing the necessary things in her basket. A whisk, rolling pin, and pie pan. Flour. Powdered sugar and a sifter. Lard. Butter. Eggs. Vinegar.

"Vinnie," she said. "What does it mean by *zest* of a lemon?"

Vinnie and Loretta both burst out laughing.

"Oh no, you don't," said Vinnie. "The cat's out of the bag, missy. Don't you play coy with us."

Lucy smiled as she put a lemon in her basket and continued shopping. She picked through a bin of strawberries and picked out the ripest of them. Then a small sack of flour. Lard. When she double checked she had all the ingredients necessary, she flipped through the dinner menus. She was going to have to learn how to cook as well, even if a little just to get them by.

"After-Church Roasted Chicken Feast." The recipe called for basting with melted butter and herbs, and a side of capers, carrots, and turnips. Lucy added a few turnips and carrots to her basket, and a small jar of capers.

"Vinnie," she said. "Have you got any chicken?"

"Do I ever! You wait right here."

The sun was setting that evening when Lucy heard Will riding into the yard. She looked around the house. There was flour everywhere. A cracked egg on the floor she'd dropped. The pie had taken longer than she'd thought; she was just getting started on dinner and she hadn't even had time to take her curlers out yet. A few stray strands of hair framed her face, sticky from bits of dough in it. One of the turnips slipped as she chopped and rolled off the table onto the floor. Outside, she heard the barn door open and close, then Will's footsteps across the yard.

The door opened and Will stood in the doorway.

She turned to him. "Hi," she said. "How was your day?"

"Fine," he said. He studied her a moment, then turned and looked back out at the property. "Why is there a chicken running around the yard?"

"Why did you tell Vinnie I was an expert pie baker?"

Will said nothing, still standing in the doorway, looking out at the yard. "Lucy, where did the chicken come from?"

"From Vinnie. She wanted to send me home with some chicken. I didn't know she meant a live one, and I couldn't say no once she came out with it clucking in its crate."

"Why'd you let it out of the crate?"

"It seemed upset, so I opened the latch and thought it would just wander off and be free. Why'd you tell Vinnie I could bake? She's expecting me to enter this pie baking contest. I've never made a pie in all my life, and it turns out it's actually quite labor intensive."

"You told me the real Emily Holloway won awards for her pies. We probably won't be here for the picnic anyway," he said. Then he went to the fireplace, knelt, and arranged the logs and kindling.

Lucy went back to chopping her turnip. "How was your day at the mill?"

"Fine," he said, blowing on the now-lit fire. Then he stood and left the house.

A few minutes later, he returned with the chicken clucking and struggling under his arm. He walked it over to the washbasin beside her and took his knife from his pocket.

"What are you going to . . ?"

He held the bird down in the sink and brought the knife to its throat, then made a quick slice across. She turned away until the fluttering stopped. The animal lay still in the washbasin, blood draining from its throat, and Will began to pluck the feathers out in handfuls. He glanced up at Lucy, studying her roller set. "I like what you've done with your hair," he said.

She smiled and watched him plucking feathers, then went back to chopping the turnip. She could feel him pause and study her again.

"What?" she asked.

"I assumed you were just being modest when you said you couldn't cook."

"I wasn't. I can't sew either," she said, pointing to her New York dress, lying across the table with the needle and thread tangled in the sleeve.

Will smiled the most handsome smile before he turned the chicken over and started plucking the backside. His hands were rough and covered in chicken blood. He pointed to *The Exemplary Housewife* on the counter. "What's that?"

"A recipe book. Well, I bought it for the recipes. It also has suggestions and advice on womanhood. Outdated, if you ask me, things like 'How to welcome him home from the field,'" she said, then she cut into the turnip and another piece skidded off the counter.

Will stopped plucking the chicken and looked around the house. "Does she say to welcome him home by having a chicken on the loose in the yard? Or to stand at the counter with curlers in your hair and flour all over your face?"

Lucy laughed and kept chopping her turnip. "She says to have dinner ready upon his arrival. And appear fresh and pretty."

Will smiled and plucked another handful of feathers. "Well I don't mind cooking. And you do look pretty," he said.

When he had finished plucking the feathers, Will chopped the chicken with a large butcher knife, putting the legs, breast pieces, and other edible parts into a large pot that he'd hung in the fireplace above the now roaring fire. To the pot, he added the turnips and potatoes, and a few chunks of butter mixed with rosemary and sage from the garden. As it cooked he sat in front of the fire, polishing his saddle. Lucy rolled out her pie dough and laid it carefully in the pie tin. Outside, the barn door creaked open, ending with a loud bang as it hit the side of the barn, then slammed shut again. Startled, she went to the window.

Will stood, grabbed the shotgun from the mantel and went to the door. "Stay here," he said, and left the house.

Lucy watched as he inspected the barn and yard. When he came back into the house he put the shotgun back.

"It's just that broken latch on the barn door. I'll fix it after dinner, if it's not raining by then."

Lucy turned her gaze back to the property. The sky was slowly clouding over.

"I've been thinking, though," said Will. "I'd feel better if you took the shotgun with you when you're out doing chores. Especially if you go any distance from the house. There's men who make a good living hunting bounties. They're ruthless and they're smart. And we're wanted dead or alive."

Lucy watched the clouds a moment longer, then looked up at the rusty shotgun that hung on the mantel. "I don't know how to work that thing."

Will blew out a long stream of smoke and took it back down from the mantel. "Want to learn?"

A little while later, they stood out on the porch, Will pointing out the important parts of the gun. The barrel. The trigger. The sight. How to cock back and reload. Every gun was different. The sight on this one was slightly high. And the trigger could be sticky.

"They call this one a short-barrel," he said. "Lighter and easier to handle than a musket."

He held up the gun, showing her how to hold it, how to aim. He had set up a row of tin cans on top of a hay bale halfway down the drive as a target. Standing just off the porch, he stood quietly, looking through the sight. Perfectly still. Finger on the trigger. Then he fired, sending one of the tin cans flying off the hay bale. He lowered the gun and handed it to her.

She took it and held it the way he'd held it, up against her right shoulder, left hand on the barrel, right index finger on the trigger. He reached over and adjusted it so it rested more on the fleshy part of her shoulder. Once she had the feel of it, she closed her left eye and looked through the sight with her right eye. She held the gun steady, aiming at one of the cans. Finger on the trigger, slowly she pulled back. The sound of it rang in her ear and the kickback into her right shoulder made her take a step back to catch her balance.

"Almost," Will said. "Reload it. Aim a bit lower this time."

She cocked the barrel back. The shell made a clicking sound as it dropped into place, which gave her a little thrill. She widened her stance slightly and pulled the trigger. This time, the can went sailing off the hay bale. She whooped for joy.

"Thatta girl," Will said, smiling.

She reloaded, then slowly brought the butt of the gun up to her shoulder, closed an eye, and lined the can into view. Something about aiming the gun with her finger on the trigger was intoxicatingly exciting. Her shoulder throbbed a little from the kickback, but to her surprise, she didn't mind it.

Will stopped her as she brought it up to aim again. His eyes focused on the road now. Lucy could hear a horse in the distance. Then a rider came into view in the driveway, coming toward the house.

"Who is it?" she asked quietly.

The rider wore his hat low, shading his face, and a black bandana, like Will did sometimes. Guns on his hips and a leather sash slung across his shoulder studded with ammunition. The horse was panting.

Will slid his gun back into his holster. "What's happened?" he asked.

The man stopped the horse near the porch and she recognized him now. Silas, the friend that had helped get her out of jail. He took his hat off and gave Lucy a nod. Then he turned to Will. "We got trouble," he said. "The house Oscar and Cal were staying at was raided by Pinkertons. They're holding 'em in jail. Gonna hang them in the morning."

"I'll saddle up Zeta," Will said.

"What about the girl?" Silas asked, eyeing Lucy. "You want me to tie her up?"

"No," said Will.

"Someone tipped off the Pinkertons, Will," Silas said.

"It wasn't her," said Will. Then he turned to Lucy. "Keep practicing with that shotgun. And don't let anyone in the house."

He started walking across the yard to the barn.

"What are you going to do?" she asked.

He didn't turn around.

Silas still sat on his horse, his hat low, but she could feel his eyes on her.

A few minutes later, Will led Zeta from the barn and they rode off. Lucy stood there thinking about how well that jail would be guarded and the danger they were riding into. She felt anxious and helpless and alone. When she could no longer hear the sound of their horses galloping in the distance, she held the shotgun up, aimed at a can, and fired. The can went soaring off the hay bale and smoke lingered from the tip of the gun. Her ear rang from the sound of it and her shoulder throbbed, but she lifted the gun again and held her finger steady on the metal trigger as she aimed. When she sent the fourth can bouncing across the yard she went and retrieved them, lined them back up on the bale and shot another round. By the time the last can was tumbling across the yard, the oppressively low clouds had darkened, and the air smelled of rain although it was eerily calm. She wanted to shoot another round but as she scanned the property, decided to save the last few shells just in case. She turned and took the shotgun back into the house with her.

CHAPTER 11

LONG AFTER THE GREY sky had darkened into the blackest of nights, Lucy sat down in front of the fire, with her hair back in curlers and Cleopatra's beautifying concoction of whisked egg whites and honey on her face. No sign of Will yet, and she was trying not to let worry overcome her. Outside, the wind had picked up, and rain was pelting the roof now. Strange noises echoed in the house. The window creaking and the rocking chair on the porch sliding back and forth. The fire even seemed to crack louder than normal. She thought about Poe's *The Fall of the House of Usher*. The way the house mirrored its inhabitants and their impending doom. It gave her chills now but there was no escaping it, so she picked *Taming Lord Ferguson* up off the floor beside her and began to read.

The story began with Caitlin, the heroine, snatched from her bedroom in the night, tied up in the back of a small wagon, crossing the highlands to the Ferguson castle. There, she was forced to wed the infamous Lord Ferguson in a small candlelit ceremony. Servants attended her, dressing her in an elegant, velvet dress. A strange headpiece that hung across her forehead. Lord Ferguson was dressed in his clan's tartan kilt, jacket, dirk, and sporran. There was a cold exchange of vows. And then he kissed her. Slowly at first, and as Caitlin began to pull away, his kiss turned passionate, his tongue parting her lips, his arms wrapping around her now, pulling her body against him. Then he carried her to the bedroom, set her on the bed, and stared at her in the firelight. Passion in his eyes. Caitlin was trembling. So was Lucy. Then Ferguson left her, going through a side door into his own quarters. Caitlin lay in bed, still trembling, knowing there would be a time when he wouldn't sleep in his own quarters.

Lucy lowered the book and stared into the flames. Outside the wind was increasingly violent and she pictured Will riding in it. She was sick with worry now and overcome with a heightened awareness of how intertwined her fate was with his, and how much she actually cared for him. She tried to continue reading but couldn't focus on the words, so she went to the sink and rinsed the concoction from her face. Then she removed the curlers from her hair, tousled it out with her fingers, and went to bed.

In her dream, she was shipwrecked in a violent storm. Barely able to see through the fog, she swam toward a harbor, terrified and disoriented. The waves were overtaking her as she stumbled up on shore. From one of the nearby docks, men shouted at her in a language she didn't understand. Then she saw him, standing alone on the shore.

Lucy sat up in bed.

The wind was howling, the windowpane rattled, and she thought she heard the front door open.

"Will!" she called out.

She got out of bed and went to the kitchen. The front door was closed.

She went out onto the porch. The wind beat her face and her skirt flailed about recklessly. She shielded her face. Lightning showed the trees bending sideways in the wind, and the thunder rumbled so loud she felt it in her chest. A giant wind gust broke a post free from the railing, and spun it into the window, glass shattering everywhere. Then a banging and loud snap from somewhere inside the house. She went back inside and stopped as she looked up to see part of the roof being carried away in the wind.

She screamed and turned and ran down the porch steps to the storm cellar at the side of the house. It was entered through a trap door in the ground, and she pulled at the handle with all her might but it wouldn't budge. The rain was coming down so hard, it was painful against her face. She tried to shield her face with her arm and pulled at the door again. This time her hand slipped and she fell backwards. She thought she heard someone call out her name, but when lightning lit up the sky, all she could see was an outline of the barn and a hay bale blowing across the drive. Her hair was whipping in the wind, and her dress was soaked through. She got back to her feet and tried to pull on the door again. It was no use. She looked around in the darkness, not sure where to take cover. Both the barn and house could collapse on her. She reached down and tried to lift the door again.

Then, from behind, someone grasped her arm and pulled her back.

It was Will.

He reached down and yanked the door open. "Climb down," he shouted.

She turned and started climbing down the ladder. He followed, shutting the trap door behind them.

Everything pitch black. She felt her way down the ladder until her feet touched solid ground. When Will reached the bottom, she felt him brush past her. He fumbled around in the dark and knocked something over, then finally struck a match and lit a candle. Hard-packed dirt walls and floor, not more than four feet wide, surrounded them in either direction. There was a wooden chair and a small shelf with the kerosene lantern, matches, and two green army blankets. Two small wooden crates sat on the bottom shelf.

Will ran his hands through his hair. Water dripped down his face. His eye was bruised and swollen, as though he'd been in a fight, but she could see no further injury. His black shirt was soaked and clinging to his body, and his chest rose and fell in long slow breaths.

"Are you all right?" she asked.

He nodded.

The trap door above them rattled violently, banging in the wind. Will snapped one of the wooden legs off the chair and climbed back up the ladder to wedge it in the door. The banging stopped. He climbed back down, went to the shelf, and tried to light the lantern. After a few attempts, the lantern wouldn't light, and he swore under his breath as he shook out the last match.

"What happened?" she asked. "Are your friends all right?"

"Take your clothes off," he said.

"Pardon me?"

"We have to hang our clothes so they can dry out overnight," he said as he handed her a blanket from the shelf.

Lucy took the blanket.

He took off his gun belt and set it on the shelf, then lifted his shirt up and over his head. She turned away. She heard him take his boots off and unzip and step out of his pants. Water hit the floor as he wrung out his clothes.

When she turned back, he was standing with a blanket wrapped around his body. His clothes draped over the shelf.

"Lucy, you're going to freeze to death," he said and took her blanket from her and held it up in front of her like a curtain. "I won't look. Hurry up. The candle's not gonna last long."

He looked away. Slowly, she started undoing the buttons. She was trembling but managed to work her wet dress over her head, then slid out of her bloomers. Stark naked and wet. She took the blanket from Will and wrapped it around herself, then handed him her clothes. He wrung them out and hung them on the shelf beside his.

While the storm raged on above them, they sat on the ground, side by side, against the cold dirt wall and huddled in their blankets in silence—the only light, the small flame of the candle casting shadows on the dirt walls. Lucy sat shivering in her blanket and tried to wring some of the water from her hair.

A branch or piece of debris tumbled across the lawn above them, and they both sat quietly, staring up at the trap door.

Will ran his hands through his hair and sat rubbing his face.

"What happened?" she asked. "Did you get them out of jail?"

"Yeah."

Lucy adjusted the blanket around her. Thunder boomed and shook the earth, and she shuttered. The candle sputtered, slowly shrinking, eventually sputtering as it neared the end of the wick, casting strange and distorted shadows all around them. Wax spilled down the holder and pooled on the ground.

"Did you find out who it was, that tipped the Pinkertons off?"

"Yes."

"Who was it?"

"He's dead."

"Did you kill him?" she asked, pulling the blanket tighter around her. Her teeth were rattling now, and her body shivered uncontrollably.

"Come here," he said quietly and pulled her onto his lap. He tucked her blanket tighter around her like a mummy, then wrapped his blanket around them both. With his arms around her, her face against his bare chest, she closed her eyes and tried to think of anything else. Her aunt. San Francisco. Putting her feet in the Pacific for the first time. Will brought a hand up and gently brushed a piece of her hair back off her face. His fingers grazed her temple and sent uncontrollable chills through her. She could hear his heart beating loudly, and let herself lean into the warmth of his skin on her cheek.

There was a loud crash above. Something collapsed. More debris tumbled across the lawn and clanked against the trap door. She thought she heard a horse whinnying. Maybe it was the wind.

"Do you think the horses are okay?" she whispered.

"No," he said, and pulled her closer against him.

"Lucy," Will whispered. "Lucy, wake up."

She was still lying against him. He gently moved her from his lap and stood up. Lucy sat huddled in her blanket against the wall. Too dark to see, she only made out the outline of him as he dressed. A small stream of light shone through a crack in the trap door. The rain had stopped. Something that felt like a centipede crawled onto her hand and she jumped. Will finished dressing and climbed up the ladder. The latch on the door clicked, and he opened it. Grey daylight flooded in. He looked down at her silence. He turned and climbed the rest of the way out. She stood and hugged the blanket around her as she stared up at the clouds, listening to his footsteps across the yard.

He let out three sharp whistles and shouted for Zeta. Then his footsteps ceased, and all went quiet. A piece of wood crashed against something with a loud crack.

"Goddamnit," she heard him say.

She went to the shelf where her dress hung. Still damp and cold. She let the blanket fall. Shivering, she slid the dress over her head. Will whistled and shouted for Zeta again. Everything still quiet. When she finished dressing, she climbed the ladder and peeked her head out. Pieces of wood and shrapnel strewn about the yard. The barn had collapsed. An evergreen tree lay on the ground amongst the wreckage. The plow still intact but on its side. The wagon lay split in half. The horses were nowhere in sight. Nor the little goat. Just the cow, standing beside the broken fence, grazing on grass as though nothing had happened.

Will stood with his back to her, hands laced on the back of his head. He lowered his hands and turned and met her gaze. She looked away, back to the house. It was still standing. The front door missing. The window shattered.

Will walked to her, still standing on the ladder. "Give me your hand," he said.

She took his hand and let him help her out.

His eyes were bloodshot. He pulled his tobacco bag and rolling papers from his pocket and sat down on the trunk of the fallen evergreen. Lucy sat down beside him. He filled the paper with a pinch of tobacco and rolled it back and forth on his thigh. When he was done, he put it to his mouth and struck a match against his pants. He sat with his elbows rested on his knees, his shoulders slumped forward. He blew the smoke out in a long stream, looked over at Lucy and then out at the horizon.

"The horses are gone," he said.

She stared at the ground, watching the heel of his boot dragging back and forth in the dirt.

Then he stood. His eyes focused on the road. "Someone's coming," he said. "Let's get in the house."

She looked out at the road. She couldn't see anyone but could hear horses in the distance now.

Will crossed the yard to the porch, and she followed him. He ripped one of the dangling hinges from the doorframe as he entered. He grabbed the shotgun from the mantel, went to the bedroom, and stood, looking out the window. She stood a few feet behind him, trying to see past him through the window.

"Did you go to Sheriff Lyman yesterday? After I left?"

"What?" she asked.

"I asked you a question."

"I didn't speak to anyone. I never left the house."

He aimed the gun out the window. The cigarette hung from his mouth, smoke billowing around the barrel. "He's coming this way with three others," he said.

Lucy peered out the window behind him to see three riders on the road, heading toward the house, with Zeta and the tan mare trailing rider-less in tow. Sheriff Lyman rode out front, his badge gleaming. She recognized another as Vinnie's husband, Thomas.

"I haven't spoken to anyone, I swear," she said.

Will lowered the shotgun and set it on the bed. Then he took off his gun belt and tucked one of his guns in his boot, the other in the back of his pants, before adjusting his clothing over both. He took one last drag of his cigarette and put it out on the windowsill. Then he turned and went to the porch.

The loaded shotgun still lay on the bed. Her heart raced. She went to the bedroom door and looked out.

Will was standing with his back to her, looking out at the property. She could now hear horses coming up the drive.

He turned back to her. "I'm going to get rid of them," he said. "Stay in the house." He went out onto the porch.

She stood there for a moment, then went back to the bed and grabbed the shotgun. Hiding it behind her, she crossed into the kitchen and hid behind the front door, peeking out.

Will was standing a few feet from the porch, his hat in his hand. He gave a friendly wave as the men rode to him and dismounted.

Lucy's hands trembled as she clenched the shotgun. The third rider she'd never seen before; he had dark skin and piercing blue eyes. Young, somewhere in his twenties. She listened as Thomas introduced him as John Stark, who ran the JS Saloon on Main Street. She couldn't make out what John Stark said as he shook

Will's hand, but it made everyone laugh. Thomas had found the horses roaming around town and knew there must have been trouble. They all turned and studied the wreckage of the barn.

"It's worse than I thought," said Thomas. "We're gonna need to build you a whole new barn. And wagon. What a shame."

Will began to protest, but Thomas cut him off.

"Tell you what, I'll ride back into town. Take the wagon to the mill and load up some lumber. Lyman and Stark, you stay here and start helping Holloway clean this up."

"No, no, don't worry," said Will. "I'll just build a lean-to from the scraps."

"No, sir," said Thomas. "It's bad enough you aren't gonna get a crop in this year. We can't leave you without a barn or a wagon. I'll let Alister know what happened; tell him you won't be back to work for a few days. I wouldn't be surprised if he donates the lumber for this."

Lucy watched as Thomas rode off down the drive.

"You got any coffee?" asked John Stark. "I haven't slept yet. Gonna need to sober up I guess."

"Course," said Will.

The sheriff and John Stark walked the horses to the cottonwood and pulled out some rope.

Will came up the porch steps and entered the house. He eyed Lucy, who stood with the shotgun hidden behind her skirts. He went to the stove, lit it, and set a pot of water on top. Then he took out his tobacco and papers and began rolling a few cigarettes out on the counter.

She peered back through the doorway. The sheriff and saloon owner were using the rope to tie the horses up to the lower hanging branches of the tree. She turned back to Will.

"How long does it take to build a barn?" she asked.

"Four or five days. Maybe a week."

"A week? What am I supposed to do? Will they be expecting meals?"

Will finished rolling the cigarettes and put them in his shirt pocket. Then he took the canister of smashed coffee beans from the cupboard and put a spoonful into three mugs. The water was coming to a boil, and he lifted it from the stove and filled each cup.

"Put the shotgun back up on the mantel where it belongs," he said.

Lucy took the gun out from behind her and set it on the mantel.

Will grabbed all three cups and went to the front door, then stopped and turned back to her. "The man who turned my friends in was helping us. Or pretending to anyway. I considered him a friend," he said. "I slit his throat and left him in an alley for the vultures. You get any ideas of telling those men who I am so you can take off with the reward money, I'll do the same to you."

He left the house and crossed the yard and handed each of the men a coffee. Will and John Stark each lit a cigarette. Sheriff Lyman went to the remains of the barn and started tossing boards into a pile. Tears flooded Lucy's eyes now, but she did not let them fall. She pictured Lyman, Thomas, Stark, and herself strewn about the ground with their throats slit. Vultures and blackbirds swarming. Will riding off on his horse, never looking back. She felt so foolish. She knew playing the role of a married couple was a farce, yet she'd let herself think he at least cared about her. But he didn't. He was a wanted outlaw and to him, she was a means to an end. She took a step toward the doorway and glass crunched beneath her feet. She picked up one of the shards of glass and ran a finger across the edge. Blood oozed from her skin, and she stood and watched it for a while, then wiped it on the skirt of her ugly cotton dress.

When Lucy was seven she dropped a vase in the dining room and she'd tried to clean it up herself, worried she'd be in trouble. There was blood on her hands when the maids ran into the room. *"Miss Lucy, Miss Lucy, no, don't touch! Miss Lucy!"* Kia, the oldest maid, screamed out. When her father found out about the incident, Kia had been blamed and fired for breaking the vase. Her mother, already not well at the time, did nothing to stop the maid from being thrown out in the street. Terrified of her father, Lucy said nothing either and cried silent tears every night for weeks. Kia had been her only friend and had mothered her the days her own was too melancholy to get out of bed. Lucy never found out what became of Kia, and she'd always regretted being so weak against her father that day.

Lucy was just about finished piling the shards of glass in the dustpan and sweeping when the steady sound of sawing, boards clanking, and laughter from the men stopped. Then, she heard a wagon coming down the road. She set the broom aside and went to the porch. Across the yard, John Stark and Lyman stood on either side of the fallen evergreen tree, each holding a side of a giant saw. Will held an armful of wood. Everyone's attention was on the road now.

The wagon was piled high with lumber. It was Thomas, but he wasn't alone. Vinnie sat beside him in the front seat, in a bright purple dress and a matching hat, waving like a queen as they turned into the yard.

Thomas parked the wagon near the other horses. Vinnie leapt down, went to the back, and lifted out two medium-sized boxes. She stacked them atop one another in her arms and carried them across the yard to Lucy, a big smile across her face.

"Hi, sweetie pie! Oh my stars, the window's shattered! And the door's gone!" Her eyes grew as big as saucers as she went past Lucy into the house.

Lucy followed her.

Vinnie set the boxes on the counter and produced a tool from her skirt pocket to work the lid off the first one. Hoping for some more of those delicious flapjacks, Lucy hadn't realized how hungry she was until now. Vinnie pulled two pairs of working gloves from the box, then a few small scrubbing brushes. Spray bottles. Rags. A dustpan. Vinnie was saying something about a ladies' aid group that met at the café every Monday. They were supposed to clean this house after Uncle Holloway died, but it still hadn't been done properly. Lucy looked around the house. She'd swept a little and wiped down a few cupboards but was certain that even with the deepest clean, the place would still look like a hovel. Vinnie moved on to discussing the lunch menu for today. The food was all on ice in the wagon—on the menu: potato salad, buttermilk biscuits, corn on the cob, roast turkey, and cranberry sauce.

"Slaughtered one of my prize turkeys this morning," Vinnie said, and made a gesture across her throat as if slicing it.

Lucy's heart raced as she listened. She could fake being able to clean, but what would Vinnie think when she saw that she could barely chop a potato?

A loud bang and shouts came from outside. Lucy rushed out to the porch. Will was holding a board up like a baseball bat, and Lyman wound up and threw a small piece of debris at him. Will swung and hit it across the yard. All the men cheered. He looked back at the house and held Lucy's eyes for a moment. An expressionless stare. Then he got into position for another pitch from Lyman.

Lucy went back into the house.

Vinnie held up a jar of bleach. "Make sure you keep this separate, in the back of your cupboard, so you don't get confused and put it in the soup. Though, it's crossed my mind to add a few drops to Thomas's dinner when I'm cross with him," she said with a giggle.

Lucy eyed the skull and crossbones and the word poison on the bottle. "How many drops would you need to kill someone?" she asked.

Vinnie let out a howl of laughter. "Oh, you do beat all, girl," she said. "Now, close your eyes and no peeking. I've got a surprise for you in this other box." Vinnie giggled. "I mean it. Close 'em!"

Lucy closed her eyes, and when she was allowed to open them, Vinnie was flinging a quilt up in the air, holding it out like a matador. "Ta dah!" Her eyes shone bright, and she was smiling ear to ear. The quilt was a patchwork of mismatched textures and patterns, sewn together in an interesting way.

"Vinnie!" said Lucy. "It's beautiful. Wherever did you find such a thing?"

"I made it, you goose," said Vinnie, handing her the blanket and the box she pulled it from. "There's new sheets in there too. Go on now. I'm sure you're excited to make your bed up. I'll get started on scrubbing the stove."

Vinnie whistled while she worked. "Hark the Herald." "Sweet Dixie." Lucy did her very best to work with the vigor of a farm girl: tucking the corners of the sheet in neatly as she made the bed, taking turns with Vinnie whacking the rug they'd dragged outside with the broom, and sweeping up the rest of the glass. She dusted cobwebs from the ceiling, washed down the table and chairs, the walls, the counters. She polished the silverware, and on her hands and knees, scrubbed the fireplace. Vinnie admired the fox as she brushed and fluffed its fur, telling it what a pretty coat it had and calling it "foxy." They had barely began scrubbing the soot-stained bricks when Vinnie noticed the time.

"Leave your sudsy water for later," she said. "We've gotta get cooking!"

Lucy left the brush in the bucket and followed Vinnie out to the wagon to unload the groceries.

Not a cloud left in the sky, and the afternoon sun was shining. Barely a breeze, the branches of the cottonwood stood still, while the horses shook out their manes at the flies. The men had started on the framework of the new barn already. Lucy followed Vinnie to the buggy.

There were two crates of groceries. Vinnie pulled out the first crate and handed it to Lucy.

From the corner of her eye, Lucy could see Will walking over to the wagon. "Let me help you with that," he said.

"We don't need any help, thank you," said Lucy.

Will took the box from Lucy.

"Well, what a gentleman!" said Vinnie. Then she lifted out the second crate, and the three of them crossed the yard to the house.

A tool belt hung low on his waist, with a hammer hanging from the side; his hair, back of his neck, and shirt wet with sweat. The muscles of his back were outlined through his shirt. Lucy knew she should divert her eyes but continued gazing at the back of him as they walked.

Inside the house, Will set the crate on the counter, then wiped his brow and looked around. "Looks good in here," he said before he turned and started to go back outside.

"Oh no, you don't," said Vinnie. "You stay put while I make you a glass of lemonade."

"I won't say no to that," he said, and sat down at the table.

Lucy stood beside Vinnie at the counter.

Vinnie took a few lemons from the crate, along with a cutting board, and began cutting one of them into small rounds. "Say," she said, "I never heard the story of how the two of you met."

Lucy took one of the lemons and an extra knife and cut it in half. "How we met?" she said. "Right. Well, it's kind of a long story. We met at a . . ."

"She was pointing a gun at me," said Will.

"What?" shouted Vinnie with a laugh. "Go on!"

Lucy turned to Will now, speechless.

"It was love at first sight," he said. "She was standing in the distance, her hair down, and her dress torn. Alone and courageous. She was the most beautiful thing I'd ever seen."

Lucy's thoughts went back to that day, dying of thirst, terrified, and in complete disarray. She studied his face now, searching for a sign he was teasing, but his gaze remained on her, a certain softness in his eyes.

Vinnie squealed. "It was love at first sight! Of course it was, just look at her," she said. Then she dumped the lemons into a glass of water and mixed in a little sugar and a few chips of ice before handing it to Will. "Okay now," she said. "Off you go. Us gals have to get started on lunch."

Lucy nicked herself three times with the knife before getting the hang of peeling potatoes. Vinnie didn't seem to notice, humming and whistling as she worked. Nor did she seem to notice Lucy's wide eyes when she handed her a glass and asked her to go and fetch some milk for the sauce.

"You mean from the cow?" Lucy asked.

"No, from one of the men." Vinnie said, then laughed so hard she had to wipe tears.

The cow was tied to the oak tree at the end of the row of horses. Lucy went and cautiously knelt beside it. Gently, she grabbed one of the udders and held the cup beneath, squeezing top to bottom, the way Phoebe had shown her. A small spray of milk came out. She smiled and felt a wave of pride as she kept going. She could hear footsteps walking toward her but didn't look up.

"Do you need help?" Will asked quietly.

"I've got it."

He stood behind her. She squeezed the teat a few more times, the glass nearly full.

The cow let out a long moo and spread its legs, and before she could ask what it was doing, it began urinating in a stream so heavy it splashed up as it hit the ground.

Lucy dropped the glass, covered her face with her hands, and fell backwards. "I swear this thing is the spawn of Lucifer."

She quickly stood, brushed herself off and looked over to see Will holding back a smile. "Right," he said. "Well, I can see you've got it." He reached down and picked up the empty cup, handed it back to her and walked away.

They picnicked beneath the cottonwood, oversized blankets laid out on the ground. The men were famished and talked about plans for the barn as they ate. They called Will "Holloway" and spoke to him with a level of respect that surprised Lucy, asking where he learned his architect skills and about his farm in Missouri. Will explained their troubles farming back in Missouri, how tobacco was finicky. Too much heat and they don't germinate. Too much rain and they harvest thin and flaky and don't sell.

"After two bad years in a row," he said, "me and the little missus decided it was time for a new start. Didn't we, sweetheart?"

"Yes, that's right," said Lucy.

"And here you are!" said Vinnie with a giggle. Then she fixated her eyes on the road. "Well, for goodness sakes," she said. "Who on earth could that be?"

Two men on horseback were riding down the road toward the property.

Lyman stood. "That's US Marshal Conrady from Denver. He's got a Pinkerton with him. I wonder what they're doing out in these parts."

"Uh-oh," said Vinnie. "One of us must be getting arrested." She jokingly put her hands up with her eyes wide and erupted into a fit of giggles.

Lucy glanced back at Will. He was stone faced, watching the men as they turned up the driveway and neared, stopping their horses just in front of the group. Both men were older, with greying hair. One had the badge of the star, United States Marshal; the other, a badge with an eagle at the top—Pinkerton National Detective Agency. The marshal had a thick mustache; he took his hat off. "Afternoon, folks," he said. "Sorry to bother you, Lyman. Folks in town said we could find you out here."

"It's no bother," said Lyman. "What can I help you with?"

"The Shanks-Kane Gang is back in these parts. Broke the Rindone brothers out of jail yesterday. It was bad. Streets were shot up from Larimer to West Fifth. Eight dead and counting."

Vinnie gasped. "The Shanks-Kane Gang, oh my stars!"

"Sorry to be the bearer of such bad news, ma'am, but I'm afraid so. Word is they're after the railroad money coming in by stage-coach in the next week or so. The railroad's already sent several Pinkerton detectives out to try and track the gang down before any more damage is done."

"What brings you all the way up here, though?" asked Lyman.

"We caught word they might be staying up around here."

Lucy felt the blood running from her face, her heart pounding so loudly she was certain everyone could hear. Will took a bite of his chicken, sitting there as though none of this pertained to him.

"You had anyone suspicious in the area lately, Lyman?" the marshal asked. "Anyone new in these parts we should know about?"

"Nothing suspicious, no," said Lyman. "Only new folks in these parts are the Holloways here, from Missouri. Had a bit of trouble in the storm last night, lost their barn."

"I see," the marshal said, eyeing Will, then letting his gaze linger on Lucy in a way that made her want to cover herself. "What'd you say your last name was?"

"Holloway," said Will. "Nelson Holloway, and this is my wife, Emily."

The Pinkerton fellow spat on the ground and studied Will. "How'd you get the shiner?"

"A piece of debris, before I got us down into the shelter," said Will.

The Pinkerton remained expressionless, still eyeing Will. "And where are you Holloway folks from?" he asked.

"Missouri," Vinnie said, not giving Lucy or Will time to answer. "And if you don't mind, our lunch is getting cold."

Both men sat quietly on their horses, eyeing Lucy and Will.

"All right then," the marshal said. "We best keep riding. Have a lot of area to cover yet. Let us know if you hear of anything, Lyman."

"Course," Sheriff Lyman said. "Good luck, gentlemen."

The marshal put his hat back on but still held his eyes on Lyman. "I mean it, Lyman," he said. "I'll remind you that harboring and abetting the likes of these men's a hanging offense. I know how you run things around here, and I've got my eye on you."

Lyman stayed quiet. The marshal and Pinkerton jabbed their spurs into their horses and rode off.

"I didn't like the looks of either of those fellas," said Vinnie. "Sometimes I don't know who to be more scared of, the outlaws or men like that who call themselves the law. No offence, Lyman."

"None taken, Vinnie. I became a sheriff to serve and protect those who need it, and sometimes that means going above the law."

Lucy clutched her skirt in her hands to hide how badly she was shaking. Even though she felt a strange comfort in her present company, her heart was still beating wildly.

Will lifted his glass of lemonade. "I just want to say cheers and thank everyone for all your help today," he said. "Want you to know how much we appreciate this."

Everyone clanked glasses and went back to eating. Vinnie told a joke about a three-legged cat. Lucy forced a chuckle and sat pushing her food around her place. Half a day laboring away in the kitchen, and now she'd lost her appetite.

Hours later, after everyone had gone home, Lucy scrubbed the bricks around the fireplace. The old wooden brush gave her two splinters and the start of a callous on her hand. The water in the pail began to turn grey; the suds gone. She felt like Cinderella, save for the evil stepsisters and stepmother. And prince. Outside, the sun was lowering over the foothills. Will was still hammering away out in the barn alone. Lucy rinsed the brush and studied the brick of the fireplace. Where there had been layers of soot, now beautiful tones of red and orange emerged.

"Lucy!" Will shouted from the yard. "Luce? Can you come out here for a sec?"

She stood, took the bucket to the porch, and tossed the water out onto the yard. Then she set it down and crossed the yard. The smell of fresh cut lumber filled the air as she neared. Will was standing amongst the framework. His hair was wet with sweat and his face was dirty. He'd stopped to roll and light a cigarette. He took a drag, then went and grabbed a two by four from the pile, hoisted it up horizontally against the framework, and nodded to the end of it.

"Hold the other side," he said.

She held the end of the board up. Will took a nail from his pocket, held it up against the board, and pulled the hammer from his belt. The board vibrated in her hands, but she kept a firm grip while he worked his way toward her, pounding nails every foot or so along the length of the board. Then he went back to the pile, hoisted another over his shoulder, and came and lifted it into place above the last. Lucy grabbed an end. Will pounded one nail in, then stopped mid-swing to wipe his brow and look at her.

"I shouldn't have spoken to you like that this morning," he said. "I was angry about a friend who turned on me and I took it out on you."

She nodded and stood holding the board in place, waiting for him to continue hammering.

"I'm sorry, Luce. You didn't deserve that."

"Thank you," she said quietly.

He hammered another nail in, then he stopped and turned to her. "I'm going to Argentina," he said. "With the money from the robbery. They say it's the new Wild West. Untouched and open for the taking."

"Why are you telling me this?"

"You asked and I never answered because I didn't trust you, but that was wrong. You've never given me a reason not to, and both of our lives depend on us trusting each other."

He lifted his shirt up to wipe his face, revealing the muscles of his stomach. "I never set out to be a bank robber," he said. "That's not how any of this started but it's what it's become. I kept fighting after the war because it felt like the only option at the time. People were displaced and starving and it was the only way I could see to help. But I'm tired of fighting. I'm so fucking tired; all I want is to leave this place and start a new life. But I can't do it without first taking back what was stolen from me."

The cow let out a long moo from where it was tied to the cottonwood alongside Zeta and the tan mare.

"A fresh start sounds nice," Lucy said. "I can picture you there, in the new Wild West, in Argentina. Who knows, maybe I'll visit you one day. I'll surprise you with a tango lesson and a night out in Buenos Aires for a Spanish opera. Your worst nightmare…"

Will laughed and shook his head as he studied her for a moment, then continued hammering a nail.

She looked around, taking in the structure of the building. It was quite something, really, how far it had come in one day. Where this morning was only rubble. It would be bigger than the old barn, and much stronger. Excited now to see it done in a matter of days, she thought of the cathedrals in Europe that took over a century to build.

"Luce?"

Will had finished nailing in the board and was holding up another, waiting for her.

"Sorry," she said as she grabbed her side of the board and held it in place. "I was just thinking about the cathedrals in Europe. Did you know it took over one hundred and fifty years to build the Cathedral of Florence? Imagine something being your life's work and never seeing it to completion in your lifetime."

"The what?"

"The Cathedral of Florence. Italy. I've dreamed of seeing it in person my whole life. Although, I'd want to step back in time, see it fourteenth or fifteenth century, under construction. All the greatest minds of the Renaissance in one place. Architects, artists, philosophers. Working together on a building so grand, it would forever change history."

Will had stopped and was studying her with a puzzled look on his face, but he said nothing. He hammered another nail in.

"Vinnie wants me to go shopping in Denver with her tomorrow."

"That will be nice for you, get a day away from here."

"She told me she's been praying for a friend like me for years. The only other younger woman in town is Ava, and when she's not busy with the café, she keeps to herself apparently. I keep thinking about how we're just going to vanish, and Vinnie will find out I was lying to her the whole time."

"I know," said Will. "I felt bad watching the men work so hard to help us today. I'll make things right after we leave, or right as I can anyway. I'll wire money for our bill at the general store, and now to Alister for this lumber he donated. Least we're leaving the place better than it was. That's something."

Beyond them, the sun was beginning to set over the foothills, a beautiful orange and pink glow in the sky. They stood watching in silence for a while. When it was nearly gone, Will lit a lantern and they went back to work.

"How do you know so much about tobacco farming?" Lucy asked as he finished pounding a nail in. "Is that what your family did?"

"They did. And the Rindones. Our county was fertile for hemp, tobacco, and a little cotton. It's a hard life though. On a good year, families barely scraped by. On a bad year, well . . . it's why I left when I was fifteen. Figured, even though I helped as much as I could, I'd been an extra mouth to feed for long enough."

"Where'd you go?"

"New York."

"You've been to New York?"

"Yeah, there was always posters and articles in the newspaper advertising for work there. I ended up doing construction, in the Five Points."

"The Five Points? The slum?"

"I'd never seen anything like it. The people. Irish, Eastern European, Italian, Chinese. There was music on every corner. Banjos and drumming. There was this trombone player named Dike that wandered the streets. And this dancehall called Almack's, owned by Blacks but the Irish went there too. The beer was cheap, the music was loud and the dancing, a mix of Irish jigs and the African shuffle. It was somethin.'"

He was quiet for a moment, then went back to hammering a nail in.

Lucy'd never dreamed of going anywhere near the Five Points, but she was picturing it now. Picturing herself in this place called Almack's, dancing an Irish jig, letting her hair down and having a beer. A few buttons undone on the bodice of her dress. Dancing with a dashing young Czechoslovakian immigrant who would later turn out to be a wealthy prince in disguise.

"What part of the city did you live in?" asked Will.

"My father's house was on West Broadway, but I mostly grew up at a boarding school upstate. My father thought it would be best, after my mother died."

"What was it called?"

"The boarding school?"

"Yeah."

"Saint Mary's Ladies Academy."

"Catholic?"

"Yes. Every day started with chapel and prayers and all that. Then basic classes. Music, history, arithmetic, French lessons . . ."

"Say something in French."

"No."

"Say, 'How are you?'"

"*Comment allez-vous?*"

Will smiled and studied her. He looked as though he wanted to ask her more but turned and grabbed another board and continued hammering.

Sometime in the middle of the night, Lucy woke alone in the bedroom and went to the broken kitchen window. She felt the cool night air wafting in. Will was working by the light of the lantern, climbing around the rafters. No harness or rope. She was glad he hadn't asked her if she was going to check the telegraph office while in Denver tomorrow. Of course, she would try to find a moment to sneak away from Vinnie to check, but what she would do—should there be a response from her father and money wired—was a question she didn't even know the answer to.

CHAPTER 12

———◆———

SHE WOKE TO THE sound of voices in the yard. Daylight shone through the window and the house smelled of coffee. She sat up, rubbed her eyes, and heard the faint sound of horses and a wagon on the road in the distance. She got out of bed and dressed, then pinned her hair loosely atop her head and pinched her cheeks. She went out into the kitchen and poured herself a half cup of coffee. She took it out onto the porch. John Stark and Will were already working on the barn, hammering away. Two wagons were coming up the drive toward the house. Thomas and Lyman in the first. More lumber piled in the back of their wagon. Following them, in a smaller buggy, a one-horse hitch, was Vinnie, waving at Lucy. As she neared, she patted the empty spot on the bench beside her.

"All aboard to Denver!" she shouted out with a giggle. "I decided where we're going for lunch," she said. "There's the most marvelous little café on Third Street. I'm so excited I can hardly stand it!"

Lucy crossed the yard to the buggy.

Will stopped unloading lumber for a moment to meet Lucy beside the buggy. She reached out her hand for him to help her up, but instead, he gently took her by the arm, pulled her to him, and kissed her on the forehead. "Have fun today," he said. Then he helped her up into the wagon.

Vinnie cracked the reins and they began to ride off. As they turned out onto the road, Vinnie let out a giggle and looked at Lucy.

"Well, I don't know what your secret is, missy, but my goodness, that man is a fool for you!"

Lucy looked back at the house. The men had all gone back to work, except for Will, who was standing where she'd left him, watching her go. Lucy turned back and looked out at the road ahead.

The streets of Denver were bustling by the time they arrived. The smell of fresh bread baking from a bakery. Milk jugs waiting on the porch of a few general stores. Women in dainty gloves and umbrellas, shading from the bright morning sun. A few wagons of men in work clothes and axes over their shoulders on their way to the mines, Vinnie told her. Vinnie drove the streets with brazen assurance, and surprisingly fast.

"Move it or lose it, sister." She giggled as a woman crossing the road on foot had to leap out of the way.

Lucy eyed the store window of a dress boutique as they rode past, then a hotel with giant, regal-looking white pillars. The Denver Hotel. A man stood outside alone, smoking a cigar in a suit and top hat. A woman came bursting out of the front doors wearing a man's long trench coat over her nightie. Curlers in her hair. The woman wrapped her arms around the man and kissed him madly. Farther down, Lucy saw a café with the sign on the window: "Fresh trout served daily." A light smell of fish filled the air as they rode past.

In New York, she'd frequented a small restaurant on West 47th owned by Spaniards. They served salt-cured tuna called *mojama*, an old family recipe that dated back to the western movements of the Phoenicians in the Mediterranean. Funny, the things she missed.

Over lunch, Vinnie told Lucy she'd been raised by her Mescalero grandmother, who was employed as a cook at a ranch outside San Antonio. The grandmother died when Vinnie was thirteen, and she was in training to take over as head cook when the circus came through town. She knew, somehow, that if she did not leave that moment, she may never do so. Suddenly, after she saw her entire life laid out before her, cooking at the same ranch her grandmother had terrified her more than leaving. She packed her bags and left within the hour with the circus performers. She was in an act involving a tightrope and a monkey, and traveled all over the West, all the way to California. There was an elephant and girls who swung from a trapeze. Vinnie could walk a tightrope and juggle anything you put in front of her, or used to be able to anyway. She'd even touched the mane of a lion. And there were mimes. Vinnie took a fancy to one of them. Clive from Atlanta. Twenty years her senior, and not that attractive. But oh, how he could make her laugh.

Lucy was shocked at the story but loved the way Vinnie lit up as she talked.

"My stars," said Vinnie. "It's been so long since I spoke of it all. I wonder whatever made me think of it now."

After lunch, Vinnie had a meeting with the bank, and Lucy used the time to make a dash to the telegraph station. Albert stood behind the desk, and he lit up when he saw her. "Well, as I live and breathe! If it isn't Miss New York City!"

Albert was wearing an outfit that reminded her of a Spanish matador. Red and silver, ruffles on the tight fitted shirt, and pants that fit even tighter and had a shine to them. His hair was slicked back.

Lucy smiled and approached the desk. "Hello, Albert. Please tell me a telegram has arrived for me."

His smile turned into a frown, and he shook his head. "No, I'm sorry, sweetie. But I see you're dressed in a new ensemble. Very country girl fresh. I love it. Anyway, it's so lovely to see you! I was worried sick when you up and disappeared. And, pray tell, did that gorgeous man ever find you?"

"Pardon me?"

"Tall, blondish hair. Wore his hat low over his face, but from what I saw, he was awfully handsome. Rugged. And spurs. He was wearing spurs. Lordy, I can't tell you how I love the sound of them spurs. I'm wearing some today, look." He held his foot out so she could see the spur around his ankle. He put a hand over his mouth and giggled. "Course, I've never ridden a horse a day in my life."

Lucy gazed up at the wall to the sketch on his wanted poster. "He was here," she said quietly. He had told her finding her was a lucky accident, but he'd been here. Looking for her. Why would he do that?

"Um-hmm. He was worried sick about you, lucky girl you. Made me tell him everything I knew, which wasn't much, other than I gathered by your smell and appearance that you'd been sleeping in the alleyway while waiting on a reply that never came."

"Right. Thank you, Albert. Thank you very much. I'll see you soon, all right?"

"Toot-a-loo, Miss Cavanagh."

Lucy tried to put Will out of her mind as she and Vinnie shopped the rest of the afternoon away. Vinnie insisted she treat Lucy to a flowered tapestry to hang above the bed and a red vase for the table—nothing could cheer a place up like fresh flowers. When Lucy tried to object, Vinnie reminded her she wasn't blessed with children in this life, so Lucy would have to take some mothering whether she liked it or not. From a fabric store, Vinnie purchased a floral pattern for a new dress for Lucy, which she also insisted she'd be happy to sew. It would give her something to do at night since Thomas, sweetie though he was, was such a man of few words. To the pile on the counter, she added a thin linen fabric to sew Lucy a nightgown. And assured Lucy not to worry, she wasn't some old fuddy-duddy and would make something that showed off her figure and a little skin for her sweetie. Though the thought of how inappropriate it would be to sleep in such attire beside a man who was not her husband made Lucy blush, she did not argue since she'd been sleeping in a dress since she'd left New York. She supposed she could just be careful to cover herself up with the quilt. They tried on hats in a hat store. Vinnie tried on a furry, overly tall one with a raccoon tail down the back, all the while trying to find a matching one for Lucy, howling over the idea of the two of them showing up back at the house looking like Lewis and Clark. Lucy tried on a small feminine top hat with a few raven feathers on the side and tulle streaming down the back. Practical to shield her from the hot Colorado sun, yet a little *avant-garde*. She wished she could afford it.

"It was made for you!" exclaimed Vinnie. Then she turned to the shopkeeper. "We'll take it. My treat."

It was almost sunset by the time they arrived back at the Holloway place. Thomas and Will were still working on the barn, and both stopped and came to the middle of the drive to meet the girls as they neared in the wagon.

"Well, what's the verdict?" asked Thomas. "Did you buy the whole town?"

Vinnie giggled. "Just about! But never mind the wiles of a woman, you two! What do you think of her new hat?"

Will smiled and met Lucy's gaze as he reached up to help her down. "It suits you," he said.

When Lucy was down from the wagon Thomas hopped up and took her spot.

"Thank you, Vinnie," said Lucy. "For today."

Vinnie smiled. "Thank you, my darling! Now, I'll go get started on your dress and nightie straight away. Toot-a-loo, you two love-birds!" Still holding the reins, she gave them a snap and drove the wagon in a big circle to turn it around.

Lucy and Will waved as they rode off down the drive. When they were out of sight, Will went to the porch and sat down on the step. Lucy followed and sat beside him. The barn was over half done; the roof completed and most of the siding. Beyond it were the first rays of a pink sunset across the entire sky. She heard baaing from somewhere and noticed the goat beside the barn, in a small make-shift pen.

"The goat came back," she said.

"I wasn't sure we'd ever see him again, but I guess this is home for him now, just like us," Will said. Then he rolled a cigarette and lit it.

"I went to the telegraph station," Lucy said.

"Figured you would."

"There was nothing from my father."

"I'm sorry, Luce."

"I sure had fun with Vinnie, though. And it didn't feel pretend, you know? She told me I'd have to take some mothering and something about the way she said it made me want to cry. She keeps bringing up the picnic. There is this blank space on the wall behind her counter for the blue ribbon that no one's ever won, and she's certain I'll be the first. It breaks my heart to think about her being at that picnic, wondering where I've gone, how she could have been so fooled. You heard her, she's sewing me a dress and a nightgown."

"What's the length of this nightgown?"

Lucy laughed. "None of your business."

"She loves you, Luce. I can see it. She might be heartbroken at first, but she'll understand. Not that I know a lot about it, but I think love is just wanting what's best for someone, even if it breaks your heart."

Lucy looked back out at the sky, it was breathtaking, the way the setting sun cast a pink glow across the sky and the peaks of the mountains. "When I was younger, a beautiful sky like this used to scared me. The nuns taught it could be the second coming of Christ, because one day, He'd descend from the most beautiful sky. The clouds would part and every knee would bend as he cast his swift and final judgement on humanity. Glorification of some and punishment of others. Lonely as this wonderful world always felt, I was still never ready to leave it. So I'd go indoors. Somehow I thought if I didn't see it, it didn't exist."

Will held the cigarette out to her. "And now?"

She took it, took a drag, and let out a long slow exhale. "We humans already glorify some and cast punishment on others. We don't need God for that. I don't believe in a final judgement anymore, nor do I fear it. I don't even know if I believe in right and wrong. I think there's just finding something to hold onto, someone to love, and doing what needs to be done to protect it." She took another drag on the cigarette and handed it back to Will. "Sorry. According to Janet, a good wife doesn't speak her mind around her husband. She says it will only annoy him."

"Who's Janet?"

"The author of that recipe book on the counter."

Will laughed and took a drag of the cigarette. "Your mind is my favorite thing about you."

They watched quietly until darkness overtook the last of the sun's rays. Then Will stood. "I should get back to work on the barn. Hoping to finish up by tomorrow."

"I know you were there," she said. "At the telegraph station. Looking for me. You made it seem as though finding me was a lucky accident, and yet you risked your life in a city where there's wanted posters of you everywhere, searching for me. I've been thinking about it all day, and I still can't figure out why you would have done that."

He stomped out the cigarette with his boot and met her gaze. "You know why," he said quietly. Then he turned and walked across the yard to the barn.

By the end of the fourth day, the barn was complete. Lucy helped Will hang the last shelf, and after he hammered the last nail in, they both stood back and admired it.

On either side of the shelves were hooks, and from them hung bridles, ropes, and an extra gun belt. Four stalls were on the left-hand side; a shovel, rake, and axe lined up against the wall. There was a carefully constructed saddle rack for each saddle. The door frame arched with a large sliding barn door that Will had made himself, artfully from the wood of the last barn, so that a part of it remained.

"Well, it's no Cathedral of Florence," Will said. "But it will do."

Lucy smiled. "You did a real fine job, Will. I'm really proud of you."

"I couldn't have done it without your help," he said. Then he looked her up and down. "Is that a new dress?"

Lucy looked down at the new dress Vinnie had sewn for her. Light blue with a floral print apron. She'd been so excited to give it to Lucy at the store this morning, along with the nightie. "Yes it's a new dress," said Lucy.

"Looks pretty on you."

"Thank you."

A horse whinnied from somewhere off in the distance, followed by three sharp whistles that made Lucy jump. She followed Will outside.

Silas was riding up the driveway on horseback.

"Good or bad news?" asked Will.

"Stage has been delayed at least another week."

Will was quiet for a moment. Then he said, "He's giving the Pinkertons more time to find us."

Silas nodded. "More time, more Pinkertons; he's even recruiting private citizens." He dismounted and led the horse to the water trough beside the barn.

Will and Lucy followed. As the horse drank, Will discussed needing more dynamite for the raid. Lucy couldn't imagine what the dynamite could be for but stayed quiet. The good news, one of General Hall's guards was a soldier they'd fought with, whom they referred to as Old Charlie. There were messengers working for them as well, riding back and forth. The Rindones, along with Irish and Silas, had all been recently staying in a safe house together, but they were now splitting up and spreading out again in case of a raid. Silas nodded in Lucy's direction and told Will she shouldn't go too far from the property alone. He asked if she knew how to use a shotgun.

Lucy kept a solemn face as the men continued talking, overwhelmed with emotion. There would be even more wanted posters, and as more Pinkertons arrived and private citizens were armed and on the search, it felt like the world was closing in on them. But staying another week meant they would be here for the annual picnic next weekend. She had six days to keep herself alive and safe from the growing number of bounty hunters while somehow learning to bake an award-winning pie that would make Vinnie, the women of Valley City, and herself proud.

CHAPTER 13

---◆---

LUCY WOKE AT DAWN with a start. She couldn't remember the dream, only the feeling of falling. Her hair had fallen from the clips in the night and felt a mess, but she hadn't slept well and needed a coffee. She wrapped the blanket from the bed around her, over her nightie, and went out into the kitchen, yawning as she walked. Will was sitting at the table with his cup of coffee.

Lucy poured a coffee and grabbed *The Exemplary Housewife* from the counter and sat at the table across from him.

He smiled as he studied her wild hair and blanket around her shoulders.

"Honestly, Lucy. You don't have to get so dolled up on my account."

She smiled and took a sip of coffee, then opened the book, paging through to the section on pies and scanning a recipe. "What do you think 'docking the dough' means?"

Will shook his head and shrugged.

"This woman is exasperating. With the recipes, she speaks in riddles, but when it comes to welcoming your husband home, she's clear as a bell: 'Don't speak too much.' 'Freshen up.' 'Tidy up.' 'Help him relax a little.' 'Take his boots off.' Honestly, what kind of men is she consorting with that can't take their own boots off?"

Will sat in his chair, smiling, but said nothing.

Lucy laughed and put the book down. "Well, don't you go getting any ideas. I'll not be taking your boots off for you; that's where I draw the line."

Suddenly, she could hear footsteps outside. Will motioned for her to stay there, then drew his gun and went to the window.

"Who is it?" she whispered.

He lowered the gun and grabbed his coffee as he watched whoever it was approach, he smiled. "I think you can put Janet's book away. Help has arrived."

Light steps ascended the porch steps, then the door opened and Phoebe entered. "Hiya, missus. And mister. Saw the barn was done. Thought you'd be back at chores and might need some help."

"Phoebe," said Lucy. "Do you know how to bake a pie?"

Phoebe looked back and forth at Lucy and Will, dumbfounded for a moment. "Does a pig roll around in his own shit? Course, I know how to make a pie. All right then, let's get at it, missus. Where's your lard?"

Will went and grabbed his hat from the mantel. Still smiling as he passed Lucy on his way to the door, he kissed the top of her head. "I'll leave you ladies to it."

Phoebe was surprisingly knowledgeable on the art of baking a pie. And a surprisingly patient teacher, never questioning Lucy's complete lack of skills in the kitchen or why she needed a recipe book for something most women here could do by the time they started learning to walk. It was curious to Lucy how Phoebe had learned so much without a mother, but she never asked, which was not difficult because she barely got a word in edgewise. Phoebe was also knowledgeable about the town and its inhabitants. She knew things people didn't talk about—like Mrs. Schmidt's deteriorating health since her stroke a few months ago, and the fact that she and Mr. Schmidt wouldn't be able to run the hotel much longer, which meant there'd be nowhere to house travelers or short-term workers for Alister Kelly's mill and no way to keep the town alive. Phoebe knew that Ava was going back to Philadelphia to take care of an ailing sister, which meant there would be no café. Not that Phoebe had ever eaten there. She'd dreamed of it plenty, though, sitting down with a real tablecloth, being served and sipping out of a glass all fancy. But her pa said that was for people who could afford not to cook, and they couldn't. She knew Wesley, who owned Grain and Feed and Livery; his wife was pregnant, but Phoebe couldn't think of her name. She knew that because her pa was filling in to help Wesley out while Wesley took his wife to doctor appointments in Denver. And that was how Lucy learned the only medical provider in the town was no longer practicing. The story, as Phoebe told it, was that Lyman had been married but recently lost his wife and child during childbirth at the hands of Dr. René Chogan. Lyman had never been the same, and Dr. René only came to town to drink at John Stark's Saloon.

The story was confirmed by Vinnie later that afternoon when Lucy and Phoebe went into town for more lard, sugar, and rhubarb. Vinnie sent Phoebe upstairs to fetch a fresh muffin and spoke in a hushed tone. Dr. René was Algonquin but raised from a young boy at one of the Catholic missions, then later went to medical school out East somewhere. He was a good doctor with a kind soul. Lyman's wife, Anna, had been Swedish, a daughter of one of the men from Alister's mill. Real beautiful girl, hardly spoke any English. During her labor, she started having convulsions and a fast heart rate; both she and the baby died. Lyman never blamed Dr. René; another doctor had even told him it was a marvel she'd lasted as long as she did and that René did everything right. But René blamed himself, and the unfortunate event was all the excuse people needed to start whispering. Not in Vinnie's store, though; she wouldn't allow it. Loretta Polly tried to start up conversation about his devil's magic once and Vinnie told her if she ever heard her speaking like that again in her store that would be the last time she set foot in it. Anna and the baby were buried in the cemetery on the far east of town; Vinnie brought fresh flowers to their grave from time to time. Vinnie never really got to know her that well, but the whole town felt the loss when she died. That same week, the young teacher who'd just arrived left and there was an accident at the mill; two workers died. A few weeks later, poor Uncle Holloway was found dead. Vinnie got teary as she spoke, then she smiled at Lucy.

"Our little town felt like it was cursed for a while there. And then you and your sweetie showed up. Some new life around here, fixing up that little farm. Gave us something to hope for again." Then suddenly her expression changed, a slow smile across her face. "Wait a second, young lady! What's with all these questions about a doctor?" She spoke in a hushed tone and gazed down at Lucy's belly. "Are we expecting?"

"No," Lucy said. "Heavens, no."

Will had no complaints over the next few days, coming home to the chores done, a fresh cooked meal Phoebe'd helped prep, and a constant rotation of pies to taste. The strawberry-rhubarb on the first night was his favorite, second to the blueberry on the third. He hadn't heard the story of the doctor or that Lyman had had a wife but felt the certain sadness about Lyman made sense now. He found it funny that Vinnie thought Lucy might be pregnant. He smiled and listened with a sweet and genuine interest as Lucy repeated stories of the day, and he laughed at things Phoebe had said.

He spoke little of his days at the mill, except there were several new workers who looked at him as though they recognized him from somewhere and he was trying to keep his distance. If he was upset about the stage being delayed or staying longer than planned, he never showed it. One evening when he arrived home later than usual, he informed her that he'd been working on building a wheelchair ramp for the Schmidts. Their ailing health was bothering him and the way Mrs. Schmidt barely got around with a walker; they'd both need wheelchairs soon and shouldn't be using those stairs, especially once winter came. He was going to leave extra early tomorrow to work on it. He was determined to have it done before the robbery.

By the time Lucy rolled out the dough for the final pie with Phoebe, she felt confident enough in her skills to bake one on her own for Saturday's picnic. The girls stood at the counter with matching roller sets in their hair. As Phoebe put the crust in the oven for the prebake, Lucy pulled a gift, something she'd had Vinnie special order in for Phoebe, from the bottom drawer. It was a book that Vinnie had helped to beautifully wrap.

"Phoebe, I have something for you," she said when Phoebe turned back around. "Vinnie helped me order it in special, just for you. But I want to tell you a story before you open it. It's the story of Charles Lutwidge Dodgson, a British fellow who, as a child, was very precocious and curious about the world, just like you. He spoke with a stammer, a stutter, which caused him to get made fun of, so he became incredibly shy and didn't make friends easily. He also suffered an illness during his youth that caused him to be deaf in one ear. Charles was lucky enough to get an education. He became a respected mathematician, but what he really loved was to dream up stories. One day, while he was with a friend and the friend's three little girls, Charles told them a story about a bored little girl who goes looking for an adventure. She follows a rabbit down a rabbit hole and meets all kinds of exciting characters. The three little girls loved the story so much, they asked him to write it down for them." Lucy handed Phoebe the gift, and she unwrapped it and stood, staring curiously at the book.

"This is the story he told those little girls. It was only recently published. It's called *Alice's Adventures in Wonderland* by Lewis Carroll. That's his pen name."

Lucy could tell Phoebe was trying to find the words, and so she bent down to be at Phoebe's level. "Phoebe, I know what you're thinking—that you don't know how to read yet. But you will. This is the start of your library because you are smart and you'll learn to read. And it's a reminder that even when you don't believe in yourself, Vinnie and I do. Anything is possible in this life, Phoebe. You can do anything you want to do and go anywhere you want to go. Don't ever let anyone tell you different."

It was the most speechless Lucy'd ever seen Phoebe. Then a slow smile came across her face. "Thank you, missus," she said, then threw her arms around Lucy. "This is the best gift I ever got! And *you* can teach me to read. I can come after doing my chores a few days a week. I think my pa will think it a waste of time, but he don't gotta know."

"Oh, sweetheart. How I wish I could. And I mean that from the bottom of my heart, it's just that—"

"It's all right, missus. You don't have to say why. I already know. Everybody leaves this place."

Later that afternoon, after Phoebe had gone home, Lucy still stood at the counter, peeling and slicing potatoes. The ham had already been cooking for three hours, and the house smelled heavenly. The "Crowd-pleasing Scalloped Potatoes" had taken her an hour thus far. After all this work of peeling and thinly slicing the potatoes, they'd better be crowd pleasing. Lucy reached over and gave the simmering sauce a whisk. Then she spread the sliced potatoes out in a baking dish and ladled the sauce over. She reread the recipe to make sure she hadn't missed anything, then sprinkled cheese and breadcrumbs on top, along with a dash of salt and pepper, and put them in the oven beside the ham. The table was set, and she had a fire going in the fireplace.

She took the rollers from her hair and tossed them in the bottom drawer. She pulled out the hand mirror and left her hair wavy and down, save for a few pieces in the front loosely pinned up, like she'd seen the women of Denver do. She pinched her cheeks and studied her complexion. Her skin was dull and lifeless. Kissed by the sun. Freckles she'd never noticed around her eyes. Her society ladies of New York would be aghast. She set the mirror down and eyed the steak on the counter that she'd bought today but hadn't had a chance to run down to the icebox in the creek. Will shouldn't be home for a while—he was finishing up the Schmidt's wheelchair ramp today after work—and she suddenly had the best idea. Empress Sisi was said to have slept with a mask of veal on her face and was known for having the most vibrant, youthful skin in all of Europe. Carefully, Lucy unwrapped and sliced the steak into four thin sheets of meat. Then she took a cucumber and cut two slices for her eyes. She lay on the floor beside the fireplace and lay the steak pieces across her face. One on each cheek, two across her forehead. A cucumber slice on each eye. The empress was also known for her routine of exercises to keep her waistline small. With all the pies she'd tasted this week, Lucy decided it might be worth a try. Lying flat on her back, careful to keep her top half still, she lifted her legs up and tucked her knees in toward her chest, then lowered them back down. "One," she said. Then she did it again and continued counting aloud. "Two, three, four . . ."

Suddenly, she heard footsteps on the porch, and then the door opened.

She took a cucumber from one eye. It was Will. Beside him, his friend, Silas, smiling.

"Lucy, what in God's name are you doing?" asked Will.

"What are you doing home so early?" she asked.

"What's on your face?"

Lucy removed the steak from her face and sat up. "Steak. Empress Sisi of Austria sleeps with veal on her face. It's the secret to youthful skin; everyone knows that. What are you doing home so early?"

"We gotta go take care of something that's come up."

"Take care of what?"

Will went to the cupboard and grabbed some jerky and a half loaf of bread. Silas was still standing in the doorway, holding back a laugh.

"Silas," Will said. "Go start hitching up that wagon."

"Wagon? Where are you going?" Lucy asked.

"To get more ammunition. We found some dynamite. I'll be back tomorrow," he said. Then he left the house.

Lucy stood and went out onto the porch.

"What about your dinner?"

He was almost to the barn, and she wasn't sure if he heard her or not, but he never turned around.

Will still wasn't home when she sat drinking her coffee on the porch the next morning. She was on her second cup when she heard the first sounds of a wagon. Lucy went and grabbed the shotgun and watched nervously as a wagon began to come into view and turned up their driveway. She lowered it when she could see the driver in an oversized peach hat and matching dress, waving wildly. It was Vinnie, and she wasn't alone. Two women Lucy didn't recognize on the seat beside her. Three more riding in the back.

Lucy stood.

"Surprise!" Vinnie shouted as they turned into the drive.

"To what do I owe the pleasure?" Lucy asked as they neared.

"I know you're already married," said Vinnie. "But we never got to throw you a wedding shower!"

Vinnie made introductions as the others climbed down from the buggy, one by one.

"You've met Loretta Polly," said Vinnie. "This is Elsa Freely, Ava, and Dolores Schmidt. Susan Kelly and Agnes Cooper."

"Well, what a surprise," said Lucy. "Please, come inside."

The pastor's wife, Loretta Polly, had the same sourpuss face on she'd had when she met Lucy in the general store, never cracking a smile the whole of the afternoon. Susan Kelly was the wife of Alister Kelly, who owned the mill in town. Ava, from the café, was sweet and shy, a widow that Lucy guessed slightly older than herself but not by much. Dolores Schmidt owned Schmidt's Hotel with her husband. Vinnie whispered that she'd had a stroke and her health had deteriorated greatly over the last six months. Agnes Cooper wore her arm in a sling and had a cast on her wrist. She told Lucy about the dreadful buggy accident she was in last week. Elsa Freely was a large woman and by far the oldest, in her seventies. She was hard of hearing but wore a huge smile on her face, even though she had no idea what was going on. It was Elsa who explained the tradition of the wedding shower. It was Dutch, and the story went as this: Once upon a time, there was a Dutch girl who lived in a simple little village. Her father wanted her to marry a wealthy farmer, but she fell in love with a lowly miller. Her father refused her dowry, unless she married the man of his choosing.

The women in the village saw her sadness. One day, they had the idea to throw a party in her honor and shower her with gifts—household items that would be in a typical dowry—so that she could marry the man of her choosing. The girl and the miller lived happily ever after. The tradition lives on in Holland. And now, because of Elsa, the tradition was brought to Valley City.

"Of course, that husband of yours is far from a lowly miller," said Susan Kelly. "Alister says he's one of the best workers he's ever had. He's thinking of making him foreman, but you didn't hear it from me. You should be real proud, though."

"Thank you," said Lucy. "I am proud of him."

The girls sipped coffee and ate little cakes while Lucy opened her gifts. Dutch spices from Elsa. A doily from Dolores Schmidt. A cross stitch from Loretta Polly that said: "Above all, keep loving one another earnestly, since love covers a multitude of sins. 1 Peter 4:8."

From Ava, a serving tray. From Vinnie, a gold brooch that had belonged to her mother, and since she was never going to have a daughter, she wanted Lucy to have it.

"No, Vinnie, I can't accept this. It should be given to family."

Vinnie smiled and pinned it to Lucy's dress. "You are my family," she said. Tears welled and rolled down her cheeks as she stood back and looked at it. She hugged Lucy and wiped her tears. "All right then," she said. "Who's hungry for more cake?"

By the time Will finally arrived home with the wagon, the women had all left and the sun was beginning to set. Lucy stood over the counter, chopping some parsley she'd picked from the garden. The ham from last night was reheating in the oven, and she had gravy simmering in a pot. Her flowers and gifts were still on the table.

She heard Will drive the wagon into the barn; then a few minutes later, he walked in the front door.

"Hi," she said.

"Hi. What's all this?"

"A few of the women from town came by today. They threw me a wedding shower. It was very sweet."

"I'm sorry I had to take off like that last night. I know you'd made dinner."

Lucy opened the stove door, took the ham out, and set it on the counter. "Did you get the ammunition?" she asked.

"Yes."

Will hung his hat on the mantel, then came and stood beside her at the counter. His eyes were bloodshot.

"Have you slept?" she asked.

"No," he said. "Can I help you with anything?"

"No, it's all right. You can sit and relax. It's almost ready."

The gravy was bubbling now, and she removed it from the burner and took the ham and potatoes from the oven.

"Vinnie gave me her mother's brooch," she said as she began to slice the ham. "I've been thinking about it all day. I wonder if I should leave it behind for her when I go. I met your boss's wife. She's a real nice lady. And the widow, Elsa Freely, what a hoot. But oh, goodness mercy, I'd blush if I repeated some of the things she said."

Will stayed quiet behind her while Lucy plated their dinner. A few slices of ham on each plate, along with the scalloped potatoes. Gravy ladled over everything. A healthy sprinkle of salt and pepper. A dash of parsley.

"I hope you're hungry, mister," she said as she lifted the plates and turned around.

Will was asleep, his head face down on the table.

She set the plates back down on the counter and went to the table and stood over him. "Will," she said softly.

He woke and sat up. "Sorry, Luce."

"Why don't you go lie down for a while?"

He stood and went to the bedroom. She put a towel over his dinner, then took her plate to the table and sat down. After taking a few bites, she stood and went to the bedroom door. He was lying where he usually slept, on the floor. Sound asleep. She went to him and took a pillow from the bed and put it under his head. Then she bent down and, one by one, took his boots off.

CHAPTER 14

THE VALLEY CITY PICNIC, which had started as a local celebration, had grown into the event of the summer, where residents of New Drayton, Dodsland, and Rosetown rode in for the event. As Will and Lucy rode up the long drive to the mill, she watched the hustle and bustle of the parking of wagons, buggies, and horses.

Lucy clutched her blueberry pie against her as they rode now, wearing the red dress from Vinnie and her hair piled up high in a loose updo. Yesterday had been the final day spent baking, alone this time, without Phoebe. She'd made two of each, for Will to sample, and he'd helped her choose the blueberry for the picnic.

They tied Zeta at the end of a long row of horses. Will helped Lucy down and held out his arm to her. "Luce, I haven't wanted to frighten you but I'm fairly certain those new workers I told you about at the mill know who I am," he said, "if I give you the signal and wave, it's time to go."

"Do you see any of them here?"

"Not yet."

"All right," she said, and took Will's arm.

"You look beautiful," he said as they walked.

She felt herself blush a little and smiled at him as she met his gaze. "You clean up nice yourself," she replied.

There was a long fire pit with steaks and chicken, pork, hare, trout—meat of all kinds smoking over coals. A few men were standing alongside the pits, tending to the meat and the fire. There were hay bales and dust and dirt, tables of potato salads, pastas, and desserts. Lucy set her pie at the pie-judging table. A band was playing, about ten of them on the stage. Guitars, fiddles and a banjo accompanied with singing, and a few beating upside down barrels for drums. The music was loud and fast, like nothing she'd ever heard before and she loved it. A giant flag hung on the wall behind them. The red, white, and blue dusty and a little faded. People filled the dance floor already. A free for all—it was hard to tell whose partner was whose with everyone spinning one another about and laughing. Will told her it was the quadrille. The only quadrille Lucy knew involved everyone dancing in a line. Women were to be poised and straight faced while they curtseyed and faced their gentleman partner, and physical touch was limited, barely brushing hands as they glided through the room.

Will took her by the arm and led her over to a table where the saloon owner, John Stark, sat with Ava. They had a pitcher of a brown liquid in front of them, and John Stark poured Lucy and Will each a glass. He'd gotten his hands on some absinthe and orange liqueur, and they were sipping old fashioneds, just like Abe Lincoln.

They ate. Lucy tried a little of everything. The steak had been cooked over the fire and was one of the best steaks she'd ever eaten. The pork was covered in a sauce unlike anything Lucy had tasted. Will told her it was adobo. Vinnie's cornbread was there. And a cold pasta salad with olives and tomatoes that was to die for. And the desserts. Real vanilla ice cream. Her pie didn't get the blue ribbon, but no one seemed disappointed, not even Vinnie who said she had a new plaque she wanted to put on the wall in its empty place anyway. Both Will and John Stark each took a huge slice so hers looked popular. Vinnie came by every so often to introduce someone new. Lucy watched as she worked the party. Vinnie knew everyone. And she was liked by everyone. As was John Stark, being the saloon owner. Lucy had to admit, he had the wittiest humor she'd ever encountered and had Will, Lucy, and Ava laughing all through dinner. He could imitate anyone and had a funny anecdote about everything and anything—and he liked to use that word. Anecdote.

By dusk, the barrels of whiskey and other beverages Lucy didn't recognize were brought out. Will found a bottle of champagne and poured Lucy and Ava a glass. The band had gotten louder, and the dance floor was packed. Ava laughed at something John said and spilled her champagne. Something about Ava's face as she frantically tried to wipe it up struck Lucy as funny, and she laughed so hard she had to wipe tears from her cheeks. John stood and took Ava by the hand and said it was time to dance. To Lucy's surprise, Will did the same and led her to the dance floor. They worked their way through, and in a crowd of people, he put a hand on the small of her back, clasped her hand, and drew her to him. And they danced. There was dust everywhere, kicked up as everyone danced, and the energy was so alive and vibrant. Everybody seemed so happy, clapping and smiling, not a care for perfect dance steps or decorum.

Will smiled as he twirled and led Lucy, then let go of her and grabbed Ava. Without missing a beat, John Stark took Lucy's hand and kept her moving. Near them, an elderly lady on the dance floor danced with a young boy, eleven or twelve. Lucy couldn't take her eyes off the woman's toothless smile and hoped she danced like that at her age, with frail hands still clapping with joy. Lucy and Ava crossed the room again, and Lucy found herself back in Will's embrace. Then the music slowed, and he pulled her closer, up against his body. She leaned in closer as they moved slowly in sync. When she gazed up and locked eyes with him, she had a sudden urge to kiss him but looked away. Vinnie stood off to the side and gave her a huge smile and a wave. Will twirled Lucy around slowly to the music. Five men stood along the back wall. No one she recognized. A rough-looking crew. One of them watching her and Will.

"Those men are staring . . ." she started to say when she was back in his embrace.

"Don't look at them," he said.

"Should we go?"

"Soon."

Will laced his fingers in hers and had her close against him again to slow their dancing to a standstill, his gaze intense, his face inches from hers. She started to pull away, but he held her against him. For a moment, he just stood there, staring at her. Then he brought a hand to her face, pulled her to him, and kissed her. It was like nothing she'd ever felt before; her body felt on fire and she reveled in the softness and taste of his lips against hers. Her hands reached up to his neck, pulling him closer.

He pulled away and studied her face. People danced around her and the music played, but all she could feel were his hands on her cheeks as she lost herself in his handsome eyes. He leaned in to kiss her again, but just as their lips were to touch, she could hear Vinnie's voice.

"You-hoo, lovebirds, come on over here. There's someone I want you to meet!"

Will smiled, gave Lucy a quick kiss on the forehead and left her to go back to the table. Lucy went over to Vinnie, who was speaking to an older gentleman she introduced as a doctor who lived in Denver. He would be the one to see if a pregnancy should ever occur; Vinnie winked as she said it. It was loud and hard to hear, but Vinnie shouted out over the music. Vinnie liked what Lucy had done with her hair. So stylish. What a scandal about her pie not winning. Loretta thought so too. But not to worry, like she said, she had a plaque she'd been meaning to fill that spot on the wall with anyway.

Lucy glanced over at Will. Elsa Freely had led him back onto the dancefloor. Elsa moved well for her size. And Will was so handsome and charming. Smiling, while carefully twirling her. Across the room, the group of rough-looking men hadn't moved, still lined up against the wall. They were watching Will. Lucy was sure of it now. Something was wrong. Will was still dancing and looked over in her direction. He gave a nod toward the door and when the song ended, he let go of Elsa and made his way over to Lucy.

"Time to go," he said.

He took her by the hand and bid Vinnie a goodnight, then he guided her through the crowd and out of the barn.

"What happened?" she asked. "Is it those men?"

"Yeah. Just keep walking."

Torches lit the fence rails along the long driveway, illuminating the lineup of buggies and horses in the moonless sky. Ava and John Stark were outside now, congregating with a few others around a fire pit, off to the side. Ava had found another bottle of champagne and she held it up now with a proud smile. Lucy and Will waved and shouted out goodbyes and continued making their way down the driveway. Suddenly, an arm came from behind Lucy and ripped her out of Will's grip. A calloused hand covered her mouth. She flailed and tried to kick, but he held her so tight she could barely breathe. Will was tackled to the ground by two men. She heard someone screaming for the sheriff. Will fought the men off and pinned one to the ground, punching him repeatedly. The other man ripped Will off his friend and threw him to the ground, kicking him in the ribs. Will got to his feet and threw a few hard punches. Then one of them pulled a giant knife from his gun belt. Before Will had turned, the man stabbed him in the back. Lucy tried to scream, but nothing would come out. The man held her tighter. She felt her ribs were about to crack and gasped for air. Will stumbled forward, then turned and kicked the now bloody knife out of the man's hands and fought him to the ground. John Stark came running over and tackled another one of the men. Then a few more men she didn't recognize gathered around. It all happened so fast. Thomas, Lyman, Alister Kelly, and a few other townsfolk came running. The man holding Lucy let go of her but gave her a violent shove, and the next thing she knew she was on the ground, the side of her face scraped and throbbing. The wind knocked out of her and she gasped for air. Someone she didn't recognize helped her up. Then Vinnie was there, looking her over. Everything was jumbled, and her head was pounding. She couldn't see Will. Thomas was shouting for someone to get the doctor. Someone shouted from the crowd that the doctor had gone home already. Will was standing, bent over with his hands on his knees. He spat on the ground.

"I don't need the doc," he said.

Four of the rough-looking men were tackled to the ground. Sheriff Lyman handcuffed one while locals helped to keep the other three down. One of them spat and fought to get up.

"You shot my brother, you son of a bitch!" he shouted out. "I know it's you, Shanks!"

Mutters came from the crowd gathering around. "Who's Shanks? That's Nelson Holloway."

Lucy went to Will and took his arm. His shirt was torn. His eye was swelling already, and his lip was bleeding. Voices behind her were arguing whether he needed a doctor, arguing over what on earth had started the fight. Then apologies to the Holloways. Those drifters should have been kicked out hours ago.

"Let's go," said Will. He had a firm grip on her hand now as they walked. Thomas caught up to them. "Holloway," he kept saying. "Holloway, you need the doc. Just hold up now."

"It's just a flesh wound," he said. "My wife'll look after me."

When they reached Zeta, Will untied her from the rail and Lucy hoisted herself up. Will struggled to climb up behind her and grasped the reins. There was blood on his knuckles, and it smeared onto her dress.

"Ha," he said, and they took off down the road. She felt him hunched over. When they reached the Holloway property, they dismounted and led Zeta into the barn. Will untied his saddlebag, then stood hunched over again, hands on his knees, and spat. He wiped his mouth with the back of his hand. Then he started undoing the straps on Zeta's saddle. Lucy went to him and helped pull the saddle off while he undid the halter. He walked Zeta into the stall and shut it behind her. He took a few steps back toward Lucy but stopped and stood bent over with his hands on his knees.

"Will, please let me fetch a doctor," she said. "They say he's always at the saloon, drinking alone. I'll hurry."

"You're the doctor."

Lucy went to him and took him gently by the arm. "Come on," she said. "Let's get you in the house."

CHAPTER 15

———◆———

BLOOD RAN DOWN HIS back. The knife wound deep and a few inches long. Just above it, on his shoulder, she saw a sort of branding she'd seen on cattle: "W.SHANKS.1.6.4."

She set the lantern back on the table.

He took a swig of the whiskey and handed the bottle back to her. "Use this to clean it," he said.

She took the bottle and went to the washbasin and fetched the dishcloth. Standing behind him again, she held up the cloth just beneath the wound and tilted the whiskey bottle over it slowly, letting the liquid pour down his skin over the wound. He leaned forward and clutched the edge of the table.

"Sorry," she said.

"Give me that bottle back."

She wet the dishcloth with more whiskey, then passed him the bottle and gently pressed the cloth against the wound.

"How bad is it?" he asked.

"Well, I'm no nurse, but it's a deep cut and you're losing a lot of blood. I don't know how to stop the bleeding, even with pressure."

"You'll have to stitch it."

"Pardon me?"

"Where's that needle and thread you were using on that dress?"

"You can't be serious."

"Go get it."

"Why don't you just let me wrap it for now and go and fetch the doctor. I don't think you saw the size of the knife."

"You see those numbers on my back?"

"Yes."

"You ever hear of the guerilla fighters in the war? Bushwhackers? Quantrill's men? Bloody Bill Anderson?"

"No."

"It was a citizen army. There existed on both sides; we ambushed each other's patrol and supply convoys, seized the mail, raided cities. We didn't have the proper tags to identify our bodies for our families, so we branded them on. Those numbers on my back prove that I fought with them."

"But what does it matter now? The war's been over for two years."

"I told you how the government left soldiers in Missouri to run out anyone who fought for the Confederacy. They passed laws making it impossible for us or our families to vote, own land, or hold office. They also had authority to imprison or lynch anyone they thought might have fought with Quantrill. Twenty-one robberies aside, yes, I'd still hang for fighting with that regiment. Most of the men I fought alongside did hang, under martial law, without trial."

Lucy held the towel against the wound, thinking about how many articles she'd read in the paper regarding the government's reconstruction of the country after the war. Everything portrayed in a helpful light.

"Go get that needle and thread," Will said.

She went to the bedroom. Her satin New York dress hung from a hook on the wall, the needle and thread hanging from the hem. She pulled it from the fabric and brought it back out to Will.

She disinfected and wet the thread in the washbasin by pouring a small amount of whiskey over it, then came back and stood behind him. He handed her the needle, and she took it and worked the thread through the open end.

"I'm sorry about this," he said.

She stayed quiet, held the lantern closer, and took a better look at the wound. There was white beneath the layer of blood seeping out. Bone maybe. She felt a wave of nausea and took a long, steady breath.

"You don't have to go too deep with the needle," he said. "Just try to get the skin tight to stop the bleeding."

She put a hand on each side of the wound and held the skin together. Then she pushed the needle into the skin. Harder to work it though than she'd thought. She worked the first stitch through and pulled the thread tight.

Will clutched the table and leaned forward.

She paused.

"Keep going," he said.

The breeze picked up outside, and the leaves of the cottonwood rattled. She looked out the window at the darkness. "Who were they?" she asked.

"I honestly don't know."

"Do you think they'll come looking for you?"

"I assume Lyman took them into custody for now."

She pulled another stitch through. Her hands were wet with his blood, causing the needle to slip. The dishcloth was also soaked in blood now, so she wiped her hands on her dress and kept stitching.

Ten stitches in total. A knot at the end to keep them tight. The bleeding slowed. She set the needle down on the table.

"Thank you, Luce."

"What do I do now?"

"Put some of the salve on it."

Lucy took the tin and dug two fingers in. She dabbed the salve across the wound, then set the tin back on the table.

"Go get the sheet from the bed," he said.

After she did as he told her, he took the sheet from her, ripped a strip off lengthwise, and handed it to her. "Wrap this around me," he said. Then he lifted his arms.

Lucy took the strip and began to wrap it around his back and chest, three times, and tied the ends of it in a knot. "Is that too tight?"

"No, that's good."

The leaves rustled again, and Zeta let out a whinny from the barn. She studied his profile. His cheekbones. The gentle slope of his nose. His long eyelashes. Falling in long, slow blinks. The side of his face was scratched from the fight, and his eye was swelling and turning blue already.

Lucy went to the window and stared out at the darkness. "How often should I change the sheet and clean the wound?"

"It feels nice and tight, as long as it stops the bleeding we'll have a look in the morning," he said. Then he stood. "I'm going to go lay down."

Lucy went over to him and started to reach for his arm.

"I'm all right," he said, and went to the bedroom. She followed him and stood in the doorway. He sat down on the bed and leaned over to start slowly untying his boots. She went to him, knelt, and took his boots off and helped him lie back. Then she turned to leave.

"Luce . . ."

"Yeah?"

"Thank you."

"You're welcome." She closed the bedroom door behind her.

She went to the counter, opened the bottom drawer and pulled out her hand mirror. The scratches on the side of her face were no longer bleeding but were tender to the touch. She wet a rag and dabbed it against her cheek, cleaning the dirt from the area as best she could, and then put the mirror away.

His saddlebag still lay on the table, half open. She went and peered inside. A bag of tobacco. Rolling papers. A knife. Bullets strewn about the bottom. A roll of paper bundled together. She pulled it out. A wad of bills. She thumbed through them and stood there in disbelief. Nearly two thousand dollars. She put the money back in the bag and continued rifling around. In a side pocket was a gun. She pulled it out and inspected the ivory handle and the initials carved into the side. It was Barnet's. She heard a noise outside and went to the window with the gun. She stared out at the darkness and listened. She spun the cartridge open, then rifled around in Will's bag again, grabbed a few bullets, and dropped them into the cartridge, then clicked it shut with a flick of her wrist. A soft snoring was coming from the bedroom now. She tucked the gun into her skirt pocket and fetched the rocking chair from the porch and dragged it inside. She tucked her book, a handful of candles, and some matches under her arm, carried the chair into the bedroom, and sat down beside Will. He still lay in the same position on his side. His snoring had stopped now, but his chest rose and fell in long slow breaths. A small amount of blood had seeped through. She gently pulled the blanket over him, then she sat down in the rocking chair and watched him sleep.

Sir Isaac Newton had been wrong. Time was not fixed nor constant; she'd never known it to move more slowly. She gauged the hours by the burning of candles. Will's blood continued to seep through the sheet, and she worried about him losing too much blood. As each candle burned down to its last flicker, she lit a new one, woke Will, used the whiskey to clean the wound, re-saturated it with the salve, then wrapped it as tight as she could with a fresh strip of sheet. The wound remained the same. No better, no worse.

Sometime in the middle of the night, she noticed him sweating in the candlelight and went to the bed to feel his forehead. Hot. She brushed his hair back gently and sat on the bed beside him for a moment. Then she stood, went outside, and crossed the property to the stream to fill a bucket with the icy cold water.

Back in the bedroom, she soaked several cloths in the water, then wrung them out and laid them across his neck, shoulders, and forehead. He stirred in his sleep, reached back, and pulled the cloth off. Then he whispered something, but she couldn't make out what he said. She waited until he was asleep again, then gently reapplied the cold cloth and sat back down in the rocker.

She woke to him moaning and thrashing. Still dark. The candle at the end of its wick, sputtering and almost gone.

"No. No. No," he mumbled. "No. No. Silas, look out! Silas!"

She stood and went to him. "Will," she said. "Will, it's all right."

He was drenched with sweat. He sat up on the edge of the bed beside her, looking around the room.

She put her hand on his shoulder. "It's all right," she whispered. "It was just a dream."

He stared down at the candle on the floor and shook his head. "No, it wasn't," he said. "There are things I've done that . . ."

The candle sputtered a few more times, then flickered out. He reached out for her in the darkness and took her hand.

"We rode into Lawrence by the thousands. It was supposed to be a retaliation, and about finding Jayhawkers. It was a fucking massacre. Everything was set aflame, homes, crops, people. And the streets smelled of it. Because they'd done it to our families, that was supposed to make it right. Since that day, nothing has mattered. I've struggled to find anything good about this world for so long. Until the day I came across you." He squeezed her hand as he spoke.

Tears flooded her eyes, and she was glad for the darkness as they slid down her cheeks. "You should lie back and get some rest," she said. Then she started to help him lie back, but he didn't let go of her hand and pulled her to lie down beside him.

"Stay with me, Luce," he said.

Her heart raced as her back was suddenly pressed against his body and his arm came around her. He held her hand still, his fingers laced in hers, and she could feel his breath on her neck. The feeling of him holding her was intoxicating, as though she were falling to a place dangerous and forbidden yet didn't want it to stop. When she thought he'd fallen back asleep, she forced herself back to reality and started to pull his arm off and roll away, but he kept her tight against him.

"Go to sleep," he whispered.

She woke to the cow mooing at dawn. Will's arm was still around her, but he was snoring softly. Slowly, she eased her way out of the bed, covered him over, made coffee, and went out to the barn. It was stuffy and dark, even in the light of day. The wagon was parked to one side and had a tarp over it tied down with rope, and she went and peeked beneath it. More shotguns. Crates of bullets. Small black round objects. Grenades maybe. And dynamite. Red tubes bundled together. "DANGER" written on the side of the crate. Lucy looked back at the house, then lowered the tarp.

The cow mooed again, and she took a bucket, went to her stall, and knelt down beside her. The udders were saggy and dirty. The smell rank. She pulled on one, and the cow mooed loudly and took a few steps back. "Come on," she said. "Stand still." She pulled a few more times, a little milk coming out each time. She kept adjusting her grip but couldn't seem to get more than a few drips each time. The cow stepped forward and mooed. The udder slipped from Lucy's hand, and she nearly fell back again.

She stood and smacked the cow on its backside. "Listen. Either you want me to milk you or not. I've got a patient in the house and chores to do. Now. Let's try this one more time."

"Give her some feed and she'll stand still," came Will's voice.

He was standing in the doorway, shirtless, the sheet still wrapped around his chest and back. The bruising around his eye had darkened overnight. Scratches on the side of his face and a fat lip. He was holding a steaming cup of coffee.

"Morning," she said.

"Mornin'."

He went to the side of the barn, opened a bag of feed, scooped some into a bucket. Then he brought it over and set it in front of the cow. His face was pale, and she could see beads of sweat on his temples, though there was a chill in the air this morning.

"Are you sure you should be out of bed?" Lucy asked.

"Keep going," he said. "She'll stand still now while she eats."

Lucy pulled on the udders a few more times, and the cow ignored her and chomped loudly on her grain.

Will went to the wagon and, moving slowly, undid a few of the ties on the tarp, then pulled it back and climbed up into the back.

"Is it all for the robbery?" she asked.

"Yeah."

He picked up one of the bundles of dynamite and studied it. Then he set it back down and moved a few of the crates around.

Lucy pulled on the udders a few more times. Milk streamed out now. She patted the cow on the hip. "That's a girl," she said.

Will kicked at one of the crates and picked up a sash, a belt-like thing studded with bullets.

"What is that?" she asked.

"A bandolier," he said, and tossed it back in the crate.

"Speaking of bullets," Lucy said, taking Barnet's gun from her skirt pocket. "I found my gun in your saddlebag."

"I know. Keep it. The two thousand dollars is yours too. I was hoping to have the last thousand by now, but it might have to be wired to you after the robbery."

Lucy tucked the gun back in her pocket and eyed the dynamite. "Do you know where the stagecoach is?" she asked.

"The last Silas reported was that it's about three or four days away now. He'll come get me when it's time."

Will stepped down from the wagon and began to pull the tarp back over it. He had his back to her now, and she could see that he'd bled through his bandage again. She set the bucket of milk aside and went over to the wagon.

"Do you always use dynamite?" she asked.

"For the stagecoaches and trains, yes. Not for a bank."

"How do you rob a bank?" she asked.

"Careful planning. Knowing when there's money in the bank. Who handles the money. What time the cashiers change shift. And a well-planned escape. Setting up safe-houses in advance for a hundred miles. Relays of fresh horses."

"How do you know how to do all that?"

"Guerrilla fighting isn't the kind of war you see in the papers. We didn't learn how to march in a line or follow orders on a battle-field. We learned the art of stealth and careful planning. Disguises. Raids. Escape routes," he said as he tossed a rope across the wagon. "Hold the other side down."

When they'd finished tying the tarp down, Will went over to Zeta's stall to open it, then led her outside and tied her to a post. He took a brush and ran it the length of the horse's back a few times. Then he turned to Lucy and held out the brush. "You want to help me brush her down?"

Lucy went to him. She took the brush and began brushing the horse while gazing at the muscles of the animal's neck and back.

"Talk to her," said Will, lighting a cigarette.

"Why?"

"When I got her, she was only half broke. The Apache chief who gave her to me said: 'If you don't talk to the animal, you will not know the animal. What you don't know, you will fear. And what one fears, one destroys.'"

"You got Zeta from a savage?"

Will produced a tool from his pocket and lifted one of Zeta's hooves, then chipped a dried piece of dirt from it. "From a chief," he said. "I spent a few years as a guide on the Santa Fe Trail. The Apache didn't want us there and were known to raid wagons around Raton Pass and Fort Union. I didn't want any trouble, so I went and asked to meet the chief, and we made an arrangement."

"You made an arrangement."

"Yes."

"What was it?"

"I gave him merchandise in turn for protection. And Zeta."

"What was the merchandise?"

"Guns."

"Guns. You traded guns with a savage."

"Talk to the horse, Lucy."

She noticed a burr in Zeta's mane and started working it out with the brush. "Let's get this hair of yours fixed up, all right Miss Zeta?"

When Will had cleaned all four hooves, he took the brush from Lucy.

"Come here," he said. After he stood behind her and put his hand over hers, he showed her how to lift the horse's leg.

"Right there," he said. "Feel that? Push and she'll lift her leg for you."

Lucy pushed on the back of her leg, and Zeta lifted it. Will helped her with both her front and hind legs, making her do it over and over until she could get Zeta to raise her hoof without his help. As she was kneeling to do so, Barnet's gun slipped from her pocket onto the ground.

Will picked it up and handed it to her. "You know how to shoot this thing?"

"I shot it once, at the coyotes."

"Let me see you grip it."

Lucy held it out with one hand, pointing at the end of the driveway.

Standing behind her, Will adjusted her elbow so it was bent, ever so slightly. Then he brought her other hand to the gun and adjusted her fingers. "A pistol isn't like a shotgun. Hold it as an extension of your body, strong and surefooted, like you're throwing a punch. Top fingers along the base, like this. Now before you put your finger on the trigger, squeeze the base as hard as you can."

Lucy squeezed with both hands, and it pulled ever so slightly to the right.

Will adjusted the fingers on her left hand. "Again."

She squeezed so hard her hands shook, but the gun stayed pointing straight ahead.

"Good. Cock it with your left thumb, right index finger on the trigger. Now aim at the top of that fence post. Both eyes open. Gaze soft, just over the sight. When you're ready, put your finger on the trigger and fire."

Lucy kept her grip steady, aimed, and pulled the trigger. The bullet hit exactly where she'd aimed, a tiny stream of smoke lingered from the top of the fencepost.

Will smiled. "You're a goddamned natural. Now go grab Zeta's saddle for me."

"Will, you're in no condition to go anywhere."

"I'm not," he said. "You are."

"You're not serious."

"I need you to go to the general store and find out what you can. If anyone seems suspicious. If Lyman has those men in custody. See if Vinnie has a newspaper. And stop by John's saloon and get another bottle of whiskey."

"Will, look at my dress. I'm covered in blood."

"You're a farmwife. Tell them you slaughtered the goat this morning."

Lucy looked over at the little goat. He had a long piece of hay in his mouth and was trotting in circles around his pen, like a little show pony.

"We need to know if those men are in custody," Will said. "If anyone seems suspicious, we can't stay here. Luce, remember that if we're found out, turned in, we hang. I want you to take that gun with you and be prepared to use it."

Lucy looked out in the direction of the town. "I'll go to town and see what I can find out. But I'm not riding the horse. I'll walk."

"Go grab the saddle. It's time you learn to ride."

The saddle, pad, and bridle all hung on hooks in the barn, and Lucy lifted them down and carried them outside.

Then, with Will talking her through it, she saddled the horse. First the pad, then the saddle. She adjusted the stirrups. Tightened the strap. She learned how to put her hand between Zeta's ears and push on her head in a way that made her lower it to slide the halter on. How to use her thumb to ease her mouth open to get the bit in. Then Will made her mount by herself. Left foot in the stirrup. Hand on the saddle. She hoisted herself up. The reins in her left hand, the slack of it in her right, behind her. Some men rode with both hands out in front, on the reins, but it made them look like amateurs. Always keep one hand back. Sit up straight and be relaxed. Keep talking to the horse. Keep your eyes out in front of her head. The horse will go in the direction of both your body, and the reins. She made a few circles around the cottonwood, getting the feel of the reins. Zeta was well trained, obeying the slightest tug of the reins. It was easier than she thought. And a little bit exciting. The power of the animal she sat on making her feel uneased and thrilled all at once. After a few laps up and down the driveway, once even trotting, she was ready, and she rode off down the driveway.

"Don't forget a bottle of whiskey," Will shouted after her.

CHAPTER 16

LUCY LOWERED HER HAT ever so slightly over her eyes as a lone wagon passed her on Main Street. At the general store, she dismounted Zeta and tied her to the porch. Three men she didn't recognize eyed her as they passed. She gave them a curt nod and went up the steps. The door chime made her jump as she opened it, though she'd lost track of how many times she'd heard it now. Vinnie was standing behind the desk and gasped when she saw Lucy, then ran out to hug her.

"Oh, my darling girl! We've been worried sick about you two. Half the town's been in here asking about you. How's your sweetie?"

"He's home resting; he'll be fine. Thank you, Vinnie."

Vinnie wore a bright red dress and hair curled in ringlets, loosely pinned off her face in a red ribbon.

"I love what you've done with your hair today," Lucy said as she grabbed a shopping basket.

Vinnie reached up, touched her curls, and giggled. "I slept with it in rags. It's something new I'm trying."

"It's very Madame Bovary."

"*Who?*"

Lucy smiled and tossed a fresh loaf of bread in her basket. While she shopped, Vinnie prattled on about the picnic and the incident. Sheriff Lyman had two of the men locked up in custody, but the whole thing still made Vinnie sick. How those men could attack her sweetie that way, mistaking him for some scandalous outlaw. But speaking of scandals, the baking competition was rigged. Elsa Freely saw it with her own eyes. Lucille Mischler, the winner from Rosetown, paid the judges off; they were certain of it. Lucy stood in front of a crate with a few meats and cheeses. It made her think of the charcuterie board she used to get at Delmonico's and she felt a sudden longing for New York City. They'd revolutionized lunch hour in the city when they started selling their famous sandwiches premade and packaged to go.

"Vinnie, have you ever thought of selling premade food items? You're such a good cook, I bet . . ."

Vinnie howled out in laughter. "Oh honestly, girl, listen to you. Premade food items." She continued to chuckle to herself.

Lucy eyed the shelves for wine, even a bottle of cooking wine but didn't see any. When she was finished, she went to the desk. The *Denver Pioneer* lay on the desk, and she glanced down as Vinnie began to bag her items. The headline on the front page: PINKERTONS CLOSE IN ON THE SHANKS-KANE GANG.

"I almost forgot," said Vinnie. She handed Lucy a piece of paper. "We're starting a petition, for next years' pie competition. We want new judges and new rules."

Lucy took the paper and pencil and began to write her name. *Luc . . .* Then she stopped and quickly changed the letters to sign the name *Emily Holloway.* Her hand shaking, praying that Vinnie didn't notice. She took her sack of groceries and tipped her hat to Vinnie.

"Thank you, *madame*," she said, and turned to leave.

"Oh no, you don't. You get back here and give me a hug."

Vinnie came rushing around the desk and gave Lucy one of her loving mama bear hugs. Lucy wasn't sure why but tears flooded her eyes, and she had to choke them back as she left the store and headed to John Stark's Saloon for some whiskey.

John Stark was sitting at a table with an older man, playing cards when she entered. John had a black eye and a fat lip. The old man had a toothless grin.

"Mrs. Holloway," he said. "You're about the last person I expected to see today. How's that husband of yours holdin' up?"

"He's fine; he's home resting. How are you, John?"

"I'm right as rain, darlin'. Just a few scratches, is all."

There was a sign on the back wall she hadn't noticed, and she focused on it now. A cartoon drawing of a scantily clad woman with giant breasts pouring out of her dress, a big smile and a big glass of wine. Beneath, it read: "BEWARE! Poker playing and loose women are permitted in this establishment!" A man sat alone near the back of the bar and held Lucy's gaze a moment before looking away. He had dark hair and eyes. Maybe in his thirties. A full glass of liquor in front of him, but he didn't seem to be drinking it. She wanted to ask if he was the local doctor she'd heard about but decided to keep her word to Will about no doctors.

"To what do I owe the pleasure?" John Stark asked. "You want to have a seat? Join me and Montana here in a game of cards?"

Montana waved at Lucy and flashed her another toothless smile.

"I'm afraid I have to get back to the farm," she said. "I was hoping I could get a few bottles of whiskey."

John Stark laughed. "That Holloway," he said. "What a guy. Sends his wife into town for whiskey. How many bottles does he want?" he asked, then went behind the bar and took a few bottles from the shelf.

"Two is fine, thank you," said Lucy. "And John, while you're back there, do you have any wine? Or champagne?"

John laughed out loud. "Not sure how things are done back in

Missouri, milady, but here, we drink whiskey." He handed Lucy the two bottles of whiskey.

"Right then. My husband will be in to pay you when he's feeling better."

"Course. Not to worry. You sure you don't want to have a drink? Play a hand?"

"No, thank you. I best be on my way. Good day, gentlemen."

Will was sitting on the porch steps, cleaning the shotgun, when she rode back up the driveway. He got up to greet her, a smile on his face.

"You look good on a horse," he said. Then he grabbed Zeta by the bridle while Lucy dismounted.

"I got your whiskey," she replied. "And some things to make sandwiches for dinner."

"Good. We'll save the goat for another night."

"That's not funny."

"Wasn't meant to be."

The goat let out a long baa and leapt eagerly around his pen.

"No one seemed suspicious," said Lucy. "Vinnie told me that Lyman's got two of the men locked up. She seemed more concerned with the pie-baking competition being rigged than the stabbing. And John Stark asked after you. Tried to get me to sit and play some cards with him and a fellow called Montana."

They led the horse to the barn and walked Lucy through how to take the bridle and saddle off and let Zeta out to pasture.

"You sure no one seemed suspicious?"

Lucy nodded. "For now, though. Aren't you worried Lyman will figure it out?"

"Course."

"What do you think we should do?"

"I think we should go inside and make some sandwiches."

Come nightfall, Lucy stood alone on the porch, looking up at the starlit sky. Will was sound asleep. She'd mixed up another Cleopatra facial mask of egg whites, honey, and crushed grapes and had it smeared across her face now. The crickets echoed in the night, and the leaves rustled softly. She was not sure of the time. Maybe nine. Or ten. Back in New York, Broadway would just be getting started. Theater and opera would just be getting out, and restaurants would be getting ready for the rush. People hobnobbing about where to eat. The street full of carriages. Servants. Members of the press. New York's socialites dressed to impress. Lord and Taylor lit up with extra candlelight for late shopping. People smoking outside the Burchard Steakhouse.

A strange feeling overcame her that she couldn't quite explain. Just over a month ago, she was one of those socialites, and now it felt like a lifetime ago. Everything quiet, save for the odd baaing of the goat. She looked out at the barn and foothills in the moonlight, and for the first time, just for a moment, she thought about how hard it was actually going to be to leave this place. Then she stood and went back in the house to check on Will.

She took her book to the bedroom and lit a candle, then sat in the rocker to read beside him. Chapter 7. Caitlin had just found out from the maid that the Lord had returned home from battle, and that he was drunk.

> *She threw the covers back and rushed to the lock the door, but she was too late. It opened, and he entered, eyes ablaze. "You're mine," he said, in a low, raspy voice. Then he grabbed her by the arm, pulled her to him, and kissed her, his tongue madly devouring her.*

Lucy ran a finger across her lips and thought back to Will's kiss that night on the dancefloor. She knew she had to put it out of her mind, but her heart began to race as she thought of it. And this book, she'd never read anything like it and couldn't believe such a racy story had been published, or ended up in Vinnie's store. Lucy continued reading.

The swelling of his loins pressed against Caitlin's thigh. He ripped her dress and cupped her bare breasts. She gasped out in pleasure now. Her womanhood throbbing. She searched for some formidable act of willpower. Stop him . . . With a sweep of his hand, he lifted her skirt and tore at her bloomers. "You're mine," he said again.

"What's on your face?"

Lucy jumped, then lowered the book. Will was staring at her.

"What do you have all over your face?"

"Oh. It's egg whites, grapes, and honey. Cleopatra used it for her complexion." She gazed back down at her book and kept reading.

"How's your book?"

"It's fine, I guess."

"What's it about?"

"It's about a girl who's sold to the lord of a rival clan. Set in the Scottish Highlands, thirteenth century," she said.

She continued reading silently.

He had her pinned up against the wall now, and she wrapped her legs around him and clutched at his back as he lifted his kilt and . . .

"Read aloud," Will said, propping himself up on the pillow.

"I'd rather not."

"Please?"

Lucy marked where she was by folding the corner of the page. Then she turned a few pages ahead. She read aloud, pausing every so often to look up from the page and find Will still awake, listening intently. The chapter ended with Lord Ferguson receiving news that he'd been recruited by Robert the Bruce, handpicked for a special army to fight English rule. It would mean fighting for a cause he believed in. It would mean he would be gone for as long as it took to defeat the English.

"She loves him, this Ferguson," Will said.

Lucy said nothing and let out a yawn.

"Luce," said Will. "You should get some sleep."

She went to the kitchen and rinsed her face but left the curlers in her hair. Back in the bedroom, she took Barnet's gun from her skirt pocket and set it on the nightstand. She gingerly climbed into bed beside him. She lay with the covers around her neck, as close to the edge of the bed as she could without falling off.

"Luce?"

"Yes?"

"Have you ever been in love?"

"No. Have you?"

"Yeah. Once."

"Who was she?"

Lucy's heart raced now, but she didn't know why. She stared up at the ceiling, at the shadows dancing in the candlelight.

Will's arm came around her and pulled her to him.

Her heart beat so loudly, she feared he might hear it.

"She was someone unexpected," he said. "Goodnight, Luce."

"Goodnight."

CHAPTER 17

———————◆———————

HIS ARMS WERE STILL around her when they woke in the morning
to the sound of horses riding toward the house. Then two sets of
feet dismounting. Spurs coming up the porch steps.

Will sat up and took his gun from beneath his pillow.

There was a knock on the door.

"Anyone there? Sheriff Lyman here."

"What should I do?" Lucy whispered.

"Go see what he wants."

"I have curlers in my hair."

"Go."

Lucy got out of bed and went to the kitchen to open the front
door. Sheriff Lyman was standing on the porch with a man she
didn't recognize. He had a moustache and dark hair that was
balding on top and stuck out on the sides. He wore little glasses
and a tuxedo.

"Morning," said Lyman. "This is Detective Goswald. He's with
the Pinkerton Agency. Is your husband around?"

"He is, but he's not feeling well, and I'd rather not wake him."

"All right," said Lyman. "Fair enough. When he's feeling better, you mind telling him to come by and fill out some paperwork for me?"

"And I'd like to ask him a few questions," said the detective.

"I'll let him know," she said. "Anything else I can do for you, gentlemen?"

"No, that's fine, Mrs. Holloway," said Lyman.

He started to walk back down the steps. The detective ran a hand along the sides of his suit coat and looked around the property. "Mind if I have a look in that barn? Word is they're storing dynamite somewhere around here."

Lucy looked at the barn, her heart racing, trying to think of a quick excuse to get rid of them.

"Come on now, detective," said Lyman. "Let's let these people be."

The detective turned back to her and eyed her up and down in a way that made her skin crawl. She hugged herself as she inched away and bid them good day.

When she went back to the bedroom, Will was standing at the window, already dressed in the grey shirt he'd been wearing the first time she saw him. He wore his gun belt and had his boots on.

"What are you gonna do?" she asked.

"I gotta get that wagon out of here."

"Where will you take it?"

"You mind putting some coffee on?"

"Sure," she said. Then she left the room, filled a pot of water, and lit the stove.

He came out into the kitchen and took his hat from the mantel. "I'm gonna go hitch up the wagon." He left the house.

When the coffee was ready, she poured two cups and went outside.

Will was out in the yard, the mare hitched to the wagon and Zeta tied to the back. She handed him his coffee. "But your wound, Will. You'll break the stitches open."

"I'll be all right. I'll be back in a few hours." Then he hopped up onto the front seat of the wagon with his coffee and snapped the reins, driving off.

Lucy stood on the porch until long after he was gone. She removed her curlers and let them drop to the porch one by one. There was an extra leather gun belt hanging beside the saddle, and she took it down and put it on. Then she went to the barn. There, she dragged a hay bale out to the middle of the driveway and lined four cans.

Back on the porch, she stood with Barnet's handgun in her hands, lined up her fingers on each side, exactly the way Will had shown her, and squeezed. Adjusting her left index finger, she squeezed again, then softened her gaze over the sight, lining up the first can.

She fired. The can went sailing across the yard. She bit her lip and held back a smile. A thrill of excitement ran through her veins.

She re-holstered the gun and drew again. And again. Faster each time. Only one miss that nicked the side of the can but didn't send it flying off. She kept going until all four cans were strewn across the yard. She went and lined them up again and fetched more bullets from the barn. Back on the porch, she spun the cylinder back, reloaded, and spun it shut. As she re-holstered the gun she scanned the property. She thought back to what Will had said about killing being in instinct, and she wondered now if she could do it. If she could take a life. Focusing back on the cans, she drew the gun from her holster, aimed, and fired.

At dusk, she sat in the rocking chair on the porch, watching the sun as it set over the foothills. Though she was excited to see it set over the Pacific too, she gazed out now with a sadness at the pink glow over the mountains, trying to burn it into her memory. And trying not to worry about Will. She hadn't asked how far he would have to go to hide the dynamite somewhere else but had a sinking feeling he should have been back by now.

"Where are you, Will?" she asked into the breeze.

Saying it aloud made her think of Shakespeare's Juliet, the scene with her alone on her balcony. Months before leaving New York, she'd come across a literary analysis on the story. It was fascinating and dissected Shakespeare's language and meaning, breaking the story down scene by scene. In that famous balcony scene, Juliet is asking the night: "*Wherefore art thou, Romeo?*" In Shakespeare's English, "wherefore" didn't literally mean "where," it meant "why." Juliet isn't wondering "where" Romeo is, but rather "why" she loves him.

Lucy sat there thinking about it for the longest time. The turmoil Juliet was going through, in love with a man she could never have.

Suddenly, she heard a horse in the distance. She breathed a sigh of relief until the lone rider came into view, riding up the driveway to the house. A grey horse she didn't recognize. He wore a top hat, a vest, and a badge. Lucy froze as he got close enough to see his face. It was the Pinkerton Detective, Goswald, from this morning.

"Evening, ma'am," he said.

"Good evening, sir. What can I do for you?"

He stopped the horse near the porch, dismounted and loosely tied his horse to the rail post. "Don't suppose your husband's awake to ask a few questions," he said.

Lucy stood. "No, I'm sorry. I'm afraid he's actually out for a few hours."

The man held Lucy's gaze, then slowly looked her up and down. He turned and looked around the property. "You say you folks are from Missouri? I noticed this mornin', you got an Eastern look about you. Something about the way you carry yourself."

"We're from Missouri."

"Talked to a man in Thompson, gave a description of Will Shanks escaping, took some poor woman hostage."

"Yes, I read that in the papers."

The man looked around again, then turned back to Lucy and spat. "His hostage was a woman he described looked like you. Real pretty little thing, apparently. Uppity, with an Eastern accent. And now we think she wasn't no hostage; she's in cahoots with him and that gang of his."

"Sir, I've told you my husband is not home. But I will let him know you stopped by and wish to speak to him. Good evening," she said. Then she turned to go into the house.

He lunged up the steps and grabbed her by the arm before she could go through the doorway. "I think I'll wait here for your husband if it's all the same to you," he said, his face eerily close to the side of hers as he spoke. Then, still holding her arm, he pushed her into the house and closed the door behind them.

Lucy tried to pull from his grasp but couldn't.

"I'm going to ask you one more time. What is your real name, and why are you helping Will Shanks?"

"My name is Emily Holloway and my husband, Nelson, will be home any moment now."

The detective reached up and touched her hair. "You said he was out for a few hours. Not very smart of him, leaving you all alone out here. Don't you think? What kind of a man does that?"

Lucy took a step back, but he held her arm tighter. "Sir, please."

The detective grabbed her other arm and pinned her forcefully against the wall, securing both of her arms above her with one hand. Slowly he ran his free hand along her face, down her neck, and cupped her breast. Lucy had Barnet's gun in her skirt pocket, and she fought now to get an arm loose.

He tightened his grip and his eyes narrowed. "You're a fighter," he said, his breath foul. "I like that."

He leaned in and kissed her, forcing his tongue into her mouth. He had his free hand on her face now, his fingers digging into her cheek. His lips left hers and he moaned as he began to lick her neck and ear.

"Sir, stop. Please," she said. She kicked at his shin, and he pinned her harder against the wall.

"That's it," he said. "Keep fighting me."

His mouth was back on hers. As he kissed her harder and harder, she felt him bite her bottom lip, drawing blood. When he pulled away for a moment, she spat in his face.

He backhanded her hard, so hard it stunned her and blurred her vision. Then he grabbed her by the arm and pulled her roughly toward the bedroom.

With her free hand now, Lucy reached down and pulled the gun from her pocket. She clicked back the safety with her thumb, gripped it tightly, put it to the side of his head, and fired. He let go of her and collapsed to the floor. Motionless.

A stream of smoke came from the end of the gun. Blood spattered the wall. She clicked the safety back and pointed it at the body. He lay on his side, and she kicked at him to roll him over onto his back. She shot him in the chest once more just to be sure. Then she put the gun back in her skirt. She wondered how far the shots could have been heard. She had to get him out of the house. Hide his body somehow. She bent over him and checked his pockets. A small wad of cash and a pocket watch. She put the cash on the table, grabbed him by the feet, and began to drag him.

Slow going. But she managed to get him through the front door. Down the porch steps. His head hit each step with a thud. Across the yard. Dragging his heavy dead weight with everything she had. She stopped to catch her breath and look around.

She continued until the body was about ten feet behind the barn, out of plain view. She gathered some foliage and broken branches and covered the body as best she could. Then she went and untied his horse, smacked it on its backside and watched as it trotted off. She went back into the house.

To a pail of sudsy water, she added a splash of Vinnie's bleach from the back of the cupboard. Lucy cleaned the wall first. It was everywhere. The bedroom door. The bricks of the fireplace. The fox even got a little on its tail. She left the door propped open to air the place. She saved the floor for last. That was the biggest task. A giant pool of blood near the bedroom door. She scrubbed until her hands hurt. The bucket of suds and water turned a foul color of red. She rinsed the brush and started scrubbing again when she heard a horse coming into the yard.

She stood and went to the door. Too dark now to see him perfectly, but she could see the white on Zeta's face. She watched Will dismount and go to the barn. Lucy went back to scrubbing. A wave of emotion overwhelmed her, and for the first time since it happened, she was shaking. She could feel her eye swelling where Goswald had backhanded her and could still taste blood on her lip. No idea how Will would react. Or what they would do with the body. Who he might have told he was coming here.

The barn door closed and footsteps came across the yard and up the porch steps. Will came through the front door.

"Hi, Luce," he said, and looked around the house. With a confused look on his face, he asked, "What the hell happened . . .?" Then he took a second look at her. His face drained of color as he studied her.

"Jesus. What happened? Who did this to you?"

"I shot him," she said, holding back tears.

"Who?"

"That Pinkerton."

Will came and knelt beside her, his eyes searching her face. He took the scrub brush from her and helped her stand. "Come sit. Let me see your eye," he said.

"I'm sorry," she whispered as she sat down. "I didn't know what to do; it all happened so fast. He forced his way into the house, asking about you. He knew who you were. When he realized I was here alone, he started putting his hands on me and kissing me. And then he was dragging me to the bedroom and . . ."

He sat down beside her. "Lucy, did he rape you?"

"No. I shot him before he could get me to the bedroom."

Will ran his hands through his hair and sat staring at the fire. Then he put an arm around her and held her against him. "I should have been here. I'm so sorry."

She closed her eyes. Tears streaked her cheeks now.

"Where's the body?" he asked.

"I dragged him out behind the barn."

Will kissed her on the side of her head and stood. "I'll be back in a while," he said. Then he stood and left the house.

She changed the water in the bucket and went back to scrubbing the floor. It didn't take long for the water to become red again. The floor was almost back to normal now, save for one stubborn spot on a floorboard that was still a dark shade of pink. Lucy stood. Her knees and back ached. She took the bucket to the porch and tossed the water out into the yard. She grabbed the lantern and crossed the yard to where she'd left the body.

Will was standing a few feet from the body, digging a hole that was already about a foot deep and the length of a body. He stopped to wipe his brow. As he turned to take another scoop of dirt, she could see he'd bled through the back of his shirt.

"Will, your back."

He stopped and looked at her but said nothing and continued digging.

She went to the barn and held the lantern up to the row of tools. Two shovels hung at the end. She took one before returning to Will and started to help him dig.

CHAPTER 18

---•---

ON EASTER SUNDAY EACH year at the Saint Mary's Ladies Academy, any new student that hadn't already been baptized into the faith was baptized in a ceremony to put them on a path to righteousness. Lucy had just turned nine years old when she sat in the front pew of the chapel with two other girls. All dressed in long white cotton gowns, one by one, they were led to the pool where the priest stood waist deep in water. Organ music played quietly, and the full congregation watched on as the priest anointed her with oil and asked her to renounce Satan. "*I baptize you in the name of the father, the son, and the holy spirit. Amen.*" The priest leaned her back into the water three times. Sister Elizabeth helped her towel off and dress and told her that her soul was delivered from evil now; she was redeemed in Christ.

"Luce," said Will. "Are you gonna finish your breakfast?"

She was standing at the kitchen window, gazing out at the property.

Will stood and took his plate to the washbasin. Then he went and took his hat from the mantel. "I'll go tack up the horses."

She watched as he crossed the yard to the barn.

It wasn't that she didn't believe in redemption, or the deep-seated desire to reclaim parts of ourselves lost along the way. But that day in the chapel, that was not it. She wasn't even sure what real redemption looked like, but she knew it had nothing to do with church, or a priest with some holy water.

There were callouses on her hands from shoveling a grave, and the reins rubbed against them now as she rode behind Will on the tan mare. Where they were riding to was an old deserted cabin, not more than forty-five minutes away. Will needed to check on what was to be their first checkpoint, where he and his men would regroup after the robbery, switch out fresh horses, and ride. The trail narrowed as they rode until there was nothing left of one, and the horses had to step over fallen trees and maneuver through brush so thick branches scraped Lucy's arms. The mare whinnied and stopped before a larger fallen tree. Lucy dug her spurs in and coaxed it to step over.

Will turned in his saddle. "Thatta girl," he said. Keep her moving. It's not far now."

The cabin was no more than a small shack that looked as though it hadn't been touched in years. The window was broken, and a tree had fallen and was leaning up against the side of it. She dismounted and followed Will into the house.

Directly inside the door was an old wooden table with two chairs. A small fireplace sat near the back and a cot in the corner. Cobwebs everywhere. A thick layer of dust and dirt on everything. Will rested his saddlebag on the table and unpacked several cans of beans and some jerky. Some basic medical supplies: gauze, tweezers, and salve. An extra canteen of water.

When he went back outside, she followed. To the back of the cabin were tied three horses. Lucy and Will grabbed buckets and filled them in a nearby stream, then carried them back to water the horses. Will fed them each a half bale of hay and some grain. He handed Lucy a brush and told her to brush them down a little while he checked their hooves.

"Where'd they come from?" she asked as she worked out a burr in one of their manes.

"A local who's helping us. We've got fresh horses at the next checkpoint; we'll leave these there for him."

"How are you getting to Argentina?"

"By boat, from the San Francisco harbor. A friend of Irish has his own ship, sails cargo up and down the west coast, all the way to Buenos Aires. He's agreed to store us on, but this delay has not made him happy. He's waiting one more week for us, which means we're gonna have to ride like hell."

"What's your plan once you get there?"

"To Argentina?"

"Yeah."

He was quiet for a while, then he said, "Buy a nice piece of land and build a home I guess. I don't know. I just want a simple life from here on out."

"If things were different, I mean if you weren't wanted, would you still go?"

He pulled a cigarette from his pocket and lit it. "If there's anything I've learned, it's that wishing things were different is the quickest way for a man to drive himself crazy."

When they rode back into the yard later that afternoon Lucy's heart skipped a beat when she saw a horse tied to the tree and a man knocking on the door.

"It's Lyman," said Will quietly. "He might be looking for that Pinkerton."

Lyman turned and waved at Lucy and Will. He came out into the yard to meet them.

"Afternoon, folks," he said. "Didn't mean to bother you. Seems the Pinkerton I was with yesterday went missing. Was wondering if you'd heard or seen anything of him." Lyman looked around the property as he spoke.

"Can't say I have," said Will. "You, sweetheart?"

Lucy looked down at the ground and noticed a faint trail of blood where she'd dragged the body across the yard, only a few feet from where Lyman stood. Her heart raced, and her hands were trembling. She could feel both men's eyes on her.

"No," she said. "I haven't seen him."

"All right then," said Lyman. "I'll let you know if I hear anything. You might get a few more Pinkertons out here asking questions; they'll want to have a look around the property since Valley City was the last place he was seen. Probably not till after that stagecoach of railroad money gets through though. It's getting close now. Last I heard, Hall was on the move again with at least ten armed guards." Lyman mounted his horse and stared out at the horizon. "You folks stay safe out here, and you come to me if you need anything, you hear?" he asked.

Will and Lucy looked at each other, then Will gave Lyman a nod. No one spoke.

Lyman spurred the horse and rode off.

Lucy and Will dismounted and let the horses into the barn. She started to undo the straps on the saddle. "Have you heard from Silas?" she asked.

"No, but something tells me I will today."

Will hoisted his saddle onto the bench, then came and helped take Lucy's off and tossed it beside the other. Then he stood there, staring at her for a moment. "Lucy, what I said back there, how wishing things were different could make a man crazy. It's because from the first moment I met you, I've wondered if things were different, if I wasn't wanted, if you and I—"

"Don't say it, Will. Don't. You'll just make it harder."

"I'm in love with you, Lucy."

"You don't even know me."

"Come with me."

"Come with you where?"

"Argentina."

She looked away, her hands still on the bridle she was undoing. Tears stung her eyes, but she held them back. "You've lost your mind."

"I'm in love with you, Luce. Look at me and tell me you don't feel it."

"It doesn't matter, Will. Even if I did feel it, it's not enough. I don't belong in Argentina any more than I belong here on this farm. I know the kind of life you want and I'll never fit in it."

"I just want you, Luce. If that means living in a city with opera and restaurants, then we'll live in Buenos Aires."

She shook her head. "I've come all this way to see my aunt. It's what I've wanted ever since . . . since my mother died."

"Where was she? All those years you were dreaming of going to live with her. Where was she? If she wanted to stay a part of your life, why didn't she try harder?"

"My father kept her away."

"People don't give up on what they love."

"You don't know my father. You wouldn't understand." Lucy felt a lump in her throat but refused to cry. "I left because I was tired of feeling alone."

"I know, Luce. I'm tired of feeling alone, too. Look, maybe your aunt was a nice dream to hold onto, an illusion that gave you some peace. And gave you the courage to leave New York. It doesn't mean you belong there, with her. I get needing answers about who your mother was, but it's not going to change who you are."

"How can you stand there and talk about illusions? Look around, Will. This whole thing is pretend. I'm not Emily Holloway, and you barely know anything about me or my real life. Or what I want."

Lucy turned and left the barn. She crossed the yard to the house. Once inside, the door shut behind her, she let the tears fall. If they were so close to the end, closer to what she'd wanted all along, why did it hurt so much?

She heard footsteps on the porch, and the door opened. She quickly dried her eyes but did not turn around.

"I know you survived for days in the Colorado wilderness alone after witnessing a horrific massacre," he said. "I know you stood and pointed a gun on a stranger when you could have stayed hidden in the bushes. I know you didn't need help from that chatterbox-of-a-little-girl, but you saw she needed a friend. I see the way Vinnie loves you. You see the good in everyone, Lucy, and you don't let the evils of this world stop you from dreaming. You're right; there's a lot I don't know about your life. But I know who you are, and I know you make me better just by being around you."

She turned around and faced him and met his gaze.

"Luce, tell me you don't feel it too, and I'll . . ."

She went to him and kissed him.

His hands caressed her cheeks. She closed her eyes. The feeling of his lips, his hands on her face, the smell of him—she reached her hands to the back of his neck and ran her fingers through his hair. Her heart raced and her body felt on fire. He was kissing her harder now, and she pulled him closer, her body up against his. His lips left hers, and he kissed her cheek, her ear, her neck. He began undoing the buttons on her dress, kissing her skin as he unbuttoned. Working his way down her neck, her collarbone. She was trembling now, her body aching for him in a way she didn't understand, but she wanted more. She wanted his body against hers, to taste every inch of him.

He stopped and they stood, faces inches apart, his kind eyes searching her face.

She took his hand and led him to the bedroom.

He took his shirt off and laid her down on the bed. On top of her now, he began to gently kiss her again. His hands roamed down over her hips, slowly pulling her skirt up over her knees, exposing her bare legs. Then he ran his hand along the inside of her thigh. She undid his belt and grasped at his hips, pulling him closer to her.

He stopped and froze as he looked up at the window.

"What is it?" she whispered.

Then she heard the faint sound of horses coming down the road.

He stood and went to the window, watching out in the darkness as he did up his belt, then put his shirt back on. She followed him out to the main room, buttoning her dress as she walked. Without a word, he grabbed the shotgun from the mantel.

"Stay in the house," he said. Then he went out onto the porch.

Lucy grabbed Barnet's gun from the counter and went to the window. Four riders were coming up the drive to the house.

Will knelt down behind the railing and raised the shotgun.

The men stopped their horses near the cottonwood tree. Someone let out a whistle, followed by three quick, loud ones. Will lowered the shotgun and stood. Then he leaned the gun against the railing and went to the riders. One by one, they dismounted. Will embraced one of them. Then he led them all to the barn.

Lucy stood watching at the window while she adjusted her skirt and drawers and buttoned up the last few buttons on her dress.

She was still standing there when they filed into the house. Dirty, tired faces. Scruffy facial hair. Guns hanging from their hips. Weathered clothing. All around Will's age. Will entered last.

"Lucy," he said. "You already know Silas. This is Irish, Cal, and Oscar."

"Pleased to meet you all," she said.

Oscar and Cal had darker features and even curlier hair than the posters, especially Oscar. Tight ringlets that he kept shorter. Cal's hair was longer and messier, with waves that brushed the collar of his shirt. Silas's clothing was the cleanest, his shirt, a button up with cufflinks. His boots were some sort of reptile skin. She took care not to stare at the scar on his left cheek, and held his gaze for a moment, still unsure how he felt about her or if he trusted her. Irish was the tallest, a lanky build with an Adam's apple, strong cheekbones, and dark eyes. He flashed her a charming smile. "It's a pleasure to finally make your acquaintance, lass," he said.

Will came to the counter and started to open the first can of beans. "The stage is gonna be right where we want it tonight. There was supposed to be a few more of us. But we'll sort it out."

"Sit down, Will," said Irish. "I'll help the lass."

Will gave Lucy a nod and went to the porch. Silas, Cal, and Oscar followed. They left the door open, and the house filled with cigarette smoke.

"Heard you're from bonnie New York," Irish said as he stabbed the knife into the can and started to work the top off. "I spent a few years there myself. I was 'bout fifteen years old, fresh off a boat from Ireland. Worked a few different jobs there, one in construction where I met Will, till one night we got real lucky at a hand at poker, decided to take our winnin's and . . .anyway. Not important. Then came the war, and well, that was that. I got some cousins immigrated to Argentina. Workin' the docks of Buenos Aries port and started their own shipping company. Said I could come down and they'd help me get started. Makin' a killing out on the high seas. That's the life for me, Luce. That's the life for me. That's my background, ya know. Shipping. Back in Ireland my great-grandfather—"

"Jesus, Irish," said Silas from the porch. "She doesn't want to hear your entire life story."

"You just mind yer business out there. Me and Luce here are gettin' along jest fine, ain't we lass?" Irish smiled and patted Lucy on the back as he popped the top off the third can and dumped it into the pot.

"You talk all you like, Irish," Lucy said. Then she reached up and grabbed some eggs from the cupboard.

And talk he did. By the time everything was cooked and they were plating up six dinners, Lucy had learned that Irish had two sisters back in Ireland but hadn't spoken to his family since he'd left and had loved one girl in his life; he'd met her in a Philadelphia whorehouse and spent only a few nights together but that was all it took. He'd joined up with the Confederate guerrilla soldiers by accident. It was too long of a story to tell and he'd save it for another time, but he fought along men who became like his brothers, for that he was thankful. He leaned in and whispered to her that Oscar and Cal's little brother, Johnny, was shot and killed in Cheyenne a few weeks back and no one speaks of it. Then he added that Will was the smartest hand at poker and one of the best horsemen he'd ever seen.

The men had begun to argue outside, and between his chatter, she tried to eavesdrop.

Irish stopped and put a hand on her forearm, ever so gently. "It's okay, lass," he said. "We had three sharp shooters back out at the last minute, ex-soldiers. I can't say I blame 'em. I'm tired of fighting too. Not to mention Will's not healed yet from that stabbing. Don't you worry none. We'll get ourselves to Argentina, one way or another. Now, where were we?"

As they plated their dinners, Irish gave a toast: "Here's to the land of the shamrock so green. Here's to each lad and his darlin' colleen. Here's to the ones we love dearest and most. May God bless old Ireland, that's this Irishman's toast!"

Silas and Irish kept watch and ate their dinners on the porch while the rest of them sat at the table. As they dined, Oscar and Cal told stories of Will when he was young. Her favorite was of a church picnic where a girl named Sally Medlock showed Cal and Will her breasts for a nickel. They talked about how in their travels later on, after they'd left home, it was Will who'd met the owner of the Santa Fe Stagecoach Company and convinced him to hire them as guides, even though they were all barely twenty years old at the time, and how much they'd all ended up loving that job. They all loved Santa Fe and had been to Mexico several times. There was a saloon in Santa Fe with half-priced whores on Sundays, a group of Apache warriors they befriended and spent a winter with, and a market just south of El Paso, in Mexico, where they'd eaten *churros* and drank Spanish coffee. There was one particular old *abuela* who was missing all her teeth and could barely walk but made the best *tamales*. Cal bet a hundred dollars that old broad was still alive. Then he turned to Lucy. "Lucy," he said solemnly. "Can I get a woman's opinion on something?"

"Of course," Lucy said.

"You think my hair's too long? I'd cut it, but it gets so poofy. My curl just isn't right if it's too short."

Oscar rolled his eyes. "Stop talking about your damn hair."

"Easy for you to say," said Cal. "You've seen my wanted poster. I look like a damn woman."

"An ugly woman," said Irish from the porch.

When they were done eating, the men retired to the porch to smoke. Though Will had told her he'd be right back in to help her with the dishes, she stood over the washbasin now, absently scrubbing plate after plate, listening to them arguing outside. Oscar and Cal called the job suicide. Irish asked what choice they had. Silas wanted to know how they would possibly execute this with no sharp shooters above. Will remained quiet.

The door opened, and Will came back into the house. He went to the counter and picked up a towel.

"I made arrangements for you, at a small bed and breakfast run by a lady I trust," he said. "I'll wire you the remaining thousand dollars I owe you within a day or two."

Lucy studied the dishwater and ran the rag over the plate.

"Luce, did you hear what I said?"

"Did you mean what you said before?"

"What I said about what?"

"About me coming to Argentina."

Will reached into his pocket and produced a small piece of paper, which he held out to her. "I had Silas check the telegraph station for you."

She took the piece of paper. It was a telegram from her father.

Trial is over. Acquitted on all counts. Money wired to Denver Stagecoach Station for your passage home. Lane will still marry you.

Postscript: I know where you're headed. Aunt Louisa passed away a month ago.

Lucy was speechless. Her heart raced as she skimmed the words again. Tears flooded her eyes.

"I'm sorry," said Will quietly. "Go home, Luce. It's where you belong. It was wrong of me to try and make you think otherwise."

"He's not my fiancé," she whispered.

"It's none of my business," said Will. Then he stood and set a small saddlebag on the table. "To pack your things."

"Will. Wait . . ."

"You said it yourself, this was all pretend."

So much raced through her mind and yet she couldn't find anything to say.

Will went to the door. Stopping before he left the house, he turned back to her. "For what it's worth, you were a hell of a wife, Lucy Cavanagh." Then he turned and left.

She took the saddlebag from the table and opened the top drawer beneath the washbasin where she kept her things. Inside were curlers, hairpins, and a brush. The deer-tooth necklace from Seymour and the brooch from Vinnie. The dagger from Esther and the girls. She wiped her eyes and sat at the table, then gazed out the window. She had no way of knowing if her father was telling the truth about Aunt Louisa. She felt lost all over again. Darkness was falling now. The men smoked on the porch. They'd been quiet for a while, but she could hear them strategizing and debating again now. Silas was the best shot—what if he was up in the tree and four of them fought on the ground?

Then suddenly they went silent, and Lucy could hear a horse approaching. The horse whinnied and came to a stop before someone dismounted.

"Where's Lucy? What's the matter? None of you ever seen a fuckin' woman before?" It was a woman's voice.

Lucy stood and went to the window. *Esther?*

"There's no one by that name here," said Will. "What can I do for you?"

"Cut the shit," said Esther, tying her horse to a rail on the porch. "Lucy? You in there?" She walked past the men into the house.

"Esther, what in heaven's name? How did you—"

"Is that any way to greet a friend?"

Lucy went and hugged her. "I'm so happy to see you. How did you find me?"

Esther sat down at the table and lit a cigarette. "I read in the paper that a girl was caught stealing from a wagon outside the Harrison. I knew it had to be you, felt just sick about it. I was working on getting a few men ready to get you out of there, and someone beat me to it. Started to piece it all together as you and Mr. Will Shanks out there started making more headlines. My mama always told me she didn't raise no fool, and she was right, Miss Cavanagh. Sorry, where's my damn manners. Do you want one?" She held out a cigarette to Lucy.

Lucy sat down across from her and took the cigarette.

"S'pose you're wondering what I'm doing here, though." Esther lit a match and held it out to light Lucy's cigarette. "Got myself into some trouble. Not sure how to fix it this time. Not sure if I want to. I don't want to talk about it. I just needed to get away from Denver for a spell. Figure things out." She picked up the telegram that sat on the table, read it, and set it back down. "So I'm not the only one in a dilemma."

"I don't want to go back to New York," Lucy said quietly.

"Then don't. You know, there's an old Cherokee saying that we can learn everything we need to know about life from watching a river, 'cause it only moves forward."

The argument between the men out on the porch became more heated. Someone hit one of the porch rails, which shook the house.

"I know the job they're pulling," said Esther. "It's been all over the papers. Pinkertons coming in worried about General Hall getting his money stolen. I was looking forward to it happening. He's been in Denver off and on for business, portrays himself in the papers as a family man, but when he's in Denver, he haunts all the brothels. Beat on Delilah last time. I don't believe in killing, but the world would be a better place without a person like that in it. And if he ever enters my brothel again, I'll do it myself." She took a drag. "I'm sorry about your aunt."

"My father lies; I don't know if it's true."

"What was he on trial for?"

"He's a thief. He's a thief, Esther, and he'll get to carry on with no consequences. Just like General Lewis B. Hall and his railroad money." She pointed at the window toward the porch. "They're not the thieves of this world, but they're the ones being hunted." Her eyes welled with tears as she said it.

"Do you love him?" asked Esther.

"It's not that simple."

Esther took a long drag. "Yeah it is. We always know what we want. It's the things that get in the way that make it complicated. Or impossible, and it fucking hurts." Esther's eyes filled with tears now, and she quickly wiped them.

"Esther, what's wrong? What's happened?"

There was another bang out on the porch that shook the house so hard, both girls jumped. It was followed by Oscar's voice. "None of this is going to bring our sisters back," he shouted. "Or make the men who strung them up, or burnt our farm down, pay. None of it."

"Have you forgotten how this all started, Oscar?" asked Silas. "You need a reminder? Blindfolded and on your knees in a lineup of good men, shot down like fucking dogs. You wouldn't even be alive if it weren't for us fighting back. Well, he's on that coach, with all his new money, and I plan to see his face when I take it back."

"No, I don't need a goddamned reminder. Fuckin' hell. Will? Will, say something."

"You're all right," said Will. "You're right that it won't bring your sisters back, and that it might be suicide. And I'm tired of fighting too, Oscar. But the general is on that stage with our money, and I want to see it through. But we'll do what we always do, and we'll take a vote. Do we ride with the five of us, or does it end here?"

Lucy took a long drag of her cigarette. Suddenly nothing she'd been crying about mattered. All the people she'd met since leaving New York—the Wills and the Esthers and the Seymours of the world—they didn't just wish the world to be different, they acted on it. She put her cigarette out and stood. Then she took the shotgun from the mantel and went out onto the porch. "You have six," she said.

"Lucy, go back in the house," said Will.

"Seven," said Esther, standing beside her now.

Lucy studied the faces of the men. "I'm not as good as any of you, but I can ride a horse and I can shoot." She turned her gaze and pointed at Will. "Will knows. He taught me."

"It's out of the question," said Will.

"Will," said Irish, "this could make the difference to—"

"I said no."

Oscar pointed at Esther. "What about the one with the mouth? Can she shoot?"

Before Lucy could say anything, she saw Esther reach into her cleavage, pull out a small pistol, aim it at Oscar, and fire. The cup he'd been drinking from went flying from his hand and tumbled across the yard.

"Jesus, you could have shot me."

"Please," said Esther. "I could have unbuttoned your shirt if I'd wanted to. I'm even better with a shotgun."

No one moved. All eyes were on Will, who stood calmly staring at Lucy.

"Can you at least let them vote?" asked Lucy.

Will nodded. "All in favor of these two as our sharp shooters, say aye."

No one spoke. The silence was deafening, and Lucy started to turn to go back in the house.

Slowly, Oscar raised his hand. "Aye. Sorry, Will."

"No. This ain't right," said Cal. "I'm with Will on this one. This isn't their fight. And it's too dangerous."

"She's been here, helping Will for weeks now," said Silas. "She deserves to ride if that's what she wants."

All eyes were on Irish now.

"What's it going to be, Irish?" Will asked.

Irish studied Lucy and Esther for a moment. Then slowly, he nodded. "Aye. They ride."

CHAPTER 19

THERE HADN'T BEEN MUCH time, but the men had outfitted the girls each with a bandolier, showed them how to use it to load fast by feel in the darkness. The weight of it was slung across Lucy's shoulder and chest now as she rode. A shotgun sat in the holder on the saddle. Barnet's gun in a stiff leather holster on her hips. Black handkerchief around her neck to pull over her mouth and nose when the gunfire started. Will rode out in front, and they rode single file in the moonlight, save for Silas who brought up the rear beside Lucy and Esther, quietly explaining the plan as they rode.

According to their latest source, there were twelve armed guards on horseback, a driver and a shotgun atop, and General Hall inside. The goal was to make them think they were surrounded and do the job before they figured out any different. The guards were being paid to guard the money, but not well enough to die for it. They were cowards and would ride off. So would General Hall if given the chance, but the goal was not to let him. Lucy and Esther's job was to keep shooting dynamite and rounds to make them think they were surrounded by an army. Will, Oscar, and

Cal would fight on the ground and take out as many guards as possible, Silas would go after the driver atop the stage, and Irish would take care of the general inside the coach and crack the safes, which he could do within a matter of minutes. They'd fill five to six empty satchels with cash and ride. It would be loud and chaotic, and there would be a lot of gunfire and smoke. No matter what, Lucy and Esther had to remain calm as the eyes from above, to keep guards from getting into the coach, to shoot any trying to sneak up from behind any of them. After, they all would ride hard to the deserted hunting cabin Will had taken her to earlier today, where they would regroup, water the horses, and ride off within the hour. No one injured gets left behind, but should a man fall in death, they stay where they lay. It's of no use to a dead man to waste time on goodbyes or fancy words or digging a grave. The most important rule of battle: Honor the fallen by carrying on living as best you can.

Lucy listened quietly. Sticks and brush cracked as they guided the horses off the trail into the brush. Eventually, they came out onto the main road.

"Any questions?" asked Silas.

"No," said Esther.

Lucy's heart was racing. She gazed ahead at the outlines of Oscar, Cal, Irish, and Will in the moonlight, the fate of their lives hanging on the accuracy of her shot. "No questions," she said.

The spot they'd chosen to do the ambush was in the middle of a long clearing, save for a few giant oak trees. It would be unexpected to General Hall and his guards, and Will and his men needed the element of surprise on their side. Stealth attacks and ground fighting were what they'd been trained to do, what they did best. The dynamite was hidden in the bushes and tall grass, dispersed methodically in a circle around where they'd attack to make their opponents feel surrounded. The men lined the road with it now and showed Lucy where, when given the signal, she would shoot first to halt the wagon and startle the horses. The men would be hidden in the ditches, and once the dynamite went off, they would attack. The horses were tied a quarter mile from where they were. When it was all over, the girls were to jump down from the tree and run like hell, then ride like hell to the cabin.

When they were all set up, Will stood beside Lucy under the tree she was to climb. "Luce, Jesus you're shaking. Look at me. You can still back out; no one will think less of you."

She shook her head no. "Help me up."

He didn't move, his eyes intense in the moonlight, studying her face. Then his hands came to either side of her face, and he kissed her.

"I didn't mean it," she said when their lips parted. "When I said it was all pretend."

Will kissed her on the forehead. "I know," he whispered.

She could hear the first sounds of the stagecoach and horses in the distance now. In the moonlight, she could see Irish helping Esther up into her tree, across the road. Cal, Silas, and Oscar lay down in the ditch, blending in with the night.

"Okay," Will said. "Use my shoulder. Ready?"

He bent down slightly, and shotgun in hand, Lucy put a foot on his shoulder and he hoisted her to the first branch, which she grabbed and then pulled herself up. Then slowly, she made her way up two more branches.

Will walked away and disappeared into the ditch. Her heart felt as though it would beat out of her chest. She wrapped her legs around the branch, securing herself. Then she loaded the shotgun, cocked it, and aimed at the dynamite, the metal shining in the moonlight. Her hands shook violently. She took a long steady breath. *You're just in the yard, shooting cans. Just breathe. You can do this.* The sound of the coach and horses grew nearer. Slowly, the cavalcade came into view, like a small army. Five or six men on horseback on either side of the stage. Two out in front. Lucy's hands were surprisingly steady now. She lifted the shotgun and focused her eye on the sight, concentrating on the dynamite. Then she heard it—three sharp whistles. She pulled the trigger. The dynamite exploded with a bang, lighting up the road. Horses whinnied, then reared and turned in circles. Riders drew their guns, looking every direction. A few fired shots into the darkness. Will and his men appeared up from the ditches. Oscar unhorsed a guard and fought him on the ground. Lucy aimed at a far bush where there was more dynamite hidden and fired. The kickback from the shotgun nearly knocked her from the tree, but the bush exploded. She aimed again and kept shooting. A few more explosions. Several of the guards turned immediately, riding off in the direction they'd come from.

Silas was atop the stage, fighting someone. Another jumped down. Several others were fighting on the ground, but she couldn't see. She cocked the gun and fired at another bush in the distance, and the dynamite exploded. She coughed from the smoke while cocking the shotgun again, then fired again at a bush behind the stagecoach, setting off another round of dynamite. She could hear firing coming from Esther's tree nearby, but she kept her eyes on the stagecoach. Two more guards rode off. Lucy followed one through the sight of her shotgun until he was out of sight.

"Safe's open," Irish shouted from inside the coach. A horse reared, and she heard a gunshot.

"Go," Oscar shouted. "I've got three of them on their knees."

Lucy could see Oscar standing over men, on their knees, hands on the back of their heads. Will, Silas, and Cal rushed into the coach. All went quiet for what felt like an eternity. Then, from somewhere in the distance, she heard horses. Coming toward them, fast. She aimed her gun in the direction but couldn't see anything.

"Hurry up, gentleman. We got company," Oscar said. "Lucy, Esther, let's go!"

She jumped down. Esther jumped down but didn't land on her feet and stumbled forward. Lucy went and grabbed her by the arm. She looked back at the men. All of five of them were running toward her, several of them tossing satchels of cash over their shoulders. Behind them, at least five horses were riding down the road, coming up on the stagecoach fast.

"Run!"

It was the fastest she'd ever run in her life. Gunfire erupted from behind them. They neared the horses, and Lucy leapt up atop the tan mare. She turned to see Silas firing shots behind him before leaping up onto his horse. Oscar and Cal leapt up on their horses. Will and Irish, still afoot, were firing behind them. In the moonlight, she saw the outline of three guards on horseback still riding toward them in the distance. More gunfire. Will turned and fired again. One of the guards fell from his horse.

Will leapt up onto Zeta. "Ride!"

Lucy spurred her horse and the mare galloped down the road, as fast as she could run. Esther rode right beside her. Clutching the reins, Lucy looked back, relieved to count all five of the men right behind her—Will and Irish in the rear, firing back at the guards who were gaining on them. Her hair whipped around her, and her body felt at one with the horse, moving in motion with the animal, her thighs squeezing the saddle with all her might. Hooves hit the ground at a rhythm that made her feel like she was flying. When she turned again, Will and Irish were holding back, lengths behind them. Will turned and fired. One of the guards fell from his saddle. As Will turned back, he raised a hand to his chest and clutched it just before slumping in his saddle. Irish reached out and grabbed him by the back of the shirt.

"Silas," he shouted.

Silas held his horse back and grabbed Will from the other side. She could still hear gunfire coming from somewhere behind them.

"Keep going," shouted Silas as they rode. "There's still a few more back there. We've got to lose them."

Lucy turned down the path toward the cabin where they'd ridden today, still out in the lead with Esther, riding as fast as she could, even through the brush as the trail narrowed. A branch scraped her face in the darkness, and she felt blood on her cheek. She spurred the horse to keep going. As they rode the gunfire slowed, then ceased. All she could hear was horses trampling through brush in the moonlight.

By the time they got to the cabin, Zeta was riderless and on a lead pulled by Silas, and Irish had Will's body laid out in front of him. Oscar and Cal went and grabbed either side of Will and pulled him from the saddle. He was still conscious and tried to speak but coughed up blood. He stood with the help of Oscar and Cal on either side. They took him into the cabin and laid him down on the cot.

Lucy lit a lantern.

Irish went to the cot, pulled out a knife, and began to cut Will's shirt off. Everyone stood beside the cot, watching. Will's breathing became raspy. Silas helped turn Will onto his side to inspect the wound. He'd been shot in the back, but there was no exit wound from his chest. He was bleeding badly. Lucy grabbed the gauze from the table and brought it to Irish, who began wrapping it tightly around Will's chest and back.

Will opened his eyes and coughed. Blood trickled out the side of his mouth. "You need to go," he said in a raspy voice. "Take Lucy with you."

Irish put his ear to Will's chest and listened. The room went silent, save for Will's raspy breathing.

Irish looked up at the men. "It's in his lung."

"Is there anything you can do?"

Lucy wasn't sure who said it. Everything turned surreal; her eyes rested on Irish as he slowly shook his head no.

Cal left the cabin. "Fuck!" he shouted into the night.

The rest of them stared at each other in silence.

"No," said Lucy. "No! We can't just let him die."

She felt an arm come around her. It was Esther.

"I've removed a lot of bullets in the war," Irish said quietly. "But not in the lungs. Even if there was a surgeon and a proper hospital, there's no telling he'd last the night."

"We have to try," said Lucy.

"The price on our heads will be double by morning," said Silas, his voice wavering as he wiped glistening tears from his eyes. "Even if he'd survive the surgery, you won't find a surgeon who won't turn him in, and we can't do that to Will. He's a soldier. Soldiers die in the battlefield, not by a noose."

"Irish," said Will, coughing again. "Go now. And take her with you. Make sure she's safe."

"I will. I promise." Irish looked up at Lucy and held her gaze. Then he stood and went outside.

Silas knelt beside Will, tears streaming down his face now.

Oscar did a sign of the cross and nodded to Will. "Goodbye, brother," he whispered. Then he left and went outside.

Lucy turned and went outside. Esther followed her. Cal, Oscar, and Irish were preparing the horses.

Silas came outside, and Lucy turned to him. "Silas," she said. "Will could have left me for dead twice, and he didn't. I can't let him die alone."

Everyone was silent, their faces all stricken in the moonlight. The only sound, the rustling of bags being cinched, a saddle untied and tossed onto a new horse. Will coughed again inside; everyone stopped for a moment, then continued packing the horses. They moved like the walking dead, going through the motions, as though none of them really knew what to do or say. It was Irish who finally broke the silence.

"She's right," he said to the men. "I say let her stay." Then he turned to Esther. "What about you? Are you coming with us?"

"I'll stay with her," said Esther.

Silas, Cal, and Oscar mounted their horses. Irish stood holding the reins of his, then looked up at the night sky. "Damn it all," he said. "I've never broken a promise to Will, and I'm not about to break this one. You three go on without me. I'll see you in San Francisco."

"Irish," said Silas, "you know what will happen to you if you don't leave now."

"Godspeed, gents," he said. Then he walked his horse back to the side of the house and came and stood beside Lucy and Esther.

The other three tipped their hats to them, turned, and rode off.

"Don't judge them for riding off like that," said Irish. "If five years of war teaches a man anything, it's how to find a way to carry on while others fall around you."

"But you're still here," said Lucy.

"You heard me in there. I promised Will I'd see you got out of here safe."

"You were a medic in the war. If we had a surgeon to remove the bullet, what are his chances of survival?"

"Slim, Lucy. And it would have to be within the next hour or two. He doesn't have much time."

"Damnit," said Esther. "Of all the lowlifes I know, not one of them is a doctor."

"I know of one," said Lucy, " . . . in Valley City."

Will coughed inside again.

"Irish," said Lucy. "I'd sooner face the noose than stand here and let him die without trying."

Irish rubbed his face and stared out at the darkness. "I'll come with you."

"No. You both stay here and keep him alive until I get back."

CHAPTER 20

―――◆―――

MAIN STREET, VALLEY CITY, was quiet. A candle burned in the window of the general store, but she didn't see anyone inside as she rode past. When she reached the saloon, she dismounted and went through the swinging doors. Not sure what time it was, she knew it was late; there were only a few patrons left. John Stark sat at a table with the doctor and two other men. He stood as she entered. Lucy pointed at the doctor. "I need him. Someone's been shot."

The doctor looked up at Lucy warily with his dark eyes but did not speak. The saloon doors opened, and she turned to see Sheriff Lyman entering.

"What's happened?" he asked.

Lucy froze for a moment. Lyman's badge gleamed in the candlelight.

"What's happened?" he asked again.

"He's been shot. It's in his chest; there's no exit wound."

"Where is he?"

"A half hour's ride from here. In a small hunting cabin." She turned to the doctor. "Please, I've heard you don't practice anymore, but he'll die."

The doctor shook his head and looked away. "Find someone else," he said.

John Stark kicked the doctor's chair out from underneath of him, causing him to fall to the floor. "René, I've been pouring you whiskey for months now, letting you feel sorry for yourself. Someone needs your help. Get up!"

Lyman approached and put a hand up to Stark. "I'll handle this, John." He held out a hand to the doctor, who still lay crumpled on the floor. "We look out for each other in this town, and someone needs your help. Stand up, René."

The doctor let Lyman help him up. When he was standing, he brushed himself off and looked around until he found Lucy. "Where'd you say he's been shot?"

"In the back. I believe the bullet's in his lung."

"All right, then. Let's go. I'll need to stop by my place."

John Stark tossed a set of keys to Montana. "Lock up for me," he said. Then he grabbed a bottle of whiskey and followed Lyman, Lucy, and the doctor out.

Will was unconscious but still alive. Irish had wrapped extra gauze around his chest and was applying pressure. Dr. René pulled up a chair and inspected Will's wound. There were no introductions made, and no one asked questions.

"We don't have much time," said the doctor. "Clear that table and pull it over here."

On the table was Will's saddlebag, bandolier, shotguns, and two large satchels of money. Lyman and Stark moved them to the floor without saying a word and carried the table over.

René began to mix a paste of leaves and powder into a small bowl. As he did so, he calmly gave instructions to the room. He'd need Irish and Lyman at his head, one on either side to hold Will down if he woke, with John Stark at his feet. Esther's job was to hold the lantern over the wound, as still and steady as possible. And Lucy was to stand directly beside him, handing him what he needed. The tools were laid out on the table, and he walked her through them. Scalpel, small and large tweezers. The bowl was for when he retrieved the bullet, and the needle for stitching him up after. Lastly, the paste to stop the bleeding.

No one spoke as they took their positions.

"Scalpel," said René. Then he placed it over Will's ribcage and took a deep breath. Everyone silent. Then, slowly, he made a steady cut across his skin. Blood instantly ran out. He handed the bloody scalpel back to Lucy.

"Both tweezers."

Will groaned and spit up some blood. Irish wiped it, keeping a hand on Will's shoulder.

René used the tweezers to open the wound and probe through tissue and muscle. Lucy felt light-headed at the sight of so much blood running down his chest, but she did not look away.

With his eyes still closed, Will tried to sit up, but Lyman and Irish held his shoulders down. "It's all right, mate" said Irish. "It's all right."

"That's it," said Dr. René. "Keep him still." His hands remained steady as he probed. Then slowly, he pinched the tweezers. "Bowl."

Lucy grabbed the bowl, her hands shaking uncontrollably as she held it out to him.

"Lyman, grab that towel, and when I say, I want you to put pressure on the wound," René said. Then he slowly lifted the tweezers out.

The sound of the bullet echoed throughout the room as it hit the tin. Blood was pouring out of Will's chest now.

"Pressure."

Will groaned again, and the men held him down while Lyman kept pressure on the wound.

René prepared the needle and thread.

After Will was stitched, René spread the concoction across the wound. "Yarrow, myrrh, and ashwagandha, to stop the bleeding and dull the pain a little. I learned a great deal in medical school, but it was my grandfather, the medicine man of my Algonquin people, who taught me concoctions such as this. The bullet and punctured lung isn't the only risk of death. Anytime the skin is broken, there is fever, shaking, evil spirits that enter the body, like venom from a snake bite. We use plants as antiseptics to help, but it's . . . What's his name?"

"Will," said Lucy. "His name is Will." She looked at Lyman, but he was staring down at Will, expressionless.

"Will's spirit will decide now to stay or to go, and we cannot interfere. If he chooses to stay and wakes, it will be at least a month before he's himself again. For now, I will go and pray."

René went outside and sang a quiet song in a language Lucy had never heard before. Haunting and soothing. Will lay on the cot, looking almost peaceful as he slept.

Stark went over to Will's saddlebag and began to rifle around in it. "I don't know about any of you," he said as he pulled out Will's tobacco and rolling papers. "But I need a smoke."

Irish and Esther followed Stark outside. Lyman got Lucy a chair and told her to sit. Then he sat where the doctor had been sitting, across from her. Will lay between them. His chest rose and fell slowly with each raspy breath as he slept.

"Are you going to arrest us?" she asked.

After a long silence, he sat back in his chair and looked up at Lucy. "Have you ever heard of something called 'The Poor Law'?"

Lucy shook her head no.

"It was a British law, passed in Ireland around the time they began to invade. Most of the population was already starving from the great famine, but instead of having mercy on them, wealthy landowners sent in middlemen, scum of the earth, who made a living raising and enforcing rent by any means necessary. The Poor Law was passed because the wealthy saw being poor as a moral issue, those suffering from it lacked the drive to work. And so, the workhouse was created to teach the poor the value of a day's work, rather than expect charity. The most I knew of my mother was that she gave birth to me in one of these establishments, but somehow placed me into foster care, which probably saved my life. Infants born in the workhouses were separated from their mothers, and their cause of death was cited as failure to thrive. I was fourteen when the foster family I was living with lost their land, and I found myself back in Dublin, entering the very establishment my mother had tried to keep me from. The work was hard, the pay dismal, and the living conditions were worse than anything I could have imagined. I'd lay awake at night with the rats crawling over my feet, the sound of grown men weeping from their bunks. My only saving grace was a middle-aged man by the name of Neal O'Nally.

"Neal worked on the docks outside the workhouse, which meant he got to check out each morning and come back each night and pay a small sum of his wages. He always snuck in some scraps of bread or extra food for me, even though he could have been whipped for it. The second winter there he developed a cough so bad, he lost a few weeks of work. They took his blankets and decreased food rations since he couldn't pay. I got up one night when I couldn't stand his crying and begging to die anymore and put my blanket over him. Took the worst beating of my life for it, and when they were nearly done, Neal got out of bed with what little strength he had, grabbed the guard's gun, and shot him in the head. As they were dragging Neal off to be executed, he pointed to his bed. When it was quiet again, I looked under the rat chewed bedroll to find a rusted money clip, in it a few bills and the license to work on the docks. The very next day I checked myself out and showed up to work on the docks as Neal O'Nally. No one ever questioned the age on the license, which was thirty-four. I was simply worker number 983410. I worked those docks and lived on the streets, freezing under any vacant bridge or alley I could find, for the better part of a year, until I'd saved up enough for passage to America."

Will moaned in his sleep, and Lucy took his hand and pulled the blanket up around him.

"There is good and bad in this world," continued Lyman, "and people are far more complicated than meets the eye. But I know good when I see it. And Will, he may not even know it, but he's one of the good ones. And so are you."

Lyman stood and went to the door.

"You didn't answer my question," Lucy said.

"Yeah I did."

At dawn, René, Lyman, Irish, Stark, Lucy, and Esther still sat where they'd spent the better part of the night. Outside, in a row leaning up against the cabin. They'd taken turns checking on Will, spending long bursts in silence, with the only sound the spark of a match to light a cigarette. Lucy wasn't sure if it was uncertainty or death looming, but when silence was broken, it was with rare honesty and candid.

Before tonight, John Stark had never said out loud that he was a deserter of the Union Army. He wasn't sure what made him say it now but he followed with a story of a general who'd made him scalp a family. He still woke up in the middle of the night, hearing the knife cutting through flesh and bone, and felt the blood and hair in his hands.

Dr. René told them about the day his grandfather, the medicine man, was captured and arrested. René was ten years old and also captured but taken with other children in the village to a mission in Eastern Canada where they tried to teach the Native American ways out of them. He'd never felt at home anywhere since. Not at medical school in Pennsylvania, or the short time after in which he'd returned to his own people.

Irish and Lyman found out they were around the same age and had both gone through the famine in Ireland. Irish, too, had hatred for the middlemen, whose job was to collect rent at any cost. His family's middleman had shown up the day they were burying their pa. His ma had already been gone a few years; it was just Irish and his two sisters. His sisters were older, already married, and working their own land. Irish was barely fifteen, too young to take on the land by himself, and he knew it. The husband of one of his sisters had to pay to buy Irish time, but in the end, it was inevitable that they'd lose the land. Irish followed the middleman and waited till he got good and drunk and was riding his horse home alone. He shot the man and took the money back, dragged his body deep into the woods, and spent the night burying a hole so deep no one would ever find him. He left for America, where he lived in New York, in the Five Points, and met Will on a construction job.

Esther and Lucy both stayed quiet until darkness began to lift and the first rays of dawn appeared on the horizon, when Esther stated matter-of-factly that she was with child. She was not a fool; she knew what she'd have to do. This world wasn't a world set up for unwed mothers, a prostitute no less, to make it on their own with a child. But just for a moment, just for a few days, she wanted to pretend that it was.

It was mid-morning when Will began to stir in his sleep and open his eyes. Lyman and John Stark had left just after dawn to go into town to take care of a few things, but the rest of them were in the cabin and went rushing over to Will. Dr. René mixed up a new paste and sat down beside Will, who was trying to say something in his sleep now. Irish stood ready, with a hand on his shoulder to keep him from thrashing. Lucy took Will's hand in hers.

René felt Will's forehead. "Will. Will, can you hear me?"

Will blinked a few times, then opened his eyes and slowly took in the room. He tried to sit up, but Irish put a hand on his shoulder. "It's all right, mate. Easy. This is Dr. René Chogan. He took the bullet out of you."

"Where's the others?" Will's voice was still raspy. "They make it?"

"They did," said Irish. "I'm sure they're halfway to San Francisco by now."

"You were supposed to be with them."

"You let us worry about that, mate."

Suddenly, Lucy heard cracking outside. A rider was coming. Irish and Esther went to the window.

"It's just Lyman," Esther said. "But he's got a woman with him."

"Lyman?!" Will asked. "The sheriff? What the fuck, Irish?"

Lucy squeezed his hand. "It was me who went for help. I couldn't just let you die."

He held her gaze with an expression she couldn't read and said nothing more.

Lyman entered, carrying a box. Behind him, Vinnie. She was wearing a red dress, and her hair was pinned up in a high bun. She looked around the cabin, aghast.

Lucy averted eye contact, instantly ashamed of all the lying to someone she cared so much for. To her shock, Vinnie came rushing over to Lucy. And hugged her. "Oh, my darling!" she said. "I barely slept a wink. How is he?" She looked at Will but didn't wait for an answer before turning back to Lyman. "Lyman, be a dear and open that box for me, would you? I made cinnamon buns." She led Lucy to the table where Lyman was opening the box. "Come on, you need your strength. And you must be Esther. Well, aren't you just pretty as a picture? My goodness to be young like you girls again. And Irish. I heard you helped save his life. Well, don't be shy everyone—eat, eat, eat. You must be half-starved, the whole lot of you."

Speechless still, Lucy took one of the cinnamon buns from the box and took a small bite.

"Lyman," said Will. "They're going to double the price on my head; I've got to worth at least four thousand dollars by now."

"Five thousand," said Lyman.

"Pinkertons won't let this go," said Will. "Not this time. They'll find me. And you'll be charged with aiding and abetting. All of you, even you now, Vinnie. You shouldn't be here."

Vinnie pulled a newspaper from the crate. They were on the front page. "According to today's paper, all seven of you were seen heading west. Pinkertons won't be looking in these parts. Not today anyway."

Lucy, Esther, Irish, and Will all exchanged silent glances, but no one spoke.

"Irish," said Lyman, "I don't know you, but I know you risked your life to stay beside Will last night. And that's enough for me. I can't promise the Pinkertons will let this go right away, but a few carefully written articles in the papers saying all seven of you were seen boarding a ship, or crossing a border, and they'll eventually move onto something else. I can pull in a favor from an old friend who writes for a paper."

After a long moment of silence, it was Lucy who finally spoke. "Why would you help us? We lied to you. We've been lying all this time, and Vinnie, trust me, there were so many times I wanted to tell you. I didn't know I'd . . ."

Vinnie looked over at Lyman, then a slow smile came across her face and she shook her head. She turned back to Lucy and let out a dramatic sigh. "Oh, honey, come now. You don't live this long to be fooled that easily."

"What do you . . .?"

"The day you arrived in that storm, a messenger had already come by with a written notice from the stagecoach company. It was addressed to Uncle Holloway, who was dead, and so I opened it. The notice was to inform of the stagecoach attack; it had been found and there were no survivors. The stagecoach company asked to accept their sincerest condolences. I stuck it in my desk drawer. I didn't have the heart to tell anyone right away. We'd all been through so much; the whole town, so excited for the Holloway's to arrive. And then, lo and behold, the two of you showed up and, well." Vinnie shrugged. "You looked like you could use some help. I kept it to myself for, I don't know, a week maybe. Then Lyman came in with a few wanted posters he wanted me to put up, so I told him. Showed him the letter from the stagecoach company."

"That's the day I rode out with the deed to the house," said Lyman.

Lucy looked over at Will, but he just lay on the cot, watching them quietly. "I don't understand," she said. "You could have arrested us, been a hero, with quite a bounty. Why in heaven's name did you let us stay?"

"I told you," Lyman said, looking at Lucy now. "I know good people when I see them. I became a lawman to help people who need it the most, and sometimes that means going above the law."

"And," said Vinnie, "it's like I said time and time again. We take care of each other around here. And you both seemed like you needed some taking care of. At least for a little while. So Lyman and I've kept it our little secret."

Everyone was quiet again for a while. Lucy tried to think back to all the moments with Vinnie, but she was too tired to think straight.

Lyman stood and came over to the table to take a cinnamon roll. "I don't expect you to make a decision today. But far as I'm concerned, the Holloway property is yours, if you want it."

"You can't mean we stay here, in Valley City," said Lucy. "People will figure it out. You two might not be turning us in, but someone will."

"You'd be surprised what people are willing to look past," Lyman said, then gestured to the bags of cash. "Especially with a generous donation of a new schoolhouse the town's been in such desperate need of." Lyman turned to Irish and Esther, who'd been taking it all in with almost as much shock as Lucy and Will. "That goes for the both of you as well. If for any reason you want to stay around these parts, I'll help you best I can."

"Oh!" shouted Vinnie, so loud it startled Lucy. "Ava's going back to Philadelphia. We need all the girls—and young people—in this town we can get! Esther, you could run the café!"

Esther smiled and shook her head. "No, ma'am. Thank you kindly, but my work's in Denver, and I best be getting back to it."

"Well, not today you're not. You're coming back to town with me. You too, Irish. Lyman and I booked rooms for you both at Schmidt's Hotel. You both need a good night's sleep. I think Lucy and the doc have got this covered."

At dusk, Dr. René changed Will's bandages one last time and rode off for the night, stating he'd be back first thing in the morning. Lucy helped him tack up his horse, then went and sat beside Will. Alone together for the first time.

Will shook his head and smiled. "I can't stop thinking about Lyman. Fucking hell. I've beat some of the best poker players in the country and I had no idea the guy was onto me."

Lucy studied Will's face. "You still want to go to Argentina, don't you?"

Will rolled onto his side, propping himself up on his elbow, wincing as he moved. "That depends on you."

"What do you mean?"

"You know what I mean. Lucy, I've loved you from the first moment I saw you. I just want you."

She looked up at the window, and for a while, neither of them spoke. He was still gazing at her when she turned back to him. "The town does need a school," she said.

Will smiled and reached his hand out to her. "All right then. Soon as the doc says I'm well enough to ride a horse, let's go home."

CHAPTER 21

———————◆———————

Six Weeks Later

LUCY REMOVED HER NEW black top hat, with the feathers on the side, and tossed her hair out in the afternoon breeze as she rode the tan mare down Main Street. She wore a new dress, from a small boutique in Denver, which she and Vinnie discovered on the up-and-coming Washington Street, called Western Dames. It was owned by a French woman, with the most beautiful accent, who'd moved here with her American husband. She was a seamstress by trade and had the most excellent eye for fashion, finding ways to combine the most *avant-garde* styles of Europe with the practicality of the West. Lucy's dress was made of a grey material, a thin cotton that felt almost linen-like, which buttoned over a white collared breast. She wore small stylish gloves, of a matching material, with leather on the palms, reinforcement for holding the reins of a horse.

She rode to the general store and tied her horse before going up the steps. The bell chimed as she entered.

"Good day," said Lucy.

"My darling!" Vinnie said, giggling as she came running around the desk for a hug. She wore a sleek, navy-blue dress, with lace around the collar, and an oversized hat, with peacock feathers, that she'd picked out at the same store in Denver. "Look!" She pointed at the cinnamon buns, fresh bread, and few little sandwiches on her counter for sale. "Premade-food items, like you were always going on about. I feel so fancy. And people are buying them! How's that handsome husband of yours? He back to work soon?"

"In a week or so, yes. Dr. René's supposed to come by the house this afternoon, or he would have come into town with me."

"A week! What a rascal! Timed that well, didn't he? They'll be done building the school by then. You should go ride by it when you leave; the bell's supposed to arrive today or tomorrow. And wait until you see the new sign on the café. Valley City is booming!" she said, then burst into a fit of giggles. "Oh, stay right there. That reminds me. I've got something for you to take home for dinner."

She came back with a chicken, clucking nervously in a crate. "This old girl's not laying eggs anymore, bless her. But she knew the rules. You don't pull your weight around here, it's off with your head. Okay, now, what else did I have to tell you? Oh, Lyman and I put an ad in the papers back East for a schoolteacher. Isn't that exciting? That adorable little neighbor girl of yours was in the other day with her pa. He's gonna let her attend school. It's a good thing I was sitting down! She said you and her have plans for a chicken coop come spring?"

"Yes, Phoebe has big plans for my little farm. Yesterday, she had us out planting a winter garden all day. I can't wait until school starts so I can get some rest," Lucy said, with a smile, as she filled her basket with a few vegetables to roast with the chicken. She paid Vinnie and grabbed the satchel along with the chicken in the crate. "Thank you, Vinnie."

"Tootaloo! Go see the school!"

The horse sidestepped as Lucy tied the clucking chicken to the saddle. "Easy, girl." She leapt up and continued down Main Street.

The vacant building beside the general store had a new sign: "Dr. René Chogan M.D." A little farther down, another new sign had finally gone up on the café. Lucy stopped her horse in the middle of the street to take it in for a moment. "ESTHER'S PLACE." Through the large front window, she could see a few patrons inside. Mrs. Schmidt and Agnus at the table closest to the window, having their morning coffee and gossip hour, which Esther complained about daily since they were both hard of hearing and had to shout across the table at one another. Esther came out from the kitchen with a tray of something and stopped to wave at Lucy.

Lucy smiled and waved back, then she spurred the horse and continued down the street.

There were ten or twelve men working on the school. Lyman, John Stark, Thomas, Dr. René, Irish, and several others Lucy recognized from the mill. The framework was done, and the men were starting to fill in the side boards and roof. It sat on a large corner acre property, with an undisturbed view of the foothills. A small play area was being built for the younger ones, with a tire swing, tree fort, slide, and teeter totter.

Lucy waved as she rode past. Then she continued on the road home.

Zeta whinnied at the gate of the corral, and the goat bleated in the pen and leapt around excitedly as Lucy rode up the drive. A few of the kittens they'd taken in from a recent litter of Phoebe's best mouser played and wrestled beneath the giant oak. Two new rocking chairs—a handmade gift from John Stark, who, as it turned out, was a fine craftsman—sat on the front porch rocking gently in the breeze, a blanket knitted by Vinnie strewn over one.

A blackbird flew down and landed on the rouge-wearing scarecrow. Several others cawed out and circled above. Lucy slowed the horse and gazed up at them, soaring across the blue sky with such ease. Sister Mary Catherine had been wrong. Blackbirds were not a bad omen, nor were they cursed by God for their intelligence. Their ability to think for themselves was what made them adaptable. Caused them to survive as a species. In a month or two, they would migrate. Quite a majestic sight, according to Vinnie, when they gathered in the fall and flew overhead by the thousands. Using innate, instinctive navigational skills to reach their wintering grounds, then returning back, by the thousands, to the exact same spot in the spring.

As Lucy neared the house, the front door opened and Will came outside. He crossed the yard to her. He wore a new pair of trousers and a black button-down shirt she'd bought him from the boutique in Denver. His hair was shaggier, touching the back of his collar, and the front able to tuck behind his ear. He hadn't shaved in at least a week, and she loved it.

He smiled at the chicken in the crate as he helped her dismount. "Welcome home," he said. Then he took her in his arms and kissed her.

We humans, Lucy supposed, migrate out of survival, too, using navigational skills. But we don't migrate on intellect or instinct alone. Not the way a bird does. We can be set off course, led in a thousand different directions from our original destination. Because we love. And that's what sets us apart. What guides us.

We love.

CPSIA information can be obtained
at www.ICGtesting.com
Printed in the USA
LVHW040438080722
722893LV00004B/116